THE PRISONER OF RAVEN'S GAZE HALL

J. C. Briggs

SAPERE
BOOKS

THE PRISONER OF RAVEN'S GAZE HALL

Published by Sapere Books.

24 Trafalgar Road, Ilkley, LS29 8HH,
United Kingdom

saperebooks.com

ISBN: 978-0-85495-790-3

The raven sits on the ravenstone,
And his black wing flits
O'er the milk-white bones...
Manfred, by Lord Byron

PROLOGUE

Dorset, 1932

Catherine put down the book. *The Devil's Dictionary: Place Names of Westmorland and the Western Dales* compiled by Bennet Lestrange. Odd, how it still brought back that sick feeling of dread. Not the book itself, perhaps, but the associations it held, and memories of the writer, of course, though the pages with their lists of names were still menacing.

'Black Tarn', a fathomless pool, obsidian-black even on the sunniest day. 'Blind Gill'. 'The Witches' Pot', 'Devil's Crag', 'Foulsyke', 'Grimshill', 'Hell Gill'... She flicked through the pages to 'Wicked Bank Fold'. She could have told you the meanings and origins of the names without looking. It was she who had typed out the handwritten manuscript for Bennet Lestrange of Raven's Gaze Hall in Yorkshire. It was she whom he had taken to see his favourite places. How charming he had seemed at first. But he was subtle as the serpent in Eden, playing upon her as if she had been some fine instrument. She remembered his long fingers, his fine hands, one curiously marked with a dark patch which had the shape of a wing. A raven's wing, she had thought once. The thought made her shudder as she remembered how she came to mistrust, then to fear him.

The book, a few yellowing bits of newspaper, a few photographs, and a pair of gloves in the bottom drawer of an old chest in the rarely used guest room was all she had left of her time at Raven's Gaze. She had never thought she would go back. That part of her life had been over long ago. And now an announcement had come — a black-edged card, telling of a death. And there was an invitation. The second in ten years. The first had been in 1919, when she had been invited to take up a private nursing post for an elderly lady. She had needed a new job and a change after all that had happened to her in the war.

She had no wish to return to Raven's Gaze. It was impossible to think that she had anything to tell about the man who was dead, the man who had very nearly ruined her life. Yet the writer urged her to come back to Raven's Gaze Hall, for there was much to be revealed. Over the years, Catherine had thought often of the mysteries which she had never fathomed and now, perhaps, the chance had come to solve them. Was it Fate, she wondered, that it should come now when there was the possibility of change? A choice between the old life and a new one. Perhaps, the new one could only be started when the old life was finally finished, all the loose ends tied up.

She looked at the black and white photograph of the house called Raven's Gaze, with its high square tower from which it had got its strange name. In the photograph, the tower was as black as it had always seemed in the rain. She remembered those shuddering curtains of rain: rain in rare winter sunlight falling sharp as knives; leaden clouds pressing down on the battlemented roof; and the wind whining in the chimney, or howling through the tossing treetops, or roaring round the tower which was like a sheer forbidding cliff, immoveable in storm and tempest. And there, nearly at the top of the tower, she could make out the slit of the lancet window where a light had always burned. The raven's eye looking out to the fells and woods. She had arrived in the dark that first time, seeing the light from the distant road, hoping it was a welcome. She could make out the faint strip of white still. She knew now that she should have taken it as a warning.

Another photograph. A man and a woman standing by a stone bench on the terrace above the lawns. A young woman whose face could hardly be made out, for she had been caught unawares, her face angled downwards, away from the man who was looking at the camera. A thin face, unsmiling, one hand gripping his stick, the other hand raised in a warding-off gesture. He hadn't wanted to be photographed, either. If a stranger looked at that photograph, he, or she would know that this was an unhappy couple. Well, she was that stranger now, and the photograph did not lie.

The third photograph *was* a lie, though. It showed the same young woman. She was on the terrace again. It had been summer — the summer of 1920. The young woman was wearing a straw hat and a light coloured, ankle-length dress with what looked like lace at the collar. Catherine couldn't see the young woman's face, but there was something tender in the bend of her head as she looked down into a perambulator, a wicker work carriage swathed in lace. There were two large wheels and two smaller ones. It looked impossibly old-fashioned — it was even then, a relic of the Victorian era. It was a charming picture in its old-fashioned way. You might imagine a proud father taking the photograph of his wife, proud because there was a son in the baby carriage. But the man who had taken it had not been proud of the child, nor of the young woman.

She looked at one of the yellowing bits of newspaper, which almost disintegrated as she touched it. Grainy photographs told the story of a mysterious tragedy. A photograph of a young man in the uniform of a lieutenant who looked out with dark, serious eyes. And another of a young woman in a nurse's uniform, starched apron, collar and cuffs, her hair smoothed neatly under the white headdress, a cape on her shoulders, and an expression of tranquillity as she looked out at the photographer — a stranger now.

That young woman was gone.

1

Flanders, 1917

Catherine Sisley was cleaning the iron bed frame with carbolic lotion, after which she would fumigate the mattress and bedding, ready for the next occupant. It was good to know her patient was being sent home to England to recuperate from his leg wound. He had been lucky. The bullet had fractured the femur of his left leg and had passed out just above the knee. He would walk again, albeit with a limp. She had liked him — a good-looking young man with brown curly hair and an open smile. She had already done the same job for Captain Anderson's bed. She was sorry about him — his abdominal wound had been so severe that despite the surgery, he had died in the night.

The second battle of Passchendaele had begun on the 26th of October, 1917. At the clearing stations, when the nurses stood in the night to watch the flashes of light and the sky lit up as if a huge fireworks display were taking place at a distance, when they heard the rumble and roar of the guns, feeling the sound in their heart's core, they knew what would come.

The first casualties arrived by motor ambulance to Casualty Clearing Station (CCS), Number 17 and the other three at Remy Farm, a collection of farm buildings, huts, and tents. Number 17 worked in tandem with CCS Number 10, one taking in a maximum of two hundred patients before handing over to the other. There would be hundreds more casualties, but for the time being, the copious paperwork was complete. Speed of treatment was the essential thing; in the reception huts, the patients were immediately stripped of their mud-caked and bloody clothes, fumigated, disinfected, and put in a clean nightshirt, then warmed in blankets and with gas heaters. Field cards were checked for treatment already given. Anti-tetanus serum was administered if needed, wounds assessed, pulse taken, bleeding staunched, bodies rehydrated as fast as possible with sterile saline solution. Wounds were irrigated with sodium hypochlorite. The operating theatres were already busy; the surgical teams worked in twelve-hour shifts.

Catherine looked at the names on her list: Adams, Lestrange, Carstairs, Evans, Jackson, Minton. As she stood in the preparation room where equipment was kept, her hands moved mechanically, placing the enamel dishes and trays on the trolley with carbolic solution, gauze, lint, bandages and safety pins. Her thoughts strayed to the china cups in her childhood home. Minton china. She remembered the tea set with its red and gold flowers. Flowers even on the inside base of the delicate cups. She remembered her delight when as a child she had been allowed a cup of milky tea so that she could see the flowers when she had finished. The china had been sold now, along with everything else from the old house. The pang of loss assailed her again, though her parents had been dead for almost twenty years. Cousin Marjorie had been as good as a mother to her. No one could have been more tender and tactful with the little girl she had been.

She thought of the photograph of Captain Anderson's little girl which she had seen in his wallet. Poor little Elsie, whom she did not know nor ever would, but whom she pitied for the news she was yet to receive. It was part of her job to write to Mrs Anderson to tell her that her husband had died. It seemed somehow a more painful task than usual now that she'd seen the photograph of Elsie, with her wide and trusting smile. She didn't have her two front teeth yet. So young and so vulnerable.

The trolley was ready, and she wheeled it into the ward where the medical officer, Major Robertson, was ready to inspect the patients. She liked the major, a compassionate man, who smiled as she came up to Lieutenant Christopher Adams's bed. His leg injury looked worse than it was — a piece of shrapnel had lodged in his thigh, but the wound had been disinfected with hydrogen peroxide at the Advanced Dressing Station and expertly dressed so that though he was in pain, he would likely recover well. His eyes told another story, however. They seemed huge in his pale face, and as blank as pale green glass. He wasn't looking at the doctor but at some distance beyond, where fire and clamour and terror reigned, and he didn't answer when Major Robertson spoke to him, asking his question several times.

Sometimes gas cases lost their voices for a few weeks and developed a terrible cough, but Adams's eyes were not burned or swollen. Major Robertson glanced at Catherine. She knew what his look meant — deaf-mutism was one of the symptoms of shellshock. Not that they were supposed to use the term, in case it was simply strain and exhaustion which rest might cure. Catherine had a feeling that Adams's case was more than that. She'd seen too often that blank stare.

She thought of the journey he had made from shell-hole to the First Aid Post, the stretcher-bearers floundering in the mud; a horse-drawn wagon bumping him to the Advanced Dressing Station at Hooge Chateau, then on the rattling ambulance here to Remy Farm. And then where? To a forward centre behind the lines where shellshock cases were treated. To Number 59 General Hospital at St. Omer? She shuddered at the thought. There had been terrible bombing there in

September. Five nurses had been killed in the raids on Number 58 hospital; Number 59 had been bombed, too.

Perhaps she could suggest the hospital at Boulogne to Major Robertson. Lieutenant Adams would not survive a night of bombing. And she doubted whether the regime of rest, hot food, and exercise would cure him. Catherine looked at the young man again. He was frozen and made no response as Major Robertson examined the wound, not even the tiniest movement. When Catherine put on a fresh dressing, it was as if she were handling a marble statue, his flesh was so cold. She made him lie down. Sleep might help, as would the quarter grain of morphia.

'Best keep an eye on him,' Captain Robertson murmured to her. 'I'll send him to Number Seven at Boulogne, but he won't be back, I'll warrant. England for him and long-term care — very long, I should say.'

They went across to look at Lieutenant John Lestrange who had received a shrapnel wound to his neck. There was a bloodstained dressing on the side of his neck which needed changing. The fragments of shrapnel would have to be extracted in surgery — as soon as possible.

John Lestrange lay quite still, only his eyelids fluttering as he heard the voices above him. It was an unremarkable face, Catherine thought, rather thin, the pencil moustache looking like an ink stain against the pallor. His mouth was clenched tight, his lips a line of pain as if he were fighting not to cry out. His eyes opened suddenly when she straightened the tartan coverlet, and she saw that they were very dark, almost black. She smiled but he only stared back at her, his mouth still clenched, and then his eyes closed again. *Not another one*, she thought. They were all so young and so damaged.

You didn't need to be in the trenches to know the truth of war. It was out there in the constant rumble of the guns like distant thunder which seemed to come closer, ready to break over their heads at any time. You heard the enemy planes which roared in the dead of night, sometimes in pairs or squadrons, terrifyingly close. You lay in bed, expecting to be blown to smithereens at any moment. CCS 17 had been bombed in August, the tents wrecked, wounded patients killed, dead men killed again.

War was out there in the flares of light shining in the night sky, warning that death was abroad. It came closer, heralded by the hollow, lonely sound of a train whistle bringing the wounded from the trenches. It was here in the rows of graves in the cemetery, in the smell of putrid flesh, in the lime pit where the severed limbs were thrown, in the foul odours of trench foot and dysentery, in the iron tang of coagulated blood, in the smell of chloroform and carbolic. It was present in the malignant violet of flesh poisoned by gas gangrene, in the bubbling discharge of gas from ravaged bodies, in the young face half blasted away, in the deadly grey pallor of dying men. In the bloodstained bandage across the blind eyes; in the haunted eyes looking into hell; in every eye.

Lieutenant Carstairs, she thought. Time to see him, though he would not see her. He had no eyes. He would see nothing again. Who would tell him?

John Lestrange recovered well, apart from an expected mild fever after surgery. The diagnosis was not shellshock. Major Robertson thought that he was certainly suffering from what was termed general nervous debility or neurasthenia. Lestrange's manner was distant, though his eyes were not blank. More absent, Catherine thought. He was something of an enigma. He smiled when she took his pulse or temperature, changed his dressing, or asked how he felt, but it was a detached smile, merely for the sake of politeness.

She asked about his family. It often cheered a patient up to talk about the possibility of going home to recuperate, but John Lestrange only answered briefly that his family was in the Yorkshire dales. That made sense. He was a lieutenant in the 57th West Lancashire Division which had been part of the action at Passchendaele. He had been in the mud which jammed their weapons, blinded their eyes, choked their mouths and sucked at their boots so that they could hardly make any progress. No wonder he had not much to say. She had met others like him whose emotional detachment was a different kind of damage from those who raved and screamed, and somehow more chilling.

He told her of a father and grandmother at home, but he doubted that he would go all that way to the north of England. He'd rather stay in France. He desired to be back on duty as soon as he could. She wondered if he would be fit enough but did not say so. She suspected that his fear of being thought a coward was as great as any fear of going back to the Front Line.

There was talk of the push in November to capture Passchendaele Ridge — the push which would drive back the Germans, the push which would make sense of the sacrifices of those first and second battles in which casualties had been enormous. Catherine had seen them, caked in black mud, shelled, shot and gassed.

Could this coming third battle atone for the dead, and the drowned, too? She doubted it, as she pictured them lying out there in the shell holes or hanging from the barbed wire under the enormous darkness. She saw that some were eager to get back to their comrades, whom they felt they were letting down. Not to seem windy, that was the thing, but others were afraid, and who could blame them? She saw it in the eyes of those who were discharged, deemed fit to return to their battalions. There were those who pleaded not to be sent back, but most said nothing.

In the officers' ward, they chaffed each other and joked with the nurses, but when Catherine was on night duty, she heard weeping sometimes and then whispering, and sometimes the dead midnight silence was broken by a harrowing cry. Someone dreaming of what had been and what was to come. In the privates' ward, the soldiers sang the old song about the barbed wire where their dead comrades had hung during the Battle of the Somme, but when silence fell, they looked away from each other. Hands plucked at sheets and sometimes a broken sob might be heard then a rough, kindly voice would shout, 'Cheero, lads, tea's up! Never say die.'

And then they were gone, the young men whose wounds she had dressed, whose temperatures she had taken, whose tears she had wiped. Gone to Le Havre or Boulogne. Gone back to Blighty. Gone back to their units. Gone to their graves. Some she forgot, but Catherine always remembered Lieutenant Adams. He had been taken, blank-eyed and still mute, to Boulogne, from where Major Robertson believed he would be transferred to a hospital in England. And Catherine remembered Captain Minton, of course, who had died from his head injury. Major Robertson had operated, but the wound did not heal, and infection took hold. The Red Cross had sent a telegram to his parents. Mrs Minton had held his hand and the captain's father, stiff in his black suit, holding his top hat like a man queuing for the opera, had wept in the corridor, turning to her, unaware of the tears running down his sunken cheeks. His only son.

Catherine didn't forget John Lestrange entirely. It was the manner of his leaving that she remembered from time to time. Major Robertson had recommended a convalescent hospital, but Lieutenant Lestrange had been collected by some French friends, a young man and a very attractive, elegant and slender young woman — a married couple, she guessed, who had arrived in a very smart car. Lieutenant Lestrange, their old friend, was going to convalesce at her house, the young woman told Catherine, before he had to return to the Front. He might have gone to the convalescent depot in Trouville by the sea, which was where many soldiers recuperated, but judging by the obvious wealth of the young couple, John Lestrange would be very well looked after. He had not been particularly sociable, preferring to smoke and read by himself, rarely talking to the other officers. He occasionally smiled in that detached way he had, but Catherine had noticed the distaste in his expression when he heard someone raving or screaming, and how he had watched with a kind of frozen intensity as Lieutenant Adams had been taken away. Perhaps it was fear in his eyes, she thought afterwards. She could not blame him for that.

'I'll look after him,' the young woman said, smiling up at John Lestrange, 'feed him up.'

Her accent was charming, her mouth wide and red-lipped, showing neat white teeth. Sabine, she was called. Sabine with short dark hair which fitted her head like a cap. She had dark, humorous eyes, and Catherine saw how John Lestrange's face was transformed as she and her companion approached him in the reception where he was waiting. He looked joyful, she thought. It was the first time she had seen that light in his eyes.

The young man, Raoul, took his bag, and the young woman took his arm, looking up fondly at John Lestrange's face.

Catherine noticed that he had left his coat and followed them to the exit. He turned at her call.

'Thank you,' he said, offering his hand. After a moment's pause, he added with a half-smile, 'You have been very kind. I hope you get some leave, too. It's been … well, good luck.'

She let go of his hand. 'To you, too.'

John Lestrange was wounded again at the Battle of Estaires in April 1918, where the West Lancashire Division held its ground against fierce German attack, but Catherine hadn't known anything about his part in that battle. By then the Casualty Clearing Stations were on the move. In March, Catherine had joined CCS 45. Shellfire, shrieking and crashing, tearing through the air, had driven them to Aveluy, then Doullens, as the waves and waves of German troops swept across the shattered land towards Arras.

Catherine also hadn't known that Captain Leo Beaufort of the 2nd Devonshire Battalion, the man she loved, had been deployed to a place called Chemin des Dames. His last letter had said that he was soon going south with the IX Corps for refit and recuperation — *And jolly well about time*, he had written. The Devonshires had been in action at the Somme and Ypres and had suffered terrible losses.

Chemin des Dames was the name of a ridge fought over by both sides in the third Battle of the Aisne, where Leo Beaufort was killed on the 28th of May in an iron hurricane of bombardment which had crushed Leo Beaufort, his Commanding Officer, 27 other officers and 552 men. The whole battalion had been awarded the Croix de Guerre for their gallantry.

Catherine only found out about his death from the newspaper sent by Cousin Marjorie in a parcel of comforts from home. Not that Marjorie knew anything about Leo Beaufort. No one did. They had met when they were both on leave in London. Catherine had stayed with her friend, Pat Sinclair, another nurse who worked at CCS 44 at Brandhoek. Catherine liked Pat, who was a sturdy, no-nonsense, practical nurse, engaged to a colonel twenty years older than she, with whom she intended to have as many children as would fill a country house — ten at least, she said. Leo Beaufort was a friend of the colonel's family, twenty-five to Catherine's twenty-four years. The attraction was mutual and instant as a flame. In a teashop in Kensington, they had stared at each other, astonished, knowing, yet speechless, until they laughed. It was joy, uncomplicated and pure.

The thought of him had sustained her throughout the long hours on duty, throughout the misery and hopelessness that came in with the waves of casualties. His letters sustained and reassured her. Her letters, he wrote, gave him hope amid the ruin and waste. *After the war ... after the war...*

And then he was dead, and the flame of love fallen to ashes.

She had been his secret. There had been an understanding with a girl before the war, he had told her, more between his parents and their close friends... Well, he'd liked her, of course. They were friends and he had drifted into that understanding without knowing what he wanted or, indeed, what Lucy really wanted. It was assumed — on both sides — that there would be an engagement, but then the war came and somehow, he hadn't wanted to commit Lucy or commit himself.

'And what about Lucy's feelings?' Catherine had asked. She had felt wounded. She should have known this before they sat in that teashop — perhaps she would have quenched that flame. As she asked the question, she withdrew her hand from his warm touch. They were sitting in the park, in the silent shade of the trees. A private space where, for a time, the war could not find them.

Leo took her hand again and held it fast. 'It's not the same — not at all the same for her — or me,' he urged, his golden eyes burning into hers, his hand now squeezing almost too tightly. 'This is once in a lifetime, my darling Cathy. It will never come again. Nothing else matters — just us, now, this moment.'

And she forgot Lucy, whose other name she never knew, and they spent three nights in a small hotel, Captain and Mrs Beaufort, but when she read the obituary, she felt she had not known him at all.

Another splendid Devonian has been killed in France. I refer to Captain Leonard Philip Beaufort, Devon Regiment, only son of Colonel Sir Philip Beaufort, J.P., and Lady Beaufort of Beech Grove House, Honiton. The deceased did excellent work during the war, being mentioned in despatches and awarded the Military Cross. He was killed in the late action at Chemin des Dames in the Battle of the Aisne. Over 500 men of the 2nd Devonshires perished at Chemin des Dames…

A stranger, she thought. Leonard, not Leo. Leonard conjured up such a different sort of person. Sir Philip and Lady Beaufort. They hadn't known her. Had splendid Leonard Philip, their only son, been ashamed of her? She looked down at the newspaper.

...known by a wide circle of friends, Leonard was a fine fellow in every sense of the word, and the news of his death will be read with the deepest regret. The greater sympathy will be extended to his parents, the remainder of his family, his fiancée, and close friends in the severe loss they had sustained...

A fine fellow, Leonard Philip. So many friends. A hunting and shooting man who would have turned fleshy with age. Not Leo. The man she loved was tall with a fine-featured face, the face of a poet, with the sensibilities of an artist. His courage was trained, tempered as steel, bendable but not breakable. She thought she had known the core of him. Perhaps she had not, and those nights in his arms had been instigated by a desperate need for release, for some comfort before he went away. Perhaps Lucy would have done just as well. Lucy, who earned the newspaper's pity, and who had the right to grieve for the man she had expected to marry.

After that, Catherine hadn't cared much what happened to her. On the move, evacuated to Amiens, with the medicines, the equipment, the personnel, the tents packed into lorries, then rattling along the rutted roads, she just concentrated on the tasks in hand. Night duty was best. Fitting her gas mask, her tin helmet, putting on the dark coat and gum boots, taking the dimmed lantern, doing the rounds, focusing on the men, reassuring, comforting, returning to the tents, falling into bed, half-waking, listening to the guns and the planes, crawling from bed to receive more stretcher cases. Stretchers in the corridors, under the tables, working in the smoky lamplight, hearing the bombs falling, not thinking, not remembering, just doing. Then doing it all again, night and day, not knowing daylight from midnight, until she was injured by shrapnel during a bombing raid and was evacuated to the Nurses' Convalescent Home at

Hardelot, ten miles from Boulogne and from there to Dorset and Cousin Marjorie.

To Dorset, with scars on her forehead and neck, and invisible scars too deep to heal.

2

'It would do you good, you know — don't waste all you've been through, all you've learned. You're not meant to waste away in Dorset, Catherine. Up and doing, that's the thing.'

Catherine looked at Pat Sinclair's broad, strong face. Her brown eyes were anxious, but she was smiling encouragingly.

'You're needed, even now, especially now with this wretched flu. We've lost nurses at the hospital. Dear Lord, it's a plague — imagine surviving the war and dying of this. It's a matter of d—'

'Don't say duty, Pat. I know, I know, but I don't want to come back to London. It's not the influenza. It's reached us — not in the numbers, of course, but everyone knows about it. Anyway, I'm thinking of taking up a post at the hospital in Dorchester, so I'll be doing my bit.'

'Good for you — I'd have liked us to be in London, though. You could have stayed with us. I'm at my parents' house in Kensington. We could have had some fun.'

Catherine changed the subject. 'What about the colonel? What'll you do when he comes back?'

'Oh, George — he's still in Germany. I'll have to give it up, of course, but not for a year or so...' Pat looked sad suddenly. 'It's a beast, though, isn't it? When I think of the ones we lost. Do you remember Captain Beaufort — you know he came with George that time?'

Catherine's heart seemed to stop; she looked down at her cup and managed to say, 'Yes, I think so.'

'Tall, rather handsome — he was killed at Chemin des Dames. George said it was a terrible business — slaughter.

Captain Beaufort — Leonard — was engaged, you know, to a girl in Devon. So sad for her. So many — so many.'

Catherine couldn't speak. *Leonard. Not Leo.* They sipped their tea in silence until Pat said, 'Ah, well, we'll never forget, but we've got to go on — otherwise it was all for nothing. I daren't think like that.'

'No, neither dare I. I must go, Pat or I'll miss my train.'

They parted at the entrance to the Dickins and Jones department store where they'd met. Catherine had said it was too far to go to Kensington. She hadn't wanted any reminder of that tea there with Leo, but nowhere was safe. Her polite inquiry about the colonel had exploded in her face. She had promised to go up again to see Pat, but it was a promise she would not keep. She could not listen to news of Lucy again, to hear of her grief at the loss of her fiancée. Pat believed that they'd been engaged. Leo had said it had been an understanding — well, it was near enough, she supposed, in landed families. To hear it again would be unbearable. She had read Leo's letters over and over, and she had believed in his love. Now, the uncertainty haunted her.

Where to go? What to do? She had told Pat that she would take a post in Dorchester, but her reason for that choice was too stupid. Honiton was near to Dorchester and she had gone to Honiton by train to look at Beech Grove House. She hadn't been able to help herself. And she had seen a very fine car drive through the impressive gateway. Sir Philip Beaufort, she thought, or Lady Beaufort. Lucy, perhaps, who belonged there, who was their intended daughter-in-law. Bound together in grief.

The anguish of loss overwhelmed her so completely that she thought she might collapse right there in the street. She must never go there again, she told herself, but she knew that if she were in Dorchester, she would go, she would torture herself. She would want to knock on the door and tell them that their son had loved her and that she had loved him. To speak it aloud, to prove to herself that Leo had loved her. Half mad, she had been, and all those feelings of loss and pain had come back with Pat's unthinking words during tea.

Nor did she want to go back to Cousin Marjorie's. Marjorie was a dear, but she didn't know about Leo. Like Pat, she thought that a new post would be just the ticket. Catherine knew that Marjorie hoped that she would meet someone — a doctor, perhaps. Catherine would marry, have children, be happy. Catherine couldn't imagine such a life. She couldn't imagine any life.

But there was nowhere else but Marjorie's cottage. And it was too cold to stand here in Regent Street. She had plenty of time to get the train from Waterloo. She had just wanted to get away from Pat. She could walk down the busy street and look at the shops; she could go to a gallery or a museum; she could walk to Waterloo. Nothing appealed and when a taxi came and a well-dressed young couple got out, she took it and looked back at the couple, the young man with his arm protectively around the young woman's shoulders. She was looking up at him. A snapshot of love. Tears sprang to her eyes. The booking hall was crowded, but Catherine already had her ticket. She didn't want any more tea. Smith's bookstall, then. As she walked, she couldn't help thinking about the ambulance trains, hundreds of them, which had arrived here, bringing the wounded from the base hospitals in France — poor, irreparably damaged Lieutenant Adams, perhaps. Where was he now? Here was where the sailors had travelled to Southampton to take ship. She stood still. And here, Leo

Beaufort had come in from Devon to take a train to Folkestone and his death. All his passion for life extinguished, his burnished eyes closed, the body she had loved mangled beyond repair. She felt her breath clot in her throat and shook her head to banish the image. She knew too much. If only she could stop thinking about him.

Someone knocked her in passing. 'Oh, I do beg your pardon,' a man's voice apologised.

'My fault. I'm in the way.' She looked up to see a face she thought she knew.

'Nurse Sisley, how extraordinary — how very nice to see you.'

John Lestrange. 'It is extraordinary — how nice to see you, too. I hope you are well.' She saw the stick. 'Oh, I am sorry.'

'Arras, September 1918 — nearly lost my leg, but a brilliant doctor saved it. I don't mind the limp. Are you all right? You look rather white.'

'I'm fine, just rather harried by the crowds.'

'You are going for a train?'

'Yes, I'm going down to Dorset. To Abbotsbury. I live with my cousin Marjorie, who brought me up.'

'Lovely part of the world. Are you still nursing?'

'Not yet — I'm thinking of a post at the hospital in Dorchester. Nothing is settled yet. You are back home in Yorkshire?'

'Oh, you remembered. I'm on my way to Euston. I've been in — I say, would you like a cup of tea? You look as though you need some, unless your train is due?'

It was the last thing she wanted — to take tea with a former patient, someone who would want to talk about the war, but how could she say no? He looked strained about the eyes, somehow. She remembered how dark they were, and the pain he had endured. And his leg at Arras, where so many had died. To refuse seemed mean. It would only be for half an hour or so. She could put up with that.

'Yes, I've half an hour, I think, but I mustn't miss my train.'

He smiled. 'I won't let that happen. I'll walk you to your platform.'

Catherine sat at the table while John Lestrange fetched the tea. She watched him. She hadn't liked him much, she remembered. He was so detached, and he had seemed so cold in his reactions to the suffering of some of the shellshock cases, but then he had been injured, and he had been at Passchendaele. However, he seemed genuinely glad to see her. She wondered if he had been in France with his wealthy friends. She asked him when he came back with the tea.

'Yes, I've just got in. I was staying with my friends, but my father thinks it's time I came home. I know he's right, but —' a fleeting look of pain in his eyes — 'ah, well, I must do my duty to him.'

After that, they talked haltingly of the lovely French countryside, the lovely Dorset landscape, the sea not far from Abbotsbury, the unseasonably cold weather — it had snowed in March, and it was bitterly cold for April. Catherine didn't dare look at her watch during the silences. John Lestrange's friendly mood seemed to have changed. His eyes had the absent look she had noted when he was on her ward. He didn't look happy.

She looked at her watch at last. 'I must go — my train will be leaving in ten minutes. You mustn't come with me. I know the station very well.'

'Yes, all right. It was lovely to see you again. I remember how kind you were. I'm sorry I was so — so ungrateful.'

'But you were not. You thanked me when you left.'

'Did I? I felt ashamed afterwards. I thought I'd been a bit of a bear in the ward.'

'It's understandable. You were in pain. Are you now?' she asked, thinking of his change of mood.

'It comes and goes — just a nuisance, really, and my neck wound healed, thanks to you. I was lucky, I know. So many were not...' He looked away across the crowded tearoom. She was about to bid him goodbye when he said, 'What happened to that lad? Adams — the one who was out of his mind?'

What an odd question, she thought, an image of blank, pale green eyes suddenly before her. 'Lieutenant Adams?' she asked. John Lestrange nodded. 'He was sent to England for further treatment. I don't know where. I hope he's...'

'Yes, I hope so, too, but some are — incurable — they say.' His mouth twisted in agony. 'So many losses — so much — damage.'

Catherine couldn't bear any more. She stood. 'I must go.'

He stood and shook her hand. His eyes had that absent look again. 'Yes, of course.' Then he surprised her again. 'Could I write to you?'

She wanted to refuse. She didn't want to hear from him. He was too damaged, too odd, a stranger, but she hadn't the heart. She gave him Majorie's address.

Then she left him. If she took the post in Dorchester or anywhere else, she'd tell Marjorie not to send on any letters from Yorkshire. Unkind, but she couldn't cope with outpourings of loss and pain, if that was what he wanted to write.

Catherine didn't take the post at Dorchester Hospital. She knew she should do her duty, but she couldn't bring herself to it. The weeks passed. She and Cousin Marjorie settled into a cosy, domestic routine, gardening, cooking, shopping, knitting, church on Sunday — a routine which filled Catherine with a lethargy of the mind which she couldn't shake off. Marjorie was glad of her company and forbore to give advice, but she did suggest that Catherine might like to join the church flower rota or teach the Sunday school. The vicar, a former army chaplain, was still young at thirty-six — and single. Catherine might partner him in tennis in the spring.

Catherine laughed. 'Partner,' she said. 'No fear.' And Marjorie laughed, too, rather ruefully. Marjorie was funny because she was so obvious, but Catherine realised the danger of becoming so entangled in village life that she might be trapped into a relationship which she had no right to contemplate — those three nights in the hotel meant that she could not engage herself to someone else. She could not live a lie. Anyway, it was time to go. Go somewhere away from the memories of Leo and the temptation of Honiton. The question was, where?

The answer came in a letter from John Lestrange. She saw that it was postmarked Hawes. *Yorkshire*, she thought, and dreaded opening it, but Marjorie had handed it to her. Not that Marjorie was inquisitive, but it would look odd if she didn't open it and odder still if she took it up to her room.

While Marjorie poured the tea, Catherine opened the letter with her knife. She need not reply for a while, and she could write platitudes about the weather and the countryside — and put him off writing again.

'Oh,' she exclaimed as she read the first paragraph.

'Bad news?' Marjorie asked.

'No, it's just surprising. An offer of a job — a private nursing job up north in Yorkshire.'

'Someone you know?'

'Yes, a man called John Lestrange, a patient of mine when I was at CCS Seventeen. I didn't know him very well, but I saw him in London when I went up to see Pat.'

'You didn't say.'

'It didn't seem important. It was just a chance meeting at Waterloo. We had tea, talked a bit, and I got my train. He said he would write to me —'

Marjorie was delighted, 'Oh, do you think he's fallen for you?'

Catherine couldn't help laughing. That was typical of Marjorie, who so wanted Catherine to marry. A spinster herself, she had a rather romantic view of the married state, which Catherine knew was born of long-ago disappointment. Marjorie's own fiancée, a curate in London's East End, had died of typhoid. However, the possibility of a love affair between herself and John Lestrange needed to be quashed immediately. 'I've no idea. I certainly didn't fall for him. He was hard to get to know — sort of closed-up. Remote. Troubled, I suppose, but then he was badly injured, and he was still troubled when I met him again.'

'Is he the patient — for the nursing?'

Catherine glanced down at the letter. 'No, his grandmother — she's elderly and infirm, it seems, and they want a trained nurse to look after her.'

'Well-off, then.'

'I imagine so. The address is Raven's Gaze Hall — what a strange name. In somewhere called Ravendale.'

'Sounds substantial.'

'Sounds remote.'

'Quiet. Peaceful, maybe. What will you do?'

'Not my sort of thing. I mean, a private nurse to a wealthy old woman! I'd be some sort of servant, and it's so far away. I'd rather stay nearer to you.'

'But it's a chance, something different — while you make up your mind about what you really want to do. I'm not blind, Catherine, dear — you don't know what you want. And why should you, after all you've seen and done? You'd take that post at the Dorchester Hospital if you really wanted it. Maybe it's too soon to join a busy ward again. This could be a halfway house, so to speak, and the distance might give you perspective. A quiet place — to restore you.'

'I don't know.'

'Does the letter say how long they want you for?'

'No.'

'Well then, say you'll do three months as a trial period to see if you and your patient are well suited.'

'Perhaps they'll want someone to commit to longer.'

'In that case, don't go. It's perfectly reasonable for you to state your terms. They might be landed gentry, but you are a highly experienced nurse who has served her country — not a kitchen maid. It's not the nineteenth century.'

Catherine laughed. 'Well said, darling. I have served my country, and I can tell them what my terms are.'

'Then you'll write and say you'll try it?'

'Let me sleep on it.'

Catherine didn't sleep much that night. She appreciated the wisdom of Marjorie's robust advice, but it was John Lestrange who alarmed her. Suppose he did have some idea about her? But, no, it was impossible. He hardly knew her. He didn't seem that keen on going back to Yorkshire, and he'd just come from his friends in France. Perhaps he was only making a duty call and wouldn't be at Raven's Gaze Hall for very long. Three months, then, and if it didn't suit, she would come home. Maybe it would help her decide what she wanted to do with the rest of her life before she became so entangled in flower rotas and Sunday School that she would not be able to break out of them.

3

Bennet Lestrange put down his pen, shook the pounce over the paper — an old-fashioned way of drying the wet ink, but he liked the ornate silver pot which he always said carelessly was Georgian, a family thing from Rosemount, his great-grandfather's estate in Ireland.

The Georgian part was true. That he had had a great-grandfather must have been true, but he'd stolen the pounce pot when he had been a student in Dublin in 1888. A poor one, a sizar, educated for free in return for menial tasks. He waited at table on his tutor and fellow scholars whose families were rich enough to pay — not that he ever mentioned that afterwards. Dublin was very far away and his father, the respectable bank clerk, was dead, as was his mother. He never thought of the meek red-headed man with his vague eyes behind thick lensed spectacles nor of his tall, dark-haired, disappointed wife who had given her son his brains and his distinguished looks. His uncle, Michael Lyons, the wealthy bachelor grocer, had made Bennet Lestrange a gentleman of means, a gentleman of leisure, a gentleman of property, but he kept the pounce pot in memory of the man from whom he had stolen it. The man who had snatched it away when the young and gauche Bernie Lestrange touched it. His history tutor. Their dislike was mutual. It gave him pleasure to imagine the man's fat childish face creased in rage at his loss. He had learned in those years that revenge was a dish best served cold, and that anger was best served on ice. The theft was his farewell to the university, to Dublin, and to humiliation. He would never clean another man's shoes again. Had he believed in God, he might have blessed Michael Lyons. As it was, he simply forgot him. The name Lestrange, he kept, the only worthwhile inheritance from the bank clerk.

He read through what he had written. Very good. A scholarly, slim volume, but with some popular appeal. That was what he was working on. A task for a gentleman — the compilation of a dictionary of place names, their locations and origins. A *Devil's Dictionary*. For Bennet Lestrange collected the grimmest and most sinister names he could find. The Devil's Pot was his latest treasure, a deep chasm up on the fells, probably two hundred feet deep, its rocky entrance possessing the strange, rather menacing appearance of the head and jaws of a human skeleton. Two cavities, almost like eye sockets were created by two stone bars across the hole down which one could see only darkness. The devil was real enough to the folk in this remote dale. If they thought him a devil, then let them. The housekeeper was well paid to keep her mouth shut about the Lestrange family. The two other servants didn't count and there was only one neighbour to worry about. Money would talk if a reckoning came.

He took his watch from his waistcoat pocket. Nearly time. He went to the lancet window of his tower room. The lamp was burning even though it was not dark yet. The leaden sky promised rain, but there ought to be no delay. The car would meet her. She should be here soon. He looked down to the terrace below and watched the figure come limping out from the porch to stand on the steps, leaning on the walking stick, waiting to greet the guest. The figure didn't look up, though Bennet Lestrange knew from the grip on the stick that the man knew that the raven's gaze was fixed upon him.

Ah, another coming out to form the welcoming party. Another walking stick. Mama-in-law. Well, the old witch would want to be there. Her grandson couldn't be allowed to mess it up. Not that Bernard Lestrange would mind. He would put it all right soon enough and the guest would be flattered, disarmed, and charmed, even, into fulfilling their wishes. Mama didn't look up, either. She'd know he was there. She stood perfectly still, too, resting easily on her stick, the pose of a woman who knew exactly what she was doing and what she wanted. Cessation of hostilities for the time being. They wanted the same thing.

He and the motionless figures below waited as dark descended. He turned up the lamp. Let her see the welcome of Raven's Gaze Hall.

It was late afternoon in February when Catherine alighted at the station. No one else got off at Hawes Junction in Garsdale. She was to be met and taken to Ravendale — wherever that was. She had studied a map. Ravendale was marked but didn't seem to be anywhere. There was a road, some scattered houses, and quite high up, according to the contours, was marked Raven's Gaze Hall. Marjorie had been enchanted by the romance of the names: Mouse Sike, Rowantree Gill, Fea Foe. 'Land of giants,' she had said, grinning delightedly.

'Starvecrow Farm, though,' Catherine had said, her finger on the map, 'sounds grim.'

But Marjorie was not to be put off. It would be an experience — quite unlike anywhere dearest Catherine had been. High Flust. Whatever could that mean? Butterbeck sounded lovely. Catherine hadn't answered. Her eyes were fixed on the remoteness of Raven's Gaze. She felt cold just looking at it.

She stood uncertainly on the platform until a man wearing a rough tweed coat and cap approached and simply asked,

'Raven's Gaze?' He nodded briefly when she said yes and led her to a car. She couldn't see much of the landscape in the gathering darkness, but felt a steep descent down a bumpy lane and onto a main road, where she made out some cottages. There was a sudden right turn into a narrower road, a glimpse of a wall by which a fingerpost indicated 'Ravendale 2', the sense of great hills, and then what seemed like a farm track up which the car rattled. It came to a sudden stop for the driver to get out and open a gate, the soaring hills now closer, the sound and faint glint of water tumbling down, distant lights — farmhouses, perhaps on the lower slopes.

'How far away is Raven's Gaze?' Catherine asked.

The driver didn't answer. It felt too awkward to repeat the question, so she continued to look at out of the window. Where on earth was she? She had never seen such emptiness, and then as the car went round a bend and began to climb, she saw a distant single light high up, as if it were hanging in the sky. The car slowed and there was an impression of looming bulk, as though they were approaching a fortress guarded by two massive gateposts with huge stone balls on them.

'Raven's Gaze,' said the driver, speaking for the first time as he drove through. 'Be there in a minute or two.' He had an odd, hoarse voice, as if he were not used to speaking. She hoped the Lestrange family would be more welcoming.

The tower, a commanding, battlemented structure, was rather forbidding, she thought, though the light seemed to shine a welcome. As the car drew to a halt, she saw that the tower was adjacent to the house, where lights shone through stone mullioned windows, and a man and a woman were waiting on the steps of the porch. The lights of the car showed her John Lestrange, leaning on his stick. He looked forbidding, too, almost scowling. The woman was older, very tall and upright, but she had a stick, too. The grandmother, Catherine assumed, noting the severe black dress reaching to the ground. No grandfather had been mentioned by John Lestrange, so she was a widow, perhaps.

John Lestrange held open the car door and Catherine stepped out to meet him. He was smiling now, saying how glad he was to see her, and introducing her his grandmother, Mrs Whitenow, who echoed his sentiments. John Lestrange took Catherine's suitcase, and she was led through the stone porch, through the huge iron-studded oak door with its heavy iron hinges, and into the hall, where a fire burned in a vast inglenook fireplace with seats at each side. It was illumined by oil lamps and candlelight.

Everything seemed to be on a huge scale — a wide staircase with large newel posts topped with massive acorn terminals rose up to the shadows above; two faintly gleaming suits of armour stood to attention at the foot of the stairs; a very long table on which stood heavy branched candlesticks filled the left-hand wall, and she could see great iron-studded doors which must lead to other rooms. The walls were covered in patterned tapestries, and the floor was stone flagged and cold underfoot, but she noticed some heavy rugs here and there and a curious block of stone tucked into a recess under the window. The smell was of age, burning wood and smoke. She heard the sound of a clock mechanism winding up and then the chimes striking the hour while she stood looking at the elderly woman in her long black dress.

Nothing seemed real. She felt as if she had stepped into a play in which the actors had forgotten their lines, though Mrs Whitenow was looking back at her with light grey eyes that had a curious glitter in the lamplight. Her face looked as if it were a mask carved from ivory, she was so still, though there was a curious half-smile on her pale lips. A distinguished-looking woman, Catherine thought, noting the crown of silver hair piled on her head. And rather formidable. She and John Lestrange seemed to be waiting, then she heard a bell which seemed to come from upstairs. Footsteps. Another character entered the scene just as the clock chimes died away. She looked up to see a tall man dressed in a tweed suit coming down, smiling his welcome.

'Miss Sisley,' he said, 'how very good of you to come.' He took her hand and bowed. 'I am Bennet Lestrange, John's father, and you have met my dear mother-in-law, Mrs Whitenow. I do hope you will be able to help her.'

He was very like John, with the same height, very black eyes and dark hair brushed back from a high, broad forehead, but he was more confident, more smiling, more charming.

'Let me take your suitcase. I'll show you to your room. We must save Mama's poor leg.'

'So, thoughtful, Bennet, dear. Take a lamp, Miss Sisley. I shall retire for my nap soon. I shall see you at dinner. In the meantime, I'll have tea sent up to your room.'

Catherine accompanied Bennet Lestrange to the stairs. She was aware of the silence below. John Lestrange had not spoken during the exchange with his father, and he wasn't speaking now, but after a few moments she heard Mrs Whitenow say, 'Go and ask for the tea, John, dear, and then I'll see you in the drawing room for a few moments.'

Catherine was on the first landing now. Bennet Lestrange stopped and pointed to a recess under the window. 'The place of skulls,' he said, 'supposedly the skulls of ancestors of the Clayburn family who lived here before the Whitenows — murderous lot, the Clayburns. Kept their victims' skulls here until some sensible person chucked them in the lake. It has a dark history, does Raven's Gaze Hall.'

Bennet Lestrange didn't wait for an answer but led Catherine up the next flight of stairs, pausing to show her the iron-studded door to a staircase leading to another floor. 'There's an ancient stone spiral staircase behind that door which leads to the servants' quarters. Lumber rooms now. Plenty of servants in the days of glory. The few we have all live out now, which is why we need you.' They carried on down a long corridor. 'Your room's next to Mama's in case she needs you in the night. Bathroom just opposite.'

He opened the door into an oak-panelled room. Catherine preceded him and put down the lamp on an oak chest. She saw that the fire was lit. Bennet Lestrange put her suitcase on the four-poster bed and lit some more lamps, which dispelled most of the shadows, though some lurked in darker corners. The light caught the highly polished panels on which were carved sprays of leaves, thistles and rosettes.

'I'll build up the fire for you,' Bennet Lestrange said, putting on more logs and arranging a mesh fireguard in front. He saw her looking round. 'The panelling is seventeenth century, as is the door there.'

Catherine saw that there was a door just to the right of the bed. She wondered whether it connected to Mrs Whitenow's room.

'It leads into what was called a "powder room" in the eighteenth century, where a lady might freshen her coiffure. I thought you might use it as a sitting room. There are a desk and chair in there, where you might want to write your letters — there is a box in the hall where we put our letters for collection.'

'Thank you. That is very thoughtful.'

'I know the value of solitude, Miss Sisley.' He smiled again. 'You might wish to escape from us sometimes into your own private space. As for the fire, Mrs Slee will make it up in the mornings, or the girl who comes to help her. You may light it whenever you need to.'

Catherine looked at the neat pile of logs and the spills in their brass jar. 'Thank you — it all looks very comfortable.' She looked at the scrolled masks and birds and a row of grotesque little faces peering back at her on the cracked plasterwork over the fireplace.

'The plasterwork belongs to the seventeenth century, too.'

'I've never slept in a room so old.'

'I hope you are not of a nervous disposition, Miss Sisley. These faces look a bit grim in candlelight.'

'I think I'll cope,' she answered lightly, 'after what I have seen at the Front.'

He smiled, but she wondered if there was a hint of irritation in the glance he gave her. His black eyes were momentarily hard in the lamplight, but his words belied that. 'Of course, my dear, you have seen much suffering. I'm sure you will cope here. Mama won't be a difficult patient. Well, I'll leave you to unpack. I'll give you the full tour another day. Ah, and here is your tea.'

Catherine got a glimpse of the woman who had knocked at the door and handed the tray to Bennet Lestrange. A thin, sallow face, a whispering 'Sir' and then she was gone.

'Mrs Slee, our housekeeper and a very good cook, as you will discover at dinner. Seven o'clock.'

Gracious, she thought after Bennet Lestrange had closed the door. What to make of them all? Bennet Lestrange was the dominating presence, that was clear. But she thought of Mrs Whitenow's aristocratic, rather severe face. She looked like a woman who could stand up for herself. John Lestrange hadn't responded to his father or grandmother. He didn't seem happy here — he wanted to be back in France with his friends, she supposed. Well, the house looked rather grim. There was something oppressive about that vast hall. A dark history, Bennet Lestrange had said. She could believe it.

Catherine saw Bennet Lestrange in the hall at seven o'clock. He watched as she came down the stairs. She felt self-conscious under his gaze, hoping that her simple black dress passed muster and at the same time annoyed with herself for caring what he thought of her appearance. She had dressed with care, remembering Bennet Lestrange's words about the servant's quarters: "That's why we need you." The high neckline of her dress and the curls on her brow concealed her scars. She wore her pearl earrings and the single strand of pearls which Marjorie had given her when she was eighteen. The dress fell to her ankles, revealing neat black shoes with a wine glass heel.

Catherine had no intention of being treated as a servant by Bennet Lestrange, who was dressed impeccably in a black jacket and trousers. Gold glinted on the starched white of his cuffs, and she noted the patterned cravat at his neck. He had dressed with care, too. She felt a nervous flutter at her throat as she reached the last stair.

She was reassured when he smiled and said he hoped her room was comfortable and then escorted her to the dining room beyond a great oak door. Another panelled room. Another vast fireplace of carved stone. A very large round table with a shine so deep that the candlelight was reflected in its surface. Places set for three. Silver and crystal winking in the candlelight. A wine jug chased in silver with matching wineglasses. And Mrs Whitenow already seated. Entirely composed, in another deep black dress and a black lace shawl, with diamonds winking at her throat and on her fingers.

Bennet Lestrange pulled out a chair and Catherine sat down. She had no idea what to say.

'I am sorry that John cannot join us,' Mrs Whitenow said. 'One of his headaches, Bennet.'

'Ah, I am sorry, too. We must do our best to entertain Miss Sisley.'

And entertain, he did, through the soup which Catherine found delicious and the tender roast chicken and vegetables, brought in by a mostly silent Mrs Slee, who nodded briefly when she was introduced to Catherine. Bennet Lestrange took charge of the food and wine at the head of the table, and she found herself relaxing as he told her that the Pele tower at Raven's Gaze had been built in 1550, at the time when the Scots Rievers raided houses in the northern counties. Its walls were six feet thick, built to withstand a siege. Supplies were kept in the basement room, now the kitchen for the house which had been built against the tower. On the tower's second floor, there would have been a solar — a living room for the inhabitants. This was Bennet Lestrange's library and study now, he told her, and the top floor was his bedroom and bathroom. It was his fancy to keep the light burning at the window in his library.

'A welcome for weary travellers,' he said. 'I hope you saw it from the road and felt it so.'

'The house has been in my family for generations,' Mrs Whitenow said. 'I married my second cousin, James Whitenow.'

'It was sold to Mr Jeremiah Whitenow in 1780,' Bennet Lestrange said with a smile at his mother-in-law.

'A distant connection of the Clayburn family, which is why he bought the house,' Mrs Whitenow explained.

'The Clayburn family owned it from 1571, having turfed out the original family — a duel fought and won by a Clayburn. You will see the armorial shields of that noble family in the drawing room, decorated with the family motto —'

'*Fide non Fravde*,' interrupted Mrs Whitenow. 'Faith not fraud. Not especially applicable. The Clayburns were not exactly noble, as my son-in-law well knows. He has no doubt regaled you with the story of the skulls. In the seventeenth century, Myles Clayburn had a reputation for violence.'

'So, he did. Sad to say that the Clayburns dwindled away as time went on until they lost their money.'

'No son,' Mrs Whitenow said.

A curt response, Catherine thought, sensing some hidden messages in the exchange between the two, despite the smiles and the politeness.

'The house was built in 1635,' Bennet Lestrange continued smoothly, 'and rebuilt after the Civil War. Jeremiah Whitenow got a bargain, I think, when he acquired it from Elizabeth, the last daughter of the Clayburns who lived here with the pigeons and the rats — and the resident ghost.'

Catherine laughed. 'Of course, you must have one.'

'The usual tale told by the credulous Dales folk. A servant cruelly wronged by a Clayburn, exercising his *droit de seigneur*. Threw herself down the spiral staircase. I haven't heard her moaning, but who blows out your candle when you go up to bed? The ghost on the stairs.'

'That's an old tale, Miss Sisley. Pay no attention. No one's had their candle blown out in my time or my husband's, unless someone has foolishly left open a window.'

'You are right, of course, Mama. No ghosts here, Miss Sisley.'

'Only the living ones.' Catherine thought that was what Mrs Whitenow murmured, but she couldn't be sure. Mrs Whitenow took a sip of her wine.

Bennet Lestrange did not answer that, though Catherine could tell by his swift glance at Mrs Whitenow that he hadn't liked her comment. He looked at Catherine, smiling again. 'But we are braced against evil spirits, Miss Sisley. In one of the attics is what the locals call a dobbie stone, which is a huge hammer hanging from a beam. It's said to prevent evil spirits or the ghost — if a house has one — from disturbing the household, so we are safe, as Mama tells us, unless the stone should fall, of course, and bring about our decline. Not likely after three hundred years, however. I am very interested in local traditions and place names, which I collect — the curiouser, the better.'

'Raven's Gaze is an unusual name for a house. Where does it come from?'

'Simply from the old tower, as far as I can determine, which is thought be built on the site of a gibbet — a hanging place, the legend being that ravens preyed upon the corpses left to rot.'

'That's a rather grisly notion,' Catherine said.

'It is indeed, but more prosaically, the name may have been left by the Danes whose battle standard bore an image of the raven. Take your pick.'

'The Danish standard, please.'

Bennet Lestrange smiled at her. 'Very sensible.'

'And are there ravens still?'

'Oh, yes. To see a raven on the roof is to know that there will be a death in the house — so the locals tell me.'

'It's superstitious nonsense, of course, Miss Sisley,' Mrs Whitenow said acidly.

'A superstition, of course, but a prevalent one amongst the locals, and one thinks of Lady Macbeth's words —' Bennet Lestrange obviously fancied himself an actor, for he declaimed, '"The raven himself is hoarse that croaks the fatal entrance of Duncan under my battlements." And she was right. His entrance was fatal.'

'That may be so, Bennet, in a play. I doubt you'll see many ravens hereabouts, Miss Sisley. They are not very common these days. You are most likely to see crows and rooks.'

If Mrs Whitenow thought that her tart response would end the subject, Bennet Lestrange simply ignored her. 'The Clayburns used it as a Christian name once upon a time; Myles Clayburn had a son called Raven — another rogue. The one who seduced the serving maid, probably. And you find it in the records from time to time, right up to the last century.'

'An unusual first name.'

'Never used now,' Mrs Whitenow interrupted sharply, 'nor ever again.'

'If you say so,' Bennet Lestrange said, and a silence ensued for a few moments. Catherine felt that sense of something unspoken again. Bennet Lestrange poured more wine and continued, 'Yes, it is rare, as is the surname, Whitenow — uncommon in these parts. It is more common in Lancashire. It can mean "white enough" or simply "servant of White" with no name of his own.'

'I suppose we all came from nothing and nowhere,' Mrs Whitenow said drily, 'even the Lestranges. From the word "stranger", I believe.'

'Yes, one of the Norman invaders. French blood in these veins, Miss Sisley.'

'Very much diluted.' Mrs Whitenow smiled as she raised her glass of white wine to Bennet Lestrange. 'And what about Miss Sisley? I'm sure she wishes to know whence she came.'

'Very good. Yes, Sisley — from the Latin Caecilia, feminine of Caecilius, meaning blind. However, there is plenty of light in your fine eyes, Miss Sisley. I am sure you can see a long way.'

Catherine felt uncomfortable under his gaze, but managed to reply, 'I think so. I have never needed spectacles.'

'Very good. I pride myself on my excellent sight. I can see a long way over the hills and beyond, even to the future.'

'Oh, indeed, dear Bennet misses nothing,' Mrs Whitenow murmured.

Bennet Lestrange smiled at Catherine. 'And as to Caecilia, one thinks of St Cecilia, too, the patron saint of musicians. Are you musical, Miss Sisley?'

'Not really. I had piano lessons as a child, but I haven't played since before the war.'

'A pity. Still, your name is like mine, from the Norman.' Bennet Lestrange raised his glass of red wine and smiled at her. 'Good blood, I'm sure.'

'I am tired,' Mrs Whitenow said a while later, suddenly putting down her glass and interrupting Bennet Lestrange's flow of words. He had begun to tell Catherine about Byron's reference to the ravenstone in his poem "Manfred", where the raven flitted over milk-white bones. Apparently, Byron's ravenstone was a stone gibbet in Germany. A bit gruesome, she thought.

If Bennet Lestrange had served at the Front, he might not be so fascinated by bones.

'I know you are enjoying yourself, Bennet, but enough talk for tonight,' Mrs Whitenow said firmly. 'Miss Sisley must be tired, too. I should like to talk to her for a few minutes alone in my room. We'll leave you to your port.'

'Very good, Mama. You are quite right. I do beg your pardon, Miss Sisley. It is thoughtless of me. You have had a long journey, and here I am rattling on when there is all the time in the world to tell you the history of Raven's Gaze.'

'I am suddenly tired,' Catherine said, 'but I should like to talk to Mrs Whitenow.' *And remind her that I am pledged only for three months*, she thought, *not all the time in the world.*

'You can light my way, Miss Sisley. There are lamps in the hall.'

'I am sure Miss Sisley will see her way — even in the dark,' Bennet Lestrange said, laughing, as he went to open the door for them.

Catherine followed Mrs Whitenow, who gave a silent nod to Bennet Lestrange as she left the room. Clearly, she did not share her son-in-law's sense of humour. The candlelight shivered in the draught as Bennet Lestrange held the door for Catherine. She caught the sardonic gleam in his eye as he bowed to her. 'Good night, Miss Sisley, and sleep well.'

Catherine noted Mrs Whitenow's difficulty in climbing the stairs. She gripped the banister tightly with her left hand, putting the weight on her right leg, and used her silver-topped stick to steady herself and raise her painful left leg. When Catherine glanced at her sharp profile, she saw how tightly compressed her lips were. They stopped on the first landing, where Bennet Lestrange had pointed out the place of the skulls. Mrs Whitenow breathed out, but she didn't speak. The next staircase was shorter, but it was clear that Mrs Whitenow was in pain and was not going to speak of it. Catherine was not surprised. She had already surmised that Mrs Whitenow was not a woman to admit weakness.

The bedroom, lit by oil lamps, was larger than Catherine's but similarly panelled. There was an enormous fireplace in which the fire was lit, and there was a huge four-poster bed in the centre with a carved oak headboard.

'That bed dates from 1584. So many births and deaths have taken place there. I shall, no doubt, die in it.'

'Not yet, I hope,' Catherine said conventionally, somewhat disconcerted by the turn of the conversation.

'My son was born in it — the heir of the Whitenow family. He died young. A fine boy who would have been a fine man. It is a great sadness to me.'

Mrs Whitenow went to sit down by the fire and motioned for Catherine to sit in the opposite chair. She felt the tiredness wash over her again but did as she was told. What was she to say about the dead son?

'My daughter married Bennet Lestrange, whom she met in London — I still think of him as the stranger, but we must rub along as best we can. My daughter died of fever not long after the birth of my grandson.' She pointed to a silver-framed photograph on the mantelpiece. Catherine could only make out the outline of a woman with a young child in her arms.

'John?' Catherine ventured, but Mrs Whitenow was staring into the flames.

After a few moments, she answered, 'Ah, John, yes, John, my grandson.'

'He looks very like his father.'

'Yes, he is a Lestrange, of course. You think them handsome?'

'Well, yes, I suppose they are. Distinguished-looking, I should say.'

'Bennet would like that epithet, I'm sure.' Catherine noted the dry tone. Mrs Whitenow continued, 'But John is not as robust as his father. His headaches worry me — some legacy of the war, I imagine. He never talks of it.'

'I think many young men keep silent about what they saw. The memories are too terrible, and I think they fear placing a burden on those they care for.'

'Perhaps you might help him. You have seen so much and looked after so many. I should like him to stay here, to be at home where he belongs.'

'I don't know if I…'

'I don't wish to burden you, Miss Sisley, but if the opportunity presents itself — should he wish to talk to you, you wouldn't turn away?'

The question felt like a trap, but politeness to her new employer was necessary. 'Of course not, but only if John wishes.'

'He spoke very highly of you and how grateful he was for your care. He thought you and I would get on famously. I am sure we will. And now, I must tell you about my wretched leg. It is an ulcer. I have had a nurse come from Hawes, but it is a long way for her, and I don't think it is getting better.'

'May I see it?'

'Tomorrow morning will be better. It is too late now, and you need a good night's sleep. I am very glad to have you here. Take a lamp to light your way.'

Catherine took a lamp and turned back to bid Mrs Whitenow goodnight. The old lady was staring at her, her pale eyes glittering.

'I think you will suit Raven's Gaze very well. Good night, my dear.'

Catherine was relieved to be alone in her room. She felt physically drained, but her mind was buzzing as she undressed. What an extraordinary evening. So many impressions. Bennet Lestrange and Mrs Whitenow, perfectly charming to her, solicitous, in fact, repeating how glad they were that she had come. But … there was certainly hostility between them. All that business about Jeremiah Whitenow getting Raven's Gaze for a bargain price as if there had been something dishonest in it. That word "acquiring" was odd. She thought that Bennet Lestrange would choose his words very carefully. And then there was Mrs Whitenow's observation that everyone came from nothing. Perhaps Bennet Lestrange was not as well born as the Whitenows. They were perfectly polite to each other, but it was the politeness which was meant to conceal dislike. She wondered if Mrs Whitenow resented her son-in-law. He was alive and her children were dead, and there was something arrogant about him, she had to admit. The stories he told were much to the detriment of the family into which he had married and whose property he seemed to command. Perhaps Bennet Lestrange held the purse strings.

And then there was John, now the heir to Raven's Gaze. Mrs Whitenow seemed fond of him, concerned about him, but the question about her turning away from a request for help had been unfair. She hoped she had not been brought to Raven's Gaze under a pretence. The ulcer on Mrs Whitenow's leg was probably straightforward, but if John were suffering in his mind and she was expected to treat him as a patient, she did not want that. She wasn't qualified for that kind of nursing, and it was not what she had signed up for. Three months, though. Not long.

She turned down the lamp on her bedside table and lay down. It was so quiet that she could hear the wood crackling and shifting in the fire, and the flames that leapt up created flickering shadows on the wall. She closed her eyes, willing herself to sleep. She was too hot suddenly and pushed the heavy counterpane off, but that didn't help. She would not sleep. She knew that feeling all too well — the exhausted body, the band of pain round her forehead, the burning wide-open eyes, and the whirling brain.

She got up, pulled back the heavy curtain and opened the iron-framed window which was set in the lights of the larger mullioned window. The cold stung her fevered cheeks. Raven-dark, she thought. No moon, no stars, and the wind soughing in the trees below. And there, down in the valley, was a pinprick of light. Some distant farm, she imagined, where someone was awake as she was. Impossibly distant. The remoteness of Raven's Gaze struck her again, along with a feeling of desolation. The ache in her heart made it worse. *Oh, Leo*, she thought, *why am I here?*

She found some aspirin in her handbag and climbed back into bed to take them. As she drifted into sleep at last, Mrs Whitenow's words about ghosts came back to her: *Only the living ones.* Whom had she meant?

4

Catherine ate a solitary breakfast served by Mrs Slee in what she called the parlour. Catherine complimented her on the previous night's dinner.

'They like their food here,' Mrs Slee responded, her sallow face expressionless. 'Nowt's wasted, though. Very careful is the mistress. Still, tha'll get on all right with 'er. 'Imself, too, I dare say.' Then she was gone.

Someone else whose words bore more than one interpretation. Catherine wondered at the addition of "himself, too." Hard to detect, but was there a hint of mockery in the phrase about Bennet Lestrange? There was a rough insolence about Mrs Slee which she couldn't understand. Neither Bennet Lestrange nor Mrs Whitenow seemed the kind of people who would brook insolence from a servant. From what Bennet Lestrange had said about the "days of glory", servants must be hard to get, even in this remote place, she thought as she went upstairs to see Mrs Whitenow, who took breakfast in her room. Words in this house were decidedly ambiguous. Slippery. Hard to tell what the speaker really meant. And what did it mean that there was no sign of Bennet Lestrange or John? Did John habitually skulk in his own room like an unwanted guest? Or, a more disturbing thought, was he actually ill and meant to be a second patient, as Mrs Whitenow had hinted last night?

Mrs Whitenow was waiting with her leg propped up on a footstool. Catherine answered her questions about how she had slept and her enjoyment of her breakfast and asked in turn if she might examine the leg. She carefully removed the bandage, under which she saw the open wound on the inside calf of Mrs Whitenow's left leg. She knew that the condition was common in the elderly, usually a result of poor circulation, and this wound was very red and the skin around it swollen.

'It is such a nuisance,' Mrs Whitenow said, 'and it doesn't seem to get any better.'

'It is infected and needs treating every day. The important thing is cleaning and keeping the fresh bandages clean. I'm sure it will improve with careful monitoring. Your doctor has left disinfectant and fresh bandages?'

'Yes, the weekly nurse made sure that there were plenty of supplies — in the top drawer of that chest.'

'Good. I'll fetch some hot water from the bathroom. I noticed a bowl in there. Presumably your nurse used that?' Catherine had noticed the familiar kidney-shaped enamel dishes, too. They had used them at the CCS, but she must not think about that. It was unfair to compare the condition of an elderly lady with the sufferings of those at the Front. Mrs Whitenow couldn't know the horror of it all. She must not dwell on those times now. She had chosen this post, and she must fulfil her duties. In the bathroom, she picked up a couple of the dishes as well.

Catherine bathed the wound gently and patted it dry with a clean towel. 'May I arrange for a good supply of towels for this? I need a clean one each time.'

'I'll arrange it with Mrs Slee. The laundry goes out to Hawes each week. I'll order more towels from the draper's shop there.'

Catherine took the gauze and calico bandage from the drawer, as well as the familiar Dakin's solution which she'd used so often on wounds — wounds deeper and more poisonous than this. She poured a quantity into one of the bowls and used the gauze to wash away the dried blood and to irrigate the wound. The only noise Mrs Whitenow made was the slightest intake of breath. Catherine placed the used gauze into another bowl and took another to dry the wound.

'It needs to air for a minute or two before the dressing goes on. I'll take these bowls back to the bathroom. The used gauzes can be burnt. I suggest this old bandage go on the fire, too.'

Catherine emptied the bowls and rinsed them with hot water. She looked in the mirror at her own white face and tired eyes. She took a deep breath and returned to Mrs Whitenow to dress the wound with more gauze. Then she wound the bandage tightly. 'The pressure is good for the sore, and you should try to keep your leg raised as much as you can until we see an improvement.'

'I can see that you are a very good nurse, Miss Sisley. I feel very fortunate that you are here.'

'Thank you. I think you will feel much better in a few weeks.' *Six weeks*, perhaps, Catherine thought, as she took the gauzes and the old bandage to the fire, and then she could probably leave. Mrs Whitenow would not need daily care after that. Her heart felt lighter and her desolation dissolved. She was free to go whenever she wanted.

'That is very good to hear. Sometimes the pain is very bad.'

'What did your doctor give you?'

'Laudanum to help me sleep, which I do not like. It makes one so heavy-headed in the morning. And morphine tablets if I need them.'

'Do you now?'

'Again, I dislike them. I shall manage.'

'Would you like a couple of aspirin? They are useful and relatively harmless. I have some here.'

'Thank you. I will take some.'

Catherine handed her a glass of water and two tablets. 'You should rest now. Please do keep your leg raised on the footstool.'

'I will. You are very thoughtful. I do hope that I didn't offend you by talking about John. I know we didn't bring you here to minister to him — it's just that I worry so.'

Catherine felt guilty then. Mrs Whitenow was just an elderly lady, anxious about her only grandson. 'Not at all. Of course, if John wishes to talk about the war, I will listen.'

'You were there, my dear, so you will understand him better than I or his father can. One feels rather at a loss.'

'I understand.'

Mrs Whitenow nodded graciously. 'I knew you would. Now, you must go out for some fresh air. Bennet will be delighted to show you round the house and grounds. You will find the air very bracing. I hope you like walking.'

'I do. I look forward to seeing everything.'

Mrs Whitenow's smile did not quite reach her pale eyes, 'Oh, Bennet is the expert now. He has all the history at his fingertips.'

Catherine fetched her hat and coat from her room and went downstairs to find Bennet Lestrange waiting in the hall to tell her about the huge block of slate under the window. A former mounting block, he told her, though how it got inside the house, he hadn't a clue. It was referred to affectionately as "the tomb". The acorn terminals on the staircase were supposed to prevent a house from being struck by lightning — another local superstition. But Raven's Gaze Hall had withstood storm and tempest for centuries, and, as far as he knew, no inhabitant had been struck down by a lightning bolt — a hefty club, more likely. He pointed to the silent figures in their armour. 'Friendly fellows, they are, no trouble at all. No one knows where they came from. Mama's illustrious ancestors, maybe. Fitznow and Fitzthen, I call them — born on the wrong side of the Clayburn blanket, I'll bet.'

He showed her the calf-bound Bible box with iron-bound corners on the huge oak chest in the hall. The box bore the initials "M.C."

'I doubt Myles Clayburn was much of a Bible reader,' he observed, 'too busy clubbing his neighbours to death and thieving their property. Clayburn probably disposed of his bride in there, as in the old poem. You know it?' Catherine shook her head. 'Samuel Rogers' "Ginevra" — a bride trapped in a chest. Nothing left of her but a few pearls, an emerald, and her wedding ring. Nothing in there now, I assure you, but some old blankets. No one has opened it for years. "Kist" by the way, is the local word for chest. It is very interesting to hear the number of dialect words used hereabouts.'

'I suppose people don't travel very far in this remote dale.'

'That is true, Miss Sisley. Thank goodness, however, for the railway. I like a trip to Lancaster or Manchester from time to time. I have business there which necessitates my absence, though this dale is where I am at home, and this house, of course.'

He showed her the drawing room with its stone floor, huge fireplace and tapestried settee and chairs — two hundred years old, but younger than the hall tapestries, which were from the Stuart times. Ill-gotten gains, naturally. The four quarrels of stained glass in the mullions dated from 1571. He told her about "Drunken Dick" Clayburn — an Oxford man like himself, a poet whose work was now lost — who had dropped dead in this very room. The drink, it was said.

'The Whitenows were a pallid lot after the wild Clayburns. Made their money in the textile trade in Lancaster.' Catherine caught the sneer in the word "trade". He obviously regarded tradespeople as beneath him. "Servant of White" — she remembered his words about the family name. Bennet Lestrange clearly thought a lot of himself.

'Not that they kept their fortune,' Bennet Lestrange was saying as they left the room. 'Now, the kitchen and the delightful Mrs Slee.'

Bennet Lestrange took her through one of the iron-studded doors and down a short corridor, through another door into the barrel-vaulted kitchen, the basement floor of the tower. Catherine noted the first steps of another stone spiral staircase which must lead up to the next floor of the tower — Bennet Lestrange's library. The smell was of herbs and hams which hung from iron hooks in the ceiling, of new bread, and of something meaty cooking. There was a huge stone fireplace with great pewter chargers on the mantel and an in-built kitchen range, the kind she recognised from Marjorie's cottage which was built on a smaller scale. *Land of giants*, she thought, looking at another huge oak table piled with crockery, mixing bowls and silver cutlery. Mrs Slee was there in her apron, stirring something in a pot. At their entrance, she turned, bobbed her head, and murmured, 'Sir.' Catherine thought she caught a glint of malice in her stony eyes.

Bennet Lestrange certainly had the history at his fingertips. He showed her the so-called "Devil's cupboard" with its carved door, dated 1694. A spice cupboard, it seemed, placed there by one "Robin the Devil", another scion of the Clayburns, notorious for fighting, whoring and gambling his fortune away.

'We're respectable now. Isn't that right, Mrs Slee?'

'Aye, so tha says.'

'I do; I do. And don't you be telling Miss Sisley any different. Mrs Whitenow needs her nursing skills, so you look after her, please.'

'Whatever tha says, sir.' Mrs Slee turned back to her stirring. Catherine noticed what thick arms and large hands she had for such a thin woman. Like a man's hands. And they were puckered with red marks — scars, she thought, wondering what had happened to this odd, taciturn creature whose manners seemed to border on insolence to her master.

But Bennet Lestrange only smiled and pointed to a huge black cauldron filled with coal. 'The witch's cauldron. Actually, a kail-pot, once used for making gallons of cabbage broth for the workers. Mrs Slee, however, is stirring her lovely chicken broth to which we look forward at lunch.'

If Mrs Slee resented the comparison to a witch, she did not show it and made no answer.

'Not given to utterance, our Mrs Slee,' Bennet Lestrange said as he led Catherine through another door into a stone-flagged corridor, where there were more doors, 'but I don't employ her for her eloquence. Her niece, Betty, helps out, too, and her brother does the garden and other odd jobs. It was he who picked you up in the car. You will see him about. No use speaking to him — he's deaf and understands nothing. However, Mrs Slee is a very useful woman to have around. We'd starve else. Her cousin at Moor Rigg farm provides all our butter, milk, eggs and chicken. One of the Garsdale farmers keeps pigs. Everything else comes from Harper's shop and warehouse at Hawes Junction. We have plenty of supplies if we cannot get out.'

'Are there times when you can't?'

'In the depths of winter sometimes — we were cut off for six weeks once. It can happen in spring, of course, but not this year, I hope.'

Catherine shuddered inwardly at the thought of six weeks at Raven's Gaze without being able to get out and with three people she hardly knew. But she'd be gone before winter.

'Boot room, gun room, cold room, various pantries, cellar door,' he said as she followed him down the stone-flagged passage, where they stopped at another staircase. 'Backstairs for the servants in the good old times. Mrs Slee and her niece use those, but you will use the main stairs, of course, my dear, as a professional lady.'

Catherine felt a frisson of annoyance at his patronising tone, but she couldn't think of anything to say, and then they were at another door at which he stopped to pluck a tweed cape from a peg. She noticed the theatrical manner in which he swirled it onto his shoulders. A large low-crowned black hat completed the portrait of the interesting man he wanted to be seen as. The word "vain" came to her unbidden as he turned to open the door and bowed her out.

They took a gravel path lined with trees to the front door, where Bennet Lestrange swept up his arm to show her the hills: West Baugh Fell, Wild Boar Fell to the north, Scargill Moor to the northeast, and to the north, there was the village of Mallerstang, where legend had it that King Arthur's father, Uther Pendragon, had lived in Pendragon Castle. There was a story that King Arthur had come back to this land at the end of his days and that he and his knights rested now in a cave deep in the rock supporting Richmond Castle. Tennyson's island-valley of Avilon, perhaps. 'A pretty tale,' he said, smiling down at her. He would take her there one day. She did feel the enchantment of the place. Lonely, yes, but magnificent, too, so unlike the much softer Dorset. She couldn't help smiling up at him — he was a very good storyteller.

His arm came back from the heights to point out the road by which she had come up, where she could see the tops of trees and the little derelict chapel which looked like a toy church from a distance. He showed her the barn with its archer holes or slits, the old dairy, and the pigeon house. Pigeons had provided good meat once. There was a curious little stone building with yet another studded oak door which had once served as a kennel for the sleuth hounds kept for tracking fugitive raiders.

'A lawless land in those times — one feels a certain nostalgia for the days of the chieftains, lords of their fiefdoms disregarding petty authority. Look closely as you are passing, and you will see the bullet holes in the door. Legend has it that they were made by a Clayburn who came home with his mastiff to find a stranger at his door. He shot him, no questions asked. We have no dogs now — I have my gun to ward off strangers. I'm a good shot.'

'I can't imagine you get many strangers coming up here.'

'No, but I like to know who is coming onto my land, and I like to keep my hand in. My neighbour, Archie Bell, holds a shoot down at his lodge, Grouse Hall. Always a treat to go there. However, I must take heed of Mrs Whitenow's wisdom and shut up for a while. She's always telling me that I go on too much. I will ask Mrs Slee to bring you coffee in the parlour, for I must get back to my work.'

He steered her back to the front porch. 'Ah, I cannot resist. One last thing to bore you with —'

Catherine felt mortified that he should think she wasn't interested. 'Please don't think that I am bored. I have enjoyed it all, and I am grateful for your time.'

'I was only teasing. Come and look.' He pointed to circular stone relief set above the porch roof, where she could just about discern some lettering.

'What does it say?'

He spoke in Latin: 'NVNC MEA, MOX HVIVS/SED POSTEA, NESCIO CVIVS.'

'What does it mean?'

His searching look discomfited her. She noticed for the first time the curiously bruised look of his long-lidded eyes. There was something dark and secret about them which gave her a sense that he knew something about her, something that she did not know herself.

'Now mine, presently his, afterwards I know not whose.'

And with those enigmatic words, he left her. *John*, she thought. It would all be his one day, but hardly soon. Bennet Lestrange looked strong and healthy. Perhaps he worried, too, about his son and the headaches, and whether John would marry and have a son to inherit Bennet Lestrange's beloved Raven's Gaze. She could understand that.

You will suit Raven's Gaze very well. Mrs Whitenow's words came back to her. She hoped they were not thinking of a match between her and John. She had better be on her guard.

Catherine took lunch with Mrs Whitenow in the parlour. The chicken soup and fresh bread were delicious.

'I take a nap in the afternoon, Miss Sisley. Of course, you are free to do as you wish. You might like to take a walk. The family library is next to the dining room, so if you would like to read, you must see what there is in there that might suit you.'

Catherine helped Mrs Whitenow upstairs and saw that she was comfortable. 'It is my job,' she said when Mrs Whitenow told her that she could manage. 'I know that you can manage, but perhaps you have managed too well, which is why the leg isn't healing as it should.'

'You are a wise girl, my dear, and I thank you. Come and have some tea with me here at four o'clock.'

Catherine went to her room and went to look out of the open window at the soaring fells. In the immense blue sky, she saw a large black bird wheeling on the wind. *A raven surveying his fiefdom?* she wondered. It was such a beautifully clear day she could hardly think of it as an omen of death as Bennet Lestrange had said. He obviously liked to thrill with his stories of the wild past with its mysteries and superstitions. His very cloak suggested that he saw himself as an actor in a drama of his own invention. She wondered about his son. How different they seemed. But John had been at the Front Line — a terrible drama of someone else's making.

She felt the fresh wind on her face and breathed in the bracing air. The north was supposed to be always rainy. The weather might change, so it made sense to go out again and get her bearings. After all, she wanted to know how she had got here.

Wearing stout boots, her tweed coat, and a felt hat, Catherine started walking down the drive, thinking that she could perhaps walk as far as the railway station. She wasn't sure why, but it seemed like a good idea to know how she might make her return journey when the time came. However, as she walked, she felt terribly exposed, as if there were eyes on her. She stopped and looked round as if taking in the scenery, and as she turned, she glanced up at the slit of a window in the tower. Was he watching? And if he were, did it matter? Bennet Lestrange had a right to look out of his own window.

However, there was no other way to go, so she set off down the path towards the stone pillars she had seen when the car turned in. Further down the hill, she saw the low, grey roof of a house. Starvecrow Farm, she read on the wooden board fixed to a post at the end of the track. She looked along the track and saw that the house seemed to be tucked into a dip at the bottom of the fell which rose behind the roof. Another large black bird rose from the chimney pot as she looked. Surely not a raven. Mrs Whitenow had said they were rare. It might be a crow or a rook. She really had no idea. As it flew up, the sound it made was rather sinister, like mocking laughter. Did ravens croak? It certainly sounded hoarse like Lady Macbeth's raven, but there were no battlements on this roof. *What a desolate place*, she thought, wondering where the upwards path behind the house went to. How odd the names were: Raven's Gaze and Starvecrow. Both black birds — carrion birds. That was a rather horrible thought.

She walked on to where the road bent round a little and felt herself breathe more easily. No one could see her now from Raven's Gaze. She had been under too much scrutiny since she arrived, which was why she was relieved to be on her own for a while. Yes, Bennet Lestrange had been perfectly charming and Mrs Whitenow appreciative, but she felt they were assessing her. Mrs Whitenow's pale grey gaze and Bennet Lestrange's dark one unsettled her. However, they were perfectly entitled to assess her. She was a stranger, and their employee. *For goodness' sake*, she told herself, *buck up. You've been in far worse places. And you've seen far worse things than large black birds.*

The road straightened again, and she saw the ruined chapel by the trees, the tops of which she had seen from above. And there was the gate in the road which the taxi driver had opened. She remembered the sign which had told her that Ravendale was two miles from the road to the station. *Too far now*, she thought, and turned into the trees. It was only a small wood, but she was curious to see where the path led. It was very still, apart from the gentle rustling of the leaves. A bird sang somewhere, a thrush, she thought. She was aware, too, of the sound of running water, bubbling over stones, and then there was a clearing full of dappled light. She thought of Bennet Lestrange's talk of King Arthur, remembering Tennyson's words about how Arthur was taken "to a chapel nigh the field." There was something rather magical about this wood — the lovely quivering light, she supposed. Shadow and sunlight.

It was then she saw the figure seated on a fallen tree, his head in his hands. Something in his attitude suggested profound misery. At first, she hardly thought he was real, a ghostly knight in mourning for his king, but then he moved. She thought to retreat. This was private grief, whoever he was. Her foot disturbed a fallen twig, and the rustle caused the man to look up.

'Miss Sisley,' John Lestrange said, standing up and leaning on his stick. He did not look like his gleaming father this morning in his old tweed jacket and battered hat. In fact, he looked older, because of the deeply scored lines of pain about his mouth.

'I am so sorry. I didn't mean to intrude. Is your head troubling you?'

'Yes, I can't seem to shift this last headache, which is why I came out. I'm sorry I wasn't there for your first dinner. Father entertained you, no doubt. He is a great storyteller.'

'Yes, I very much enjoyed hearing the history of the house. He took me round this morning, too.'

'You met Mrs Slee?'

'I did. Her dinner last night was very good.'

'We're lucky to have her. She's a very good cook — my father likes the good things in life. I expect my grandmother told you about my headaches.'

'She did. She obviously worries about you.'

'Grandmother worries too much. Of course, I think about — then. So must you. I noticed your scar. Shrapnel?'

'Yes, a raid on the hospital, but it's not the same as for you and all those others.'

'Isn't it? We have the same scars. And not just the visible ones... You saw dreadful things —' He pointed in the direction of the house. 'They didn't... He didn't.'

'Does that make it worse?'

'I suppose it does... I don't want to talk about it to him. I'm not ready to talk about the future — yet.'

'I understand. That's why I couldn't commit to more than three months here.' She took the opportunity to give a gentle reminder.

The lines of pain turned into a smile. He looked younger now. 'I didn't do wrong by asking you to come?'

'Not at all. I think it will be a ... kind of break for me while I work out what I want to do next.'

'We're alike in that. Everyone seems in such a rush to advise, prompt, urge — you know what I mean? They don't understand a thing about it.'

Catherine knew what he meant. She thought of Marjorie, the tennis club and the vicar, but Marjorie had understood something of what she'd been through because she was wise and sensitive. However, she didn't say that. It would not be tactful and in any case, she didn't want to share confidences with John Lestrange, especially about invisible scars. She didn't know him well enough. She only said, 'I do. It's very hard to decide — we didn't know what future we would have.'

'Or if we would have one at all...'

She remembered that feeling. They had just been thankful to get through the days and nights, not daring to think ahead, not daring to think what it all meant and where and when it would end.

The silence was punctuated by birdsong. She thought of how sometimes in a quiet dawn or at twilight when the guns were silent for a while, you'd hear a bird singing and be astonished that it should sing in that ruined land. Did the bird know something you did not? It offered some hope there in the heavens above the blasted waste where hope had perished with the thousands of dead. She saw that John was listening, too, and no doubt thinking the same thoughts.

He looked at her with such desolation in his eyes. 'My brother and I used to come here. It's where we decided that we should join up — how little we knew. He was never to come here again... Nothing can ever be the same.'

'I'm so sorry. I didn't know — your — father and grandmother haven't mentioned him.'

'No. He was the favourite.' His laugh was bitter. 'They're left with second best. None of us speaks of him — I'd rather you did not say I told you.'

'I won't say anything.'

'Thank you.' He looked up to the high branches where the bird sang, and down again at her, 'And your patient? Do you think you will get along?'

Safer ground, she thought, and he knew it, too. 'Oh, yes. I can treat her leg. It will be much improved in a few weeks. When I go, it will be enough for her to have the local nurse once a week.'

'That is good.'

'She's very stoical.'

'She always has been. She and my father — two strong personalities. My father wants me to be here, to run things eventually. It should have been my brother. We own most of the farms in the dale and there's property in Ireland, and in Manchester and Lancaster. He's a wealthy man.'

'You're not ready?'

'Not yet. I will take over one day, but he always seems to be in the best of health. He's only fifty-five, and he has the business at his fingertips. I feel old in comparison. It's extraordinary — one went into it young and light-hearted and came out older, worn out...'

Catherine felt that, too, and she thought John Lestrange would find it hard to be under his dominating father's eye all the time after what he had endured, after the responsibilities he had been given. He had been a lieutenant with a platoon under his command. He had faced death daily and endured the deaths of his brother and his comrades. 'What would you like to do?'

'I have friends in London, and friends in — from — those days. It's...'

'Your father would prefer you to be here?'

'Oh, he's willing to let me off the leash for a week or so. I'm off to London tomorrow. There's a doctor in Harley Street. I'm consulting him about the headaches.'

'Oh, good. Well, I ought to get back. Mrs Whitenow wishes me to have tea with her.'

'I'll walk back with you.'

5

February became March. Catherine hardly knew how, because her days settled into a routine. Breakfast alone in the parlour, an hour with Mrs Whitenow, letters to write to Marjorie and Pat Sinclair in the little room next to her bedroom, a light lunch at which Bennet Lestrange sometimes appeared, an afternoon walk, tea with Mrs Whitenow, dinner with her and Bennet Lestrange. That was the only time she felt uneasy. She always felt as if they knew something she didn't, as if, as at that first dinner, there were meanings in their words she could not quite fathom. Their low voices often ceased when she came into the dining room, but, of course, they'd have private matters to discuss, she told herself. Once she heard John's name and his father's impatient, 'He ought to be here. Time's going on.' Mrs Whitenow hadn't replied. Catherine could not imagine sticking it out for another two months. She marked the days off in her diary. They seemed to be long days — and lonely ones.

'I do wish John would come home,' Mrs Whitenow said to Catherine one morning after she had dressed her leg. 'I didn't want him to be off again, and I hope he isn't tiring himself out in London.'

'He said he has a doctor in Harley Street.'

'Yes, he's supposed to be very good. He's expensive — expensive enough to cure the headaches, I hope.'

'Well, John seems to have faith in him and that will make a difference.'

'Of course, you are right, my dear Catherine. I have placed my trust in you, and I feel so much better. And it is good of you to talk to John. I don't want to seem impatient with him. It's just that I would like to see him settle to something. I think I understand something of what he has been through, but if he were to take an interest in the estate, it would give him a sense of purpose.'

'Would he like to pursue some other career, do you think?'

'He has never said so. Bennet would be delighted if John took an interest in something, even if it were not the estate. He has only ever wanted to see John happy and successful, and, of course, to settle down here — eventually. Bennet does not want to hurry him.'

'He was successful in the war — I mean, he was in the thick of it, leading his men into battle. Most of the lieutenants I came across were very young and very brave. Some were barely out of school and yet taking command of a platoon of men often older than themselves.'

'What a wise head you have on your young shoulders. I shall tell Bennet what you have said. Probably neither of us understands fully what John endured — or you, I should think.'

'Give him time. There is much to get over — the loss of —' Catherine sensed suddenly that she had stepped on thin ice. Mrs Whitenow was staring at her with an expression that was suddenly cold. A warning to step no further. She stumbled on — 'friends — so many losses. This new life takes a lot of getting used to.'

'Do you feel that?'

'Not exactly. I knew I should come back to nursing, but I wasn't sure in what way. I nearly took a post in a hospital in Dorchester, but then John's invitation came and my cousin, Marjorie, persuaded me that it would be the change I needed before I committed myself to a hospital.'

'And how do you feel now?'

'It's too soon to say. I feel as if I have only just arrived.'

'Well, you know you can stay for as long as you want to — even if I am very much improved. I do like having you here. We might have a beautiful summer in which you can just enjoy being here.'

'You are very kind, Mrs Whitenow, thank you.'

'We shall be very quiet for a day or two. My son-in-law has taken an early train to Manchester. He should be back tomorrow, but we will take dinner as usual.'

Catherine went back to her own room, feeling a little aimless. She looked out at the rain sweeping down the fell. She had a letter from Pat to read, and she owed Marjorie a letter and another to a nursing friend in Manchester. Pat's letter made her heart ache. She had written to say that her colonel, George, had come home on leave and that they were going down to Devon to see Sir Philip and Lady Helen Beaufort — Catherine would remember that their son, Leonard, had been killed in 1918. George had been very fond of him, and the Beauforts were, of course, still devastated...

The letter dropped onto the desk, and she stared blindly out of the window at the rain. *Leonard.* Oh, how far away Leo seemed, unreal as a dream. She didn't even have a photograph of him and when she tried now to summon up his beloved face, he would not come. She looked round the little room at the panelled walls, the fireplace with its carved stone mantel, the bookshelf, the rug beneath her feet. She was a stranger here, a stranger everywhere, a stranger to herself. It was as though she did not know who she was. She had known herself when she had been Nurse Catherine Sisley in the war. She had been terror-stricken at times; she had been filled with horror and pity, but she had known what her purpose was and to whom, in her heart, she belonged. To Marjorie and to Leo, to her patients, her colleagues.

She must go out, she thought, rain or no rain. She must walk fast and far. She must not sit here and weep, though she was tempted to fling herself on the bed in the other room and succumb to her grief and loss. She put on her mackintosh, hat and boots, and went out into the corridor. She was aware of the silence of the house. Only the clock was ticking in the hall, ticking into a future that seemed as much a blank as it had during those terrible days when if one thought of the future at all it was as if one were seeing only an unfathomable darkness ahead.

She paused at the door to the spiral staircase, which Bennet Lestrange had said led to the servants' quarters. It was surprising, she thought, that a man as wealthy as Bennet Lestrange had no servants to live in. No servants at all, really, only Mrs Slee, who lived in her cottage behind the house, and her niece who came from some other farm, and the silent gardener who had merely nodded vacantly when she walked by. The house had a dark past — perhaps the local people simply didn't want to live in it. In the gloom of the corridor, where it seemed suddenly cold, she could even imagine the ghost coming down from above to linger on the staircase. *Nonsense*, she told herself, but found herself lifting the door latch and putting her foot on the bottom step of the spiral, aware of a sudden rush of cold air coming down the steps.

She came to a long corridor lit by a skylight through which a grey, watery light spilled down. There were several doors which she supposed led into the servants' old rooms. It was bitterly cold. She thought of the poor girl who had fallen down the stairs, the girl who had been seduced by her titled employer, one of the wild Clayburns. Catherine had laughed at Bennet

Lestrange's tale. It hadn't sounded true, but here in this desolate corridor with its dark walls and stone floor, she could almost believe it. The first two doors opened to show little rooms with iron bedsteads, a couple of straight-backed chairs, a chest of drawers in each, and rolled-up rugs. She imagined young girls huddled in those iron beds, listening to the wind and rain, thinking of their drudgery tomorrow. One girl afraid of a saturnine face with hard eyes and hard hands, of footsteps blundering up the steps. She closed the doors. This was hardly improving her mood.

The next room was bigger, more of a lumber room where boxes and tea chests were stacked, but there were two white-painted beds — children's beds, she thought. John's and his brother's? The beds were stacked with more boxes. There was another skylight in the roof, and she saw that the sky was lighter now. The rain was stopping. She ought to go. She looked round the room and realised that in here the panelled walls were painted white. There was a white painted fireplace with a tarnished brass fireguard, and a narrow mantel over which hung an old cuckoo clock, the bird hanging down on its broken spring, and there was a rocking horse in the corner with a rather bedraggled mane and tail, wild eyes, and alarming nostrils. She had never had a rocking horse as a child. Not that she'd wanted one. They had always looked a bit nightmarish to her. This one did, too. There was a wicker perambulator, too, which looked as if it belonged to the last century. A nursery?

She felt the tragedy of it. A nursery where children played had become a lumber room, abandoned to dust and moths. She noted the cricket bat on the floor beside one of the beds, and the long leather bag out of which a sweater spilled and what looked like a school scarf with red and blue stripes. Perhaps Mrs Whitenow's son had played here, too. She wondered what had happened to him. How old had he been when he died? She wouldn't ask, of course. Mrs Whitenow had offered no more information after that first night, and, clearly, the death of John's brother was not to be spoken about. They had obviously been close, from what John had said about their joining up together. Two motherless boys. She didn't imagine Bennet Lestrange as a particularly loving father, and Mrs Whitenow seemed too austere. Strong personalities, John had said. Perhaps he felt crushed between them. No wonder he did not care for Raven's Gaze and preferred to spend time away.

It wasn't just the cold that made her shiver or the smell of unused things. There was sadness in this room, a sense of loss. Ghosts, certainly. Not the ghost of some tall tale from the distant past, but the recent ghosts of those who had lived and suffered in this room. She remembered that Mrs Whitenow had murmured those strange words, *living ghosts*. Had she meant herself and Bennet Lestrange? Had they been made ghosts by their losses? Not that there was anything ghostlike about Bennet Lestrange. He did not seem haunted at all. He relished the old tales, but maybe that was a way of avoiding the recent past, the deaths of his son and his wife.

She shouldn't stay. It was not her past to wonder about. She made her way to the door and froze when something hard skittered away from under her foot. When she bent down to look, she saw a toy soldier, a little lead figure in a red coat, holding a rifle in his hands. She pictured two little boys playing toy soldiers, imagining the battles they might win, whooping with joy as the opposing army's soldiers fell. Not knowing what would come. She turned to slip it into the long leather bag. Boys' things. There was no trace of John's mother here. No doll or toy to suggest that a little girl had shared this nursery.

She shut the door and went quietly down the stairs. She closed the staircase door and turned to find Mrs Slee standing there with her arms full of sheets.

'Explorin', are thee?' she said, her eyes narrowing. There was something disapproving in her tone.

Catherine was stung but controlled her impulse to retort that it wasn't Mrs Slee's business and answered breezily, she hoped, 'Yes, Mr Lestrange told me that the servants' quarters were up there. I was curious.'

'Nowt to see but rubbish up there. They should get rid o' the lot.'

'Won't those two rooms be used again?' Catherine was determined to keep up the conversation. She deliberately omitted any reference to the nursery.

'Nay, girls don't want to be skivvies nowadays — the war changed all that. An' besides — well, there's no need just for them two. I manage with our Betty's 'elp. I'm not 'avin' 'er goin' off to some factory. Did'st tha see the owd nursery?'

Catherine felt the heat at her cheeks. 'Yes, I peeped in. Nothing but lumber.'

'Well, I shouldn't be pokin' about up there, miss, if I was thee. Mrs Whitenow wouldn't care for it, an' the last room in that passage ain't safe. Plaster's comin' down, so be warned.'

'Oh, I didn't mean to be nosey, and I certainly have no need to go up again. Thank you for telling me. I shouldn't like to offend anyone.'

'Nay, well, tha'll excuse me for sayin', I 'ope.'

'Of course.'

Mrs Slee sidled away, leaving Catherine feeling rather uncomfortable. She really did hope she wouldn't cause offence to Mrs Whitenow. At the same time, there was something about Mrs Slee that disconcerted her. A warning to keep away from the old nursery? Well, she wouldn't go up there again. It was too sad.

Catherine did not visit the abandoned nursery again and Mrs Slee didn't mention the matter. Catherine felt relieved that she didn't seem to have told Mrs Whitenow, who did not refer to the upstairs rooms, but she felt uncomfortable, feeling that she had seen what she ought not to have seen, and she was afraid to speak of the nursery to Mrs Whitenow. It wasn't her business. And she felt awkwardly in debt to Mrs Slee, who had kept her secret.

However, she couldn't help thinking about the nursery, especially at night when she lay in bed, listening to the wind moaning and whistling. It was at night that sadness and emptiness possessed her, for she thought of Leo, too, and Raven's Gaze always seemed alien at night when she passed the suits of armour. Their closed visors gleaming in the lamplight gave the fleeting impression that they held the secrets of Raven's Gaze. On the stairs, her oil lamp threw huge shadows on the walls and on the place of skulls, and she always felt the cold most intensely when she passed the staircase to the old nursery. She was not afraid of ghostly tales, but she felt the strangeness of the house, its great age, and its secrets that she was not allowed to know. She missed Marjorie most at these times and longed to be home at the cottage, with its cosy rooms and familiar shabbiness.

Then John came back for a few weeks, looking better, more relaxed, and Bennet Lestrange organised excursions for the three of them. Catherine wondered if Mrs Whitenow had spoken to Bennet Lestrange about John and the need to give him time, for things seemed to be easier between them and at dinner the atmosphere was more comfortable. Bennet

Lestrange even asked about John's friends in London and what they had been up to, and John had spoken of his old schoolfriend, Freddie Hunter, and his fiancée, Alice, and how they had been house-hunting in Hampstead where they had visited Keats's house and taken a boat on the river to Richmond. Mrs Whitenow spoke of her visits to an aunt who had lived in Hampstead. Catherine told them about Pat Sinclair, who lived in Kensington and was to marry a colonel. She felt a pang then, but no one noticed.

The days were very often fine and if not, then Bennet Lestrange took them to some of the great houses and ancient churches in the area, telling them the ghost stories — the story of Wharton Hall, whose owner had been ruined by a visit from James I in 1617, and the one about Kirfit Hall, supposedly visited by Henry VIII when he was wooing Katharine Parr, and supposedly haunted by Anne Boleyn, who came to disturb the sleep of her executioner. John didn't say very much, but Bennet Lestrange could talk for all of them in his precisely pedantic way. He was always particularly charming to Catherine on these occasions, and John seemed content to smile and nod. Then John went away again, and she was sure that his father and grandmother were exercising the patience which John had hoped for. She remembered Bennet Lestrange's impatient words, and she felt rather pleased that perhaps she had played a part in John's improved health and spirits.

She sometimes went for a walk with John when he came home. They walked slowly because of his leg, but he didn't talk about it, though she guessed he was in pain. She would suggest that they sat for a while, and he would give her a look of gratitude for her tact. He didn't talk about the war very much, nor did he tell her about his friends in London. She once asked him about his friends in France, telling him that she remembered the young couple who had come for him.

'Couple?' he asked.

He didn't answer for a moment but looked up at the clear sky. She wondered if she had awakened some memory he regretted. It was often hard to know what was the right thing to say to John, but then he said, 'Oh, yes, of course, Sabine and Raoul. I haven't been back for a long time. Someday, perhaps … I don't know. There's father and grandmother…'

They walked on in what she thought was a rather strained silence until he turned to ask whether she was happy at Raven's Gaze, but he didn't ask how long she might stay. She smiled and said that she was enjoying her work, but she didn't refer to her going, either. Not the right moment, she thought, hoping to re-establish the mood of easy friendship that she felt had developed between them.

'I'm off to London, though, tomorrow. Is there anything I can bring back for you? Some books, perhaps?'

During John's absence, Bennet Lestrange asked Catherine if she would accompany him on one of his research trips. He told her about his work on his dictionary of place names and how the legends attached to the odder ones piqued his interest.

He drove her along a road that was parallel to the railway, which he told her went to Kirkby Stephen and on to Carlisle. He parked the car by some poor-looking cottages, and they walked up the fell.

'Now, a little further on we find the Devil's Bridge, spanning Hell Gill,' he told her. 'Superstition has it that the Devil flew down the fell and dropped his stones there, creating that hollow which the locals call the Kail Pot.' He laughed sardonically. 'One thinks of Mrs Slee up here, communing with her coven from Hag End — now there is a name to conjure with — the den of our fragrant Betty and her tribe. It is further down the fell towards Raven's Gaze, but I doubt you will be invited. They are a close lot who do not take to strangers, but they like my money. The devil is real enough to folk in this remote dale. Old superstitions flourish amongst the ignorant.'

They stood on the Devil's Bridge under which the water seethed and tumbled over huge stones which might well have been dropped by the Devil, Catherine thought. What a wild and desolate place. She looked round at the empty fells soaring above and back at the deep water, feeling that it was a place where you could believe in devils and witches. They walked on to a place called The Devil's Pot, where he pointed to the curious entrance which resembled a human skull. It was rather horrible, she thought, looking through the holes like eye sockets.

'Probably two hundred feet deep,' he said as they looked down into unfathomable darkness. 'Who knows how many unwary travellers have vanished into that darkness? How many bones lie there, forgotten? The mist comes down very quickly hereabouts. It would be easy to miss one's way.'

'I shouldn't like to come here at night,' Catherine said, feeling a sickening dizziness as she stepped back from the aperture from which a smell of decay rose.

'No, indeed. And you should not walk alone up here at any time. I shall always come with you if you wish to explore, and, naturally, the house is yours to treat as your home, except the top floor, if you please. It is not safe up there.'

She felt her cheeks redden. So Mrs Slee had told him. 'I did go up there. I am sorry. Mrs Slee told me it wasn't safe. I shall not go again. I was just curious.'

He smiled. 'If there is anything else about which you are curious, you only have to ask. I may not answer, of course. We all have our secrets — I am sure you have yours.'

He turned away as if nothing odd had been said, and she was forced to follow him back down the track to where the car was parked. He paused by the cottages to wait for her, and said, 'Rattenrow Cottages — where the people live with the rats — time they were pulled down.' He turned abruptly into a lane and took another path which seemed to lead to a rather tumbledown farmhouse.

'That is the Slee residence, Black Tarn Farm,' he said. 'No one there now, but Mrs Slee comes home when she is fed up with us or —' he smiled at her — 'has some black purpose on hand. And over here is the famous Black Tarn from which the house gets its name.' He led her to the edge of the water. It was as still and silent as Hell Gill was seething, and very, very black. It looked fathoms deep. 'They believe in witches up here.' He laughed. 'It is not only the sheep that have cloven hooves.'

Catherine looked down into the water, and she could imagine sinking down and down into its obsidian depths. There was something magnetic about its dark stillness that was disturbing.

'Not a place for swimming,' Bennet Lestrange said, 'full fathom five — fathom is a Viking word, of course. One fathom is six feet, so more than five fathoms, I should think. A place for drowning oneself — or someone else, if one had a mind to it.'

She felt his eyes on her and wondered what purpose he had in bringing her to these sinister places. To show off his superior knowledge, of course, but she felt it wasn't just that. It was as if he liked to unsettle her or catch her out somehow, which was why he had mentioned her visit to the attics. She had that sense again that he knew something about her that she did not know herself, and she wondered what secrets he had — dark ones, perhaps, concealed under his heavy-lidded eyes. He had his equal in Mrs Whitenow, she thought, but that didn't stop his barbed comments to her. And John seemed oppressed by him. Bennet Lestrange liked power, she concluded, her earlier unease about him returning. She couldn't help wishing herself somewhere else other than alone with him in this bleak moorland.

'Come,' he said, turning away from the water and pointing over to the west. 'There is a place called Raven Thorn over there and Raven's Nest is over to the north-east, Ravenshall to the east, which means raven's hill, and Raven's Castle to the south.' He laughed his mocking laugh, which was echoed strangely by calls from the air, then pointed upwards. 'Two up there. Look.'

Catherine looked up to see the two black birds soaring on their long wings in the immense sky, exchanging their harsh cries as if they were talking to each other.

'A conspiracy of ravens, eh? Plotting their dark deeds and croaking their dark secrets. Some can talk, you know. One wonders what they have to say about us.'

That you are one of them, Catherine thought, seeing the mark on his hand and still keeping her eyes on the sky. It was as if the birds had come at his bidding. She didn't want to look at him.

Bennet Lestrange turned to walk down the track, still speaking. 'There are plenty of crows hereabouts, too. As in a murder of crows, of course. As in a conspiracy, the word murder is a collective noun. Such phrases date back to as far as the fourteen hundreds and are called terms of venery, which are mentioned in a medieval volume entitled *The Book of Saint*

Albans, a facsimile of which I have in my library. I regard myself as a scholar of these things. A lonely calling in these parts, of course.' He stopped again and pointed. 'There is Crowshaw over to the east, and there is Crackpot Hall over in Swaledale.'

Something was expected of her. Admiration of his scholarship? 'Crackpot?' she asked, forcing a smile.

'The name means crow's pothole, though the gossips say that they are all mad over there. Down below is Starvecrow, the farm near Raven's Gaze. Wretched place, and wretched people, too.' He pointed again, showing her the oddly named Black Blote Hill, the word "blote" meaning desolate, and Hag Syke, which, despite its grim sound, merely meant a clearing.

'I am fascinated by the names and their origins. Up there are the so-called Giants' Graves — probably the site of some ancient settlement of which only the pillow mounds are left. It is extraordinary to think of the people who walked these hills before us and looked up in fear at the black ravens wheeling above them and down into the fathomless black tarns and the deep potholes.'

And that was how she came to type up his notes for what he called his *Devil's Dictionary*. He gave her a typewriter for the little writing room. She wasn't particularly skilled with the machine, but the notes were fascinating, she found, and she was delighted to write to Marjorie about the odd places with their curious, often poetic names. Butterbeck, she wrote, was a stream by alder trees. And then there was Hagg Worm Haw. The term "hag worm" which meant "adder hill" seemed to her almost Shakespearean, as did the comical Gawklands which, astonishingly, meant place of the cuckoo. Not that Bennet Lestrange was much interested in comedy, his taste being more for the sinister. Somehow, she wasn't surprised by that. There was something unsettling about him, she thought, especially in the relish he took in names such as Starvage Ridge and Hunger Hills, which certainly sounded a bit grim.

The reading and typing filled up some of the rain-swept afternoons before the customary tea with Mrs Whitenow. Bennet Lestrange appreciated her work and told her so when he gave her the notes. He didn't invite her up to his tower room and she was rather glad of that. She did not want to be alone with him because he still had an odd habit of looking at her from under his half-closed eyes, which discomfited her. It was as if he were testing her, and she never knew if she had passed the test.

However, sometimes he joined the tea and was so good-humoured and so complimentary about her help that as time went on, Catherine became more at ease with him — especially in the company of Mrs Whitenow, who was equally gracious. She thought less of leaving and more of how she was enjoying the peace and quiet, and how much better she felt for the long walks and the undemanding task of looking after Mrs Whitenow. She looked better, she thought, examining herself in the old-fashioned looking glass in the bedroom — less tired and strained, and there was a healthy colour in her cheeks. Even the scar under her fringe was less livid. Her hair looked glossier and fuller, and she slept better, only feeling the ache of sadness when she thought of Leo as she fell asleep.

She was glad to walk alone sometimes, though, enjoying striding along the paths, breathing in the bracing air. She went to the railway station, but without the restless feeling that had marked her first weeks at Raven's Gaze. Once she came across some boys playing in one of the streams which they called becks in the dales. She had waved and they waved back before they continued their building of a what looked like a dam. They looked rather poor and ragged but were clearly enjoying themselves. She wondered where they lived.

And she walked again by the farm called Starvecrow, where she saw washing on the line flying in the stiff wind. There was a perambulator outside — so someone lived there. It had seemed so deserted before. It occurred to her that she hadn't spoken to anyone but the inhabitants of Raven's Gaze for weeks, and it hadn't mattered. She didn't see much of Mrs Slee, who was as taciturn as ever. That conversation in the corridor was the longest they'd had. Her coffee had been served once or twice by Mrs Slee's red-haired niece, Betty, who was just as uncommunicative. A sullen mouth rather spoilt what might have been a pretty face. She would not be sorry to bid farewell to those two when the time came for her to leave.

Now she looked again at the perambulator and noticed a wheelchair at the front door. She thought there was a young man asleep in it in the early spring sunshine. She turned away quickly and walked on, but she couldn't help wondering about that young man. Her heart turned over. A casualty of the war? But John hadn't mentioned him, and surely it would be natural to do so.

She thought she would mention it to John, who was home just then. The opportunity came when he was driving her to see Pendragon Castle — Bennet Lestrange had gone to Manchester. But she thought better of mentioning the young man in the wheelchair. She didn't want to encourage any more talk about the war — it might lead to intimacies she didn't want. Instead, they talked of the legend that this was the castle of Uther Pendragon, and that Arthur slept under Richmond Castle.

She continued to gaze at the ruined castle, starkly outlined against the purplish grey sky, but rather romantically brooding with its backdrop of high fells. She heard John murmur, 'So all the noise of battle rolled away…'

'Oh, yes, Tennyson,' she said, '"Morte D'Arthur". I loved that at school.'

'So did I. I thought of the death of Arthur when I was sitting in the wood that day — something about the light and the quiet.'

Catherine did not say that she had had the same thought, but the notion that they should have felt the same at that moment was disconcerting. She only asked, 'Was there really an Uther Pendragon in these parts?'

'If he existed. The castle might have been built on some ancient stronghold belonging to a chieftain resisting the invading Anglo-Saxons. As for Arthur, it seems he slept on in Richmond or wherever, while the rest of us were slaying dragons.' The war again, but John's tone was light. 'Let's not talk of the war,' he went on. 'It's such a stirring day, despite the cold. Let's not think about the past —' he grinned at her — 'or the future. Let's savour this moment.'

Catherine thought of Leo again. He had told her that their moment was all that counted. She had lost him, and he seemed very far away, like someone remembered from a dream. Her knight of old. He had liked Tennyson, too.

'Lunch,' John said, looking up at the sky. 'Those clouds presage rain. There's a nice warm pub in Kirkby Stephen — bread and cheese and a pint of ale would suit me very well.'

'And me,' Catherine said.

The he was gone again. Catherine found that she missed his company. She had enjoyed the day at Pendragon Castle and the pub lunch. It had seemed very uncomplicated — two friends on an outing. She liked him, she decided. He made no demands on her, and he did seem less strained in her company, though there was still reserve, she thought. Not that she minded. No doubt he had his own secrets. Catherine had hers, but for now their friendship was pleasantly easy. And Mrs Whitenow seemed pleased that John looked so much better.

'You have done him good, Catherine,' she said, 'not just by keeping him company, but by teaching Bennet and me to be patient with him.'

6

April. Time to consider her future seriously, Catherine thought. Time slid by very easily and she had slipped into the life of Raven's Gaze, rarely disturbed by thoughts of ghosts in the nursery. The stories of its dark history were just tales told by Bennet Lestrange to amuse and edify. She realised now that he couldn't help lending drama to his stories and he liked to be the centre of attention. He was vain, as she had thought, but as long as she and John listened and smiled at his stories, Bennet Lestrange seemed satisfied, and she enjoyed the work he gave her, which gave purpose to her days. It was fascinating to find out the history of this remote place, where so few people lived and in which Bennet Lestrange and Mrs Whitenow seemed so self-contained.

But she felt the loneliness of it on some nights when sleep eluded her, and thoughts of the future intruded. She knew that she couldn't stay forever, even though the discomfort of her first, rather disconcerting impressions of the family relationships had faded. Those early dinners were bound to have been awkward. They hardly knew her, and she had no doubt seen things that weren't there, and the contents of the old nursery were private things. It wasn't for her to speculate on the tragedies they had endured. How she would have hated questions about her own loss — some things could not be talked about with strangers, and she was, after all, a stranger at Raven's Gaze, and an employee, though Mrs Whitenow did not treat her as such. She was always appreciative of Catherine's ministrations, and her leg was much better. But she couldn't stay. It would be too easy and now there was doubt in her mind about John. She was looking forward to his return too much. It wasn't that she was falling in love with him — more that they got on well and she found she could relax with him as she could not with Bennet Lestrange, But she didn't want to need John's company, and she didn't feel about him as she had felt about Leo.

Yet, how could she? Letters had sustained their passion — letters written in the knowledge that death might come at any minute, any hour, any day. How real had it been? Would that blaze of love have survived after the war? She hadn't known him. There had not been time. And what she had read of him in the newspaper after his death had been so strange, so unlike him, that she had hardly believed the man in the obituary was the man she had loved. Perhaps the actual Captain Leonard Philip Beaufort would have been a different man altogether. It was impossible to know.

She felt at ease with John. She enjoyed his company, and life at Raven's Gaze was certainly soothing after all the upheavals and perils of war. But could she stay merely because she was more at peace? Because her intense grief about Leo had lessened to a dull ache, and because the work was undemanding. She should return to real nursing. Looking after Mrs Whitenow was too easy. She needed to be challenged again. Yes, she must resolve to leave at the end of her contract. It was time to write to Marjorie and tell her.

With the decision made, she wrote the letter and felt immediately more certain. Then she went downstairs for tea with Mrs Whitenow. It was time to tell her. She couldn't help hoping that Bennet Lestrange would not be at tea. She felt that he would be displeased — she was useful to him, and, she admitted, he was one of those people whom you wanted to please because you were slightly fearful of him.

'I do understand,' Mrs Whitenow said kindly. 'Of course, I am much better, thanks to you, but I shall be very glad to have your company for the next few weeks. You have been a delight, and I know Bennet thinks the same. John will be back in a few days, and he will be equally sorry, but we must not stand in your way. It would be unfair to keep you here with little to do. Still, it is a great pity that…'

'What?' asked Catherine, as Mrs Whitenow's words tailed off.

'Nothing, dear. You must do what is best for you. Never mind what we would like.'

Catherine felt obscurely disappointed when she went back to her typing. Silly, she told herself. What had she wanted? That Mrs Whitenow would beg her to stay so that she could put off her decision and tell herself that she was needed? *Make up your mind*, she told herself. *Face the future. Post the letter.*

Catherine was glad she had already told Mrs Whitenow when after tea Bennet Lestrange knocked at her door and asked her to come up to the tower. *He must know now*, she thought, but she couldn't tell by his face whether he was displeased. She followed him down the stairs to the first landing, where a door led into his library. There were shelves stacked with leather-bound books, and a very handsome desk upon which papers were spread. A gentleman's study, she thought, noting the silver candlesticks, the silver inkwell, the blotter with its chased silver corners, and the curious-looking silver object which looked like a sugar sifter. The room smelt of leather, wood and pipe smoke mingled with the smoke from the log fire in huge hearth, and the brandy in the crystal glass at his elbow.

He smiled as he asked her to sit down. He sat at his desk, at ease in his dark velvet jacket and his patterned silk cravat, but he didn't speak. She folded her hands on her lap. Somehow, she knew she must not show her nervousness. She was entitled to go. Her three months were almost up. *You're not the servant girl in the tower,* she told herself, as she watched him pick up the sugar sifter object. She noticed how he seemed to caress it with his long hands. He liked his valuable possessions, she thought. He saw her looking and said, 'This is a pounce pot.'

'Oh, I thought it looked like a sugar sifter.'

'It is a Georgian piece which I inherited from my grandfather, who inherited it from his father. It is filled with fine powder made from cuttlefish bone to dry ink. I like to use it as a reminder of my grandfather, who left me his library and his choicest treasures and was very kind to me when I was a boy at Rosemount, his country house in Ireland ... a lovely place. Alas, it no longer exists.' He sighed. 'Ah, well, a long time ago, my dear.'

'It is very beautiful.'

'Yes, I like beautiful things — things which are not flawed. This is still perfect.' He put down the pot and said, 'So, you are leaving us.'

'I think I must. Mrs Whitenow will not need my nursing for very much longer.'

'You have done a very good job, my dear, and I thank you, too, for your help with my work. I shall be very sorry to see you go, but I do understand. This is a rather an isolated place. I can see that you might want a different life.'

'It's the future, you see, Mr Lestrange. I must think about what I am going to do for the rest of my life — in terms of my nursing career, I mean. I ought to think about returning to a hospital.'

'Ah, yes ... your future. One never knows, of course. You are a very good nurse, and I hope you will be successful. I admire your clear-sightedness and your independence. So refreshing — in a young woman. However, you know that if you wish to stay longer, you are most welcome. Mrs Whitenow will miss you.'

'Thank you, that is very kind, but I mean to go at the end of my three months. My cousin Marjorie will be glad to see me home.'

'I am sure she will. Now, let me show you the view from my lancet window. It is a treat you must see before you go.'

He stood behind her as she looked out of the window, his heavy hand resting on her shoulder. 'Look down and you will see the roof of Starvecrow Farm, the road to Garsdale, and the railway line going north to Kirkby Stephen by Hellgill Force, and south to Dent, the highest railway station in England. Over to the east, there is Hawes, of course, and Stag's Fell.'

The view was breathtaking — the fells seemed endless and empty and the height of the tower dizzying. The question she was about to ask died on her lips as she turned to face Bennet Lestrange. He was so close to her that she felt imprisoned suddenly, but he stayed before her, unmoving. She felt his brandy breath on her mouth, and his dark eyes with that considering look under his bruised lids made her feel suddenly naked under their gaze, his mouth unsmiling, his wing-marked hand imprisoning her. The experience lasted a few seconds too long. Then he stepped back, saying lightly, 'See what you will be missing.'

She pretended to look again and noticed the binoculars on the sill — the watcher, she thought. He must see everything. She waited until she was sure of her voice. 'I shall not forget it, Mr Lestrange. I have enjoyed my time here, but I must go.'

She sidestepped him and went to the door. 'Thank you for showing me.' She closed the door and found herself letting out a long breath. He had not spoken again, but she had felt his eyes on her as she'd left the room. She had never been so close to him before, and he had disturbed her because she felt as she had felt up on the moors that she had glimpsed something dark in him, something predatory in his black eyes — ravenish, she thought, if there were such a word. And that pause on the word "future" — as if, despite his assertion that she was a good nurse, he doubted her chances of success. He was wrong. She was going to shape her own destiny. She hurried downstairs to put her letter in the box.

Returning from a solitary walk a few days later, Catherine passed by the entrance to Starvecrow Farm, before which a small boy sat in the path. She stopped when she saw that he was examining his knee. She looked down to see that his knee was grazed and that his ragged breeches were wet through.

'That looks nasty. Can I help?'

Two extraordinarily dark blue eyes in a very dirty face looked back. 'Pushed, miss. Yan bletheren clumpet, Billie Moffet. Clouted 'im an' 'e pushed me in't beck.'

She recognised him as one of the boys she had seen playing in the water. 'You ought to go in and have it cleaned.'

'I will in a minnit. Our dad's badly.'

'I'm sorry to hear that.'

'Coughin'. Our ma's getten syrup.'

At that moment, a thin-faced young woman came down the path with a child on her hip, a woman with her hair tied up in a scarf, wearing an apron speckled with blood, and with red hands and dirt in her nails. 'Our Joe, what's tha bin up to?'

'In't beck wi' Billy Moffet.'

'Pair o' gowks — get tha sen inside by the fire.' Two equally arresting dark blue eyes turned to Catherine. 'Oh, sorry miss, forgettin' me manners.'

'No, I see that you're busy. Joe said your husband is poorly.'

'Nowt new, miss. TB 'tis. Nowt to do about it, 'cept the syrup. You're the nurse from Raven's?'

'Yes, can I do anything for you?'

'Come in if tha wants. Tek a look at him — poor devil. The war, see. Lost a leg. Cannot help hisself. Never spoke a word since he came back. His mind's gone... I'm Annot Syke. Me husband's Ted, an' tha's met our Joe,' the young woman said as she led Catherine along the rough track.

The farmyard was full of mud, a stinking manure heap, bits of machinery, cartwheels, and a dog kennel. A few hens pecked listlessly at bits of grass on the edges. The house did not look prosperous on closer inspection. Starvecrow seemed appropriate. The roof sagged, the chimney pots were crooked — no raven or crow, she was glad to see — and some slates were missing. The windows, small and mullioned, looked ancient, and the oak front door was propped open with a huge stone. Annot Syke's clogs rang on the stone-flagged floor as she went inside. The room was low-ceilinged and dark, except for the fire blazing in the great hearth where on a grate an iron pot bubbled. Catherine made out hams hanging from the hook, a huge table littered with plates, knives, a loaf of bread and a work basket spilling out bits of mending; several chairs, a couple of stools, oil lamps, and candles in bottles. There was a tall, curved wooden settle which she knew was placed with its back to the door to prevent draughts. It must have been hundreds of years old, it was so knotted and scarred. She saw that the wheelchair was placed on the other side of the fire.

'There,' Annot said, and within the barrier of the settle Catherine saw as she moved further into the room that a bed been placed there, and in it lay Mr Syke. He was asleep, but she saw his skull-like head on the pillow, the flush in his thin cheeks, the spittle on his bluish lips, and how his skeletal hands twitched restlessly at the blanket, where she saw the hollow where one of his legs should have been. His eyes opened suddenly, but he saw nothing. They closed again and her heart twisted in pity.

Annot poured some hot water from the kettle into a bowl and used a rag to clean up Joe's knee. 'T'aint that bad.' She took a bottle and dabbed the cut. Catherine smelt witch hazel. 'Now then, upstairs, my lad, an' tek them wet things off. Keep your eye on Clemmie for us.' Joe picked up the little girl, opened a door, and Catherine heard him limping up the stairs. Annot went behind the settle and returned some moments later. 'Ted's still asleep, miss. I gave him a mixture from Grizel Knipe. She lives up at Rowantree.'

'Oh, what's in it?'

'Black treacle, aniseed an' a drop o' laudanum. Grizel makes up the medicines for all the dale folk. 'Tis the laudanum gives him a rest at night. I cannot always get him upstairs.'

'How do you manage?'

'Owd Dandy Knipe comes sometimes an' we lift him upstairs. He was too badly this time. Best he stays there now.'

The words spilled from Catherine's mouth before she realised the futility of them. 'What about the doctor?'

'We never get the doctor — we've to do all naturally up here. Grizel makes the syrups for everyone — an' she'll lay 'em out when the time comes.' Annot looked back at the bed. 'T'will be better when — aye, well, 'tis all to be said. Will tha tek a drop o' tea?'

On her way up the track to Raven's Gaze, Catherine stood and breathed in the fresh air. Starvecrow reeked of unwashed bodies, steaming wool, woodsmoke, sickness — and poverty. Bennet Lestrange had said it was a wretched place. Wretched people, he had said. Clearly, he had no sympathy for the sick man or his wife and children who lived so near them. You could see the roof of Starvecrow from Raven's Gaze, so he and John must know about Ted Syke, crippled in the war, but they had never mentioned him. That boy, Joe, in rags, and Annot, gaunt and old beyond her twenty-seven years, but with steel in her bright eyes and the remnants of youth and prettiness. She had poured out her story to a stranger because she'd had to.

Catherine had seen men like Ted Syke many times; she had smelt blood and gas, and gangrene, and she had handled severed legs, but the pity of it all wrung her heart. To have survived and come back to that — no doctor, no air, no proper care. Annot was not hard-hearted. She was a realist. It was in her fierce, dark blue gaze. Ted had no life at all. He'd lain there unresisting when he had woken and coughed again, and Annot had given him more syrup. It would kill him in the end, she knew that, but what was she to do? Catherine had no answer.

'T'bairns,' Annot had said, 'I've to think of them. Our Joe's a good boy, but what's for him in this place? School at Lunds is tuppence a week, an' I don't always have that, an' it's such a walk over there. Our Clem's but a babby still — what's for her? Thank God, there'll be nay more. When Ted's gone, I'm sellin' up. Goin' to Leeds. Me sister's there — a widow, but she cannot tek Ted an' Joe won't go without me. I can get work there — I'll do owt. I cannot stand this place. It's never been no good.'

Annot told Catherine that she had come to Ravendale as a bride in 1910. Ted Syke had inherited Starvecrow from an uncle. They should have known better by the name, but Ted thought he were to be a landed gentleman. More fool him —

an' Annot for believin' it. Joe were nine years old now — weren't meant, Annot confessed. Jest fell to him, an' her pa made him marry her. Course, she was willin' — to get away from drudging service in a big house. An' Ted were a nice-lookin' lad, set to be a schoolteacher. Clever with his books, but that weren't to be. Ted thought they'd make a go of the farm, but it were never any good. Starvecrow were about right. Nowt thrived. Ted were no farmer. He couldn't get on with it. Weren't born to it like folk in the dale, so when the war came, it seemed like a chance. Ted wanted to go. No one knew it'd be so long and that a man could come back like that. Will Bents from Nouse Bottom were killed in 1916, and the lad from Raven's Gaze. Better for them than this. Ted were reported missin' in the September. Thought he were dead. But he were found an' after the hospital, he were brought back in the October. She should have been glad, but he was in such a state, an' then there was the T.B. Annot couldn't help wishing... Another winter would be terrible...

Catherine remembered Bennet Lestrange's talk of being snowed in. She shuddered to think what life would be like in the squalor of Starvecrow. She had given Annot five shillings. Annot had shaken her head, but Catherine said, 'For young Joe and your little girl.' And Annot had looked away as she murmured, 'Good of you, miss.' It wasn't much good, she thought. Such a paltry sum in the vastness of their poverty and misery.

She slipped upstairs and into her room, where she looked round at the comfort of it. She could sit by the window and look out at the soaring hills and then go down to a delicious tea, and then there'd be supper and glinting crystal, shining silver, and polite conversation and afterwards the ease and luxury of fresh sheets under a thick counterpane. And tomorrow and tomorrow… No, she thought, it was time to go. It was time to do something useful. She could do no more for Mrs Whitenow. She couldn't do anything for Annot Syke, except perhaps leave a few things every now and then at the farm gate when she passed, coming back from Harper's shop. She couldn't think of anything else.

Having tidied her hair, Catherine went down the first flight of stairs. On the landing, she saw that Bennet Lestrange's tower door was open. She heard him talking. *To whom?* she wondered. He didn't sound pleased. She couldn't help stopping to listen, for she heard a sound as if someone had banged a hand down hard on a table and then his voice again — not loud. He spoke with a kind of controlled anger.

'I will not tell you again. I have waited long enough. Time is going on and you're wasting it. So, do something about it. We had a bargain, and you must keep to it. If you do not, there will be consequences.'

She didn't wait to hear a reply but hurried on as quietly as she could. She was sorry to have heard Bennet Lestrange and was rather glad that she had not been on the receiving end of those icy words. Yet she wasn't entirely surprised after her experience in the tower. She remembered his dark gaze. He could be a menacing figure, and there had been something ruthless in that threat to the unseen listener.

'Oh, yes, Annot Syke,' Mrs Whitenow said, frowning and putting down her delicate china cup on the gleaming table where the silver shone, and the neatly cut sandwiches and cake waited. 'A great pity they ever came here. Her husband could never take to farming. Poor man, I don't think he has any idea that the red-haired child isn't his. The child was conceived while he was away at the Front. Clementine, she calls it. Rather fanciful. A proud girl, and a stubborn one. Bennet offered help, but she refused. She must bear the consequences, I'm afraid.'

'Oh, dear,' Catherine said, rather inadequately, she thought. She wasn't shocked by the revelation about Annot. She felt wrong-footed by the idea that Bennet Lestrange had offered to help them when she was going to suggest her scheme of leaving gifts at the farm. She gathered her wits. 'I got the impression that Mr Syke is in a very bad way, and they can't afford a doctor.'

'Mrs Slee told me that Grizel Knipe is helping with the nursing.'

'Yes, Annot told me that. I just wondered if I might do something.'

'I hope you are not thinking of offering to nurse him.' Mrs Whitenow's tone was sharp, but she must have seen some protest in Catherine's face, for her tone changed. 'I'm sorry, Catherine, if I seem hard-hearted, but do think. Syke has tuberculosis. It would be dreadful if — think about John. After all he's been through. He is not strong yet.'

Wrong-footed again, Catherine thought, but she wasn't going to capitulate entirely. 'I understand completely. I just thought I might leave some things for her — groceries, perhaps — to help out.'

Mrs Whitenow was gracious. 'I'm sure we can spare some provisions, provided you leave them outside the house. Annot Syke might accept them if she believes they come from you. She's not exactly keen on us. Rather a chip on her shoulder, has Annot. She did some cleaning for us and the red-headed father worked for us, a good-for-nothing labourer and dishonest, but I think she may have blamed us for his leaving rather suddenly. Anyway, all that is over. Ah, here is John, home at last from his travels. Come and have some tea, dear.'

Mrs Whitenow explained Catherine's concern about the Syke family and the scheme for helping them at a distance. 'I have warned Catherine that Syke has tuberculosis.'

'I quite understand that,' Catherine said, 'but I do think they need help.'

John turned to Catherine. 'You met them?'

'Only Annot really. She invited me in, and I saw her husband — very briefly.'

'I hope you will not think of going into the house again, my dear. I should not like you to become ill.'

John must have seen something in her face, for he cut in quickly, 'But a difficult situation, all the same, and Annot is difficult woman to help.' He smiled at Catherine. 'But I like your scheme. Good of you to think of it.'

'As long as you leave any gifts outside the house,' Mrs Whitenow insisted again.

'Naturally, I would not think of putting any of you in danger,' Catherine said as politely as she could.

'Very well. Now, I am going to my room. I'll leave you to enjoy your tea.'

John opened the door for his grandmother and moved to the window, where he stood staring out while Catherine poured more tea. There was something about the set of his shoulders that suggested he was unhappy. She thought of Bennet Lestrange's acid tones and wondered if John had been the recipient, and whether Bennet Lestrange's newfound patience was wearing thin, and he was telling John to take up his responsibilities. The silence was uncomfortable, but she could hardly get up and walk out.

'Do you want tea?' she asked.

'Oh, yes, tea, thank you.' But he continued to gaze out of the window.

'I felt very sorry for Mr Syke,' Catherine said.

'Yes, it's — impossible. They're not liked. Off-comers, you see. It means they don't belong here. Syke was a rather useless farmer —'

'But now —'

'I know. He was a useless soldier, too. Not in my company, but I knew what he was. Got himself a blighty one. Cowardly little beast —'

'John!' she exclaimed involuntarily. 'He's lost his leg. He's a wreck of a man —'

'I'm sorry — I'm sorry. I don't mean to — I know he's in a dreadful state. He couldn't have imagined — when he put himself in the firing line, but Annot despises him. She knows what he is. She thinks he should have died in the war. She's hard as nails, that one.'

Catherine ignored that. No doubt John disapproved of Annot's affair. She was more interested in what could be done for Ted. 'You've spoken to her about him.'

'Of course, we offered assistance. I went down to speak to her, but she wouldn't listen. Didn't want our charity, she said.'

'Do you think she'll accept the things I leave?'

'More fool her if she doesn't. My God, that stinking farm — she ought to get out of it.'

'How can she, with Ted the way he is?'

Catherine was angry. John seemed to have no pity. Of course, Annot thought it would have been better if Ted had died in the war, but she wasn't hard. Catherine had seen her tenderness with her children and her careful treatment of her maimed husband. She didn't care what John thought of her at that moment.

'Well, I'll do what I can,' she said firmly. 'I hate to think of those children without enough food, and whatever you think of Ted Syke, he isn't the only one who was branded a coward. I saw many young men for whom it was all too much — shot at dawn, some of them. That was terrible, and people are beginning to realise the injustice of it all. I know you were incredibly brave, but many were not. How could they help it?'

John was staring at her, his black eyes ablaze and his face suddenly white. She was astonished at his anger, but she didn't care. He ought to remember what she had seen and done.

She saw how his hands shook as he sat down, but his eyes were regretful now. 'I'm so sorry. I was thoughtless and stupid. You're right. It's just that we tried. I suppose I was offended by her — as if that mattered. It's my fault — I haven't — I sometimes think I'm not right, either. My head is sometimes so — I didn't want to see him — I couldn't bear —'

'Don't,' Catherine said, pitying him and regretting her own show of temper. 'I shouldn't have spoken to you like that. I should have remembered — your loss. I know that it will take a long time for you, for all of us, to think straight.'

'That's it,' he said. 'I know you understand, but I am sorry about Ted Syke. Forgive me.'

'There's nothing to forgive. We'll part friends.'

'Oh, yes, in a few weeks. Grandmother will be sorry, and so will I. I hoped — I hoped we'd have more time to — our walks have been very pleasant...'

'Thank you, but I need to go home. It's time I found a post in a hospital, and Cousin Marjorie is expecting me.'

'I understand... Still, it's been such a pleasure to have you here... And the days out with father — he's at his best when he has an audience, and he likes you, too.'

No, she thought suddenly, *Bennet Lestrange does not like anyone.* She had no idea what he really thought of her. She knew only that she had made the right decision to go.

7

After breakfast, Catherine went up to Mrs Whitenow. Her ulcer was very much better; the redness had faded, and the infection was in abeyance.

'Do you feel that it is better?' she asked.

'I do. The pain is much less, thanks to you. I hope the nurse from Hawes will know what she is doing.'

'I could speak to her and tell her what treatment I've been giving to make sure that she treats the ulcer with care.'

'Yes, I'm sure John would take you to Hawes. As to the matter of Annot Syke, I've spoken to Mrs Slee, and despite her animosity towards Annot, she has made up a basket for you to take to Starvecrow. I cannot have you spending your money. It is my responsibility.'

Catherine hid her irritation as she lingered by the chest of drawers, putting away dressings and bandages. So, it was Mrs Whitenow's responsibility suddenly. She hadn't seemed to care much before. And a basket, indeed, as if Catherine were some servant despatched to deliver Lady Bountiful's largesse to the poor of the parish.

However, she turned and said lightly, 'That is kind. It will save me a walk to Harper's shop.'

'Good. Why not go now? It is such a fine morning.'

'I will. I'll just wash my hands before I go.'

'But don't go into the house — think of infection.'

Catherine resisted the temptation to retort, closed the door quietly, and made her way to the bathroom. How insistent the woman was. Of course, she knew the dangers of tuberculosis. She wouldn't be going near Ted Sykes, but she was not going to hurt Annot's feelings by refusing an invitation to step into the house.

Catherine found Mrs Slee in the kitchen, stirring something meaty in a pot. There was a basket on the table. Catherine noted the heap of black feathers beside it, thought of ravens, and wondered what on earth Mrs Slee had packed for Annot.

'Missus says tha's takin' this to Annot Syke.'

'Yes, her husband is very poorly.'

Mrs Slee looked at her coldly, her mouth a thin line of disapproval. 'Hm,' she said, 'I 'ope she's civil to thee. She's an uppity creature, that one. No better than she —'

Catherine interrupted. She had no wish to discuss Annot's reputation again. 'I feel very sorry for them. Mr Syke is in a poor state.'

'Aye, well, it's a bad do — not that 'e were much good for farmin' or soldierin', so they say.'

Catherine's blood flared, but before she could reply, Mrs Slee had turned back to her oven. Dismissed, Catherine thought, looking at the krail pot. Heartless old witch with her cauldron and feathers.

She was glad to get outside and breathe the fresh air. If hostility had a smell, it would smell like Mrs Slee, from whose very breath bitterness came. Thank goodness for Grizel Knipe and Owd Dandy. They sounded like kindly people.

As she walked down the track, she thought about the restless atmosphere at Raven's Gaze, where moods were always shifting from warm to cold, like the restless weather of the dale today, the wind nipping her cheeks while the sun deceived with its bright light. She remembered Bennet Lestrange in the tower, smiling, then standing too close to her, his black eyes seeming to take her skin off. She could still hear his cold anger at his listener. It must have been John, who had looked upset when he had come in to have tea. John's moods were changeable, too. She thought of his anger and contempt for Ted Syke — then his apology, which had seemed heartfelt, though she hadn't forgotten the cruelty of his words. And Mrs Whitenow's coldness about Annot Syke had been surprising — and deeply unfair. Mrs Whitenow knew the terrible consequences of the war. Catherine was sure that the basket would not have been sent if she had not proposed to help the Syke family, and she could not forget how Mrs Whitenow had harped on about her not going into the house, as if she hadn't wanted Catherine to have anything to do with Annot. And Mrs Slee didn't like Annot at all. What had Annot done that they were all angered by her very name? Surely not the illegitimate child and the farm labourer — that could hardly be extraordinary in these parts.

Annot was in the yard, ragged brown tendrils of hair escaping her scarf, her rough-patched skirts billowing and her sleeves rolled up, revealing sinewy arms which at that moment were waving wildly at the black bird which rose on its ragged wings from the sagging roof, uttering its hoarse cry. She turned to see Catherine at the gate and came across, lifting her skirts, showing her bare legs as she squelched through the mud in a battered pair of men's boots.

'Visitin' the poor, milady?' she asked, but she was smiling.

'Was that a raven?' Catherine asked.

'Crow — ravens is bigger. 'Tis after the grain. Cheeky beggar. He can get his own dinner.' She pointed to a bucket. 'This is for t'chickens. We don't see ravens about much these days. Someone up at Raven's Gaze tellin' stories?'

'I asked about the name and Mr Lestrange told me that ravens are an omen of death.'

'Oh, he would. Always tellin' me Starvecrow'll be the death o' me. Wants ter buy it, but I'm not sellin' — not yet, any road. In me own time. I don't care what he says. I'm mistress here — such as it is. Just let me scatter that grain an' I'll see what's in t'basket.'

Catherine waited. Annot would survive, she thought. There was something implacable about her. Proud, Mrs Whitenow had called her. Annot had a right to be. She met her troubles with an inner strength. So, her red-haired Clementine was someone else's. Such things happened. She'd had an absent husband whom she did not love, who had failed at everything, even being a soldier. Who was Catherine Sisley to judge? She might have found herself with child after those three nights in the hotel. Who was anyone to judge?

When Annot came back, Catherine told her that Mrs Whitenow had sent the basket.

'That's a turn up — not that I want owt from them. Still, as tha've brought it, I ain't such a fool as to say no. An' it's one in the eye for Ma Slee.' Annot lifted the basket's cover, took out a pie and sniffed. 'Rook pie, I'm guessin'. Good enough for the poor. She wouldn't serve that to her ladyship. Sent it with her best wishes, did she?'

So that explained the feathers. More black birds. Thank goodness Bennet Lestrange was not here to lecture on the history of rooks. Catherine wasn't surprised at Mrs Slee's choice of delicacy for Annot, but she couldn't help smiling at Annot's irony. 'Mrs Slee was not exactly cheerful.'

'Sour old cow. Told you I'm no better than I should be, I'll bet.'

'Mrs Whitenow said they'd tried to help before.'

'Oh, aye, only because Mr Lestrange wants this place. He sent that John, but I told him to sling his hook — I know what he thought of Ted. Ted might not have been much of a soldier, but he doesn't deserve what happened. John Lestrange wouldn't come in to see him. He's the coward. Anyroad, I don't want their charity, thanks very much. They ain't all what they want to be seen, an' Missus looks down that long nose at little Clemmie. Suppose she told you Clemmie's not Ted's.'

Catherine felt herself blushing. 'She did.'

Annot's shrewd gaze saw. ''T'ain't tha fault. I don't care. Clemmie's here now, an' 'tis my job to look to her an' our Joe. Nowt else matters. They've got their secrets at Raven's Gaze an' I'll keep mine. Nowt to do with them.'

'Good for you, Annot.'

'Nowt I can do for Ted. 'Tis what it is. Tha were a nurse out there. Seen them like Ted afore.'

'I have — it's tragic.'

'What's brought you to this godforsaken place? There mun be better things to do than dance attendance on that owd woman.'

'I shall be leaving at the end of the month. It was only temporary. I'm hoping to take a post at a big hospital, probably in Dorset where I was brought up.'

'Good for you as well. Tha's best out o' that lot. But if tha wants to bring owt else, I shan't stop you. I ain't proud.'

'There's this, too.' Catherine took a bottle from her pocket. 'Laudanum. Don't give him too much.'

'I won't. I want him to go, but I shan't hurry him. I've learned patience if nowt else in this benighted place.'

Catherine walked back. She felt better. There was something invigorating about Annot. She was so frank. You looked into those fierce eyes, and you knew what you were getting, unlike — that was it, she thought, you couldn't be sure of those three at Raven's Gaze. They had secrets, Annot had said. So she knew that, too. Catherine had been conscious from the beginning that Raven's Gaze was a house of secrets. Even John, with whom she felt most comfortable, seemed always to be holding back. His brother was never mentioned, nor his mother. It was as if the past were locked away and the key hidden in a forgotten drawer. There was something they could not face, and whatever secrets they had kept them at a distance from one another.

Annot, however, poor and uneducated as she was, had the greatest tenderness for her children. She was determined to care for them — to give them better lives in the future. She had courage, too, and here was Nurse Catherine Sisley who had been in the thick of war and now was pandering to one old lady who would do very well without her. Annot had said she must have better things to do. She had, and there was not much longer to wait.

She strode up the fell. If Bennet Lestrange were watching from his tower, then let him. Catherine Sisley was free to do as she pleased.

Marjorie's letter was full of cheerful news about the church fete, the prize she had won for her cake, the roses coming, Mrs Ainsley-Greene's handsome young nephew, and the young vicar's prowess at tennis — Catherine smiled at that; Marjorie was still hoping, it seemed. And she expressed her delight that Catherine was coming home. Marjorie had missed her so. She quite understood that looking after an elderly lady whose leg was much improved was hardly the job for an experienced nurse like Catherine. Marjorie had been looking in the newspapers, and there were posts advertised. Would she like Bournemouth? Or Sherborne? A lovely town, and not too far away for Catherine to come home when she could.

In her latest letter, Pat Sinclair had suggested London again, but Catherine knew she would not go there. However, she thought she might like Bournemouth — a long way from Honiton. No temptation to visit the house of Sir Philip Beaufort. Not that she would. That wrenching grief did not visit so often — she wouldn't get over Leo, but she couldn't allow her life to stop. Pat Sinclair was right in telling her that she should not waste away in Dorset. Not in Yorkshire, either. Bournemouth's Royal Victoria Hospital was a busy one. It might suit her very well. Sherborne was lovely, but the only hospital she knew was the asylum — she didn't think she was ready to deal with mental cases. But she was ready to work in a busy ward, and she was longing to see Marjorie again. And as for the tennis-playing vicar, and the handsome nephew, she was armoured against any approaches. She had loved once and there could be no one else. Certainly not John Lestrange. He was too unpredictable, and there was too much beneath the surface of Raven's Gaze. She would be happy to go.

During her last weeks, Catherine was very careful to behave as if everything were unchanged. John had not referred to their conversation about Ted Syke, and she had not mentioned Annot to him or to Mrs Whitenow, who hadn't offered any more baskets, though Catherine had taken a few things to the farm and had spoken to Annot, who did not speak of Raven's Gaze again, only of her hopes for Joe and Clemmie, and Ted's worsening condition. 'Nowt to do for him,' she had said, looking at the hills and back at Catherine. 'An' thanks for the medicine. It helps him to sleep. Sleep's best, Grizel says, but I wonder what he dreams of. Imagine — such days an' nights of agony an' he can't speak owt of it.'

Catherine had no comfort to offer, but she gave her more laudanum. This time, she did not tell Annot to be careful. She thought of the men who had wanted to die, their mute mouths open and their eyes speaking with anguished appeal, knowing she had the means. She had turned away then.

Bennet Lestrange did not speak of the Sykes at all. He continued to give her papers to type up and was always pleasant to her, but she detected a kind of false good humour between him and John when Bennet had taken them on a trip to Kirkby Lonsdale. She had watched them at lunch. Bennet had been his usual dominating self, enlarging on the legend of the Devil's Bridge and the prevalence of devils in the dales. However, when John spoke of going down to London the next day, she had seen how Bennet Lestrange's brow had darkened and how his lips had tightened. His hand had clenched round his glass of ale.

But he had spoken pleasantly enough. 'Of course, you must do what you want, John, but I hope you will be back before Miss Sisley leaves us.'

'Naturally, I will,' John said, but she didn't miss the hint of irony in his voice.

What did it matter? Catherine thought. Why was Bennet Lestrange so annoyed? She could say goodbye to John tomorrow before he left for London. Again, she had the sense that the seemingly innocent words meant more.

John went the next day, and Catherine thought she would take the opportunity to go down to Starvecrow. Perhaps she'd be able to persuade Annot to take some money for the children. She didn't tell Mrs Whitenow that, merely saying that she would go to bid Annot goodbye.

Mrs Whitenow asked her to stay for a moment, telling Catherine that she was feeling breathless, rather faint, and did Catherine have any idea what might be wrong? Catherine took her pulse, which was perfectly normal. However, she asked if Mrs Whitenow were anxious about anything.

'Only John, my dear. I wish he wouldn't — I mean, is it good for him to keep going to those friends in London? They must remind him of the war. Ought he to try to put it behind him?'

'I don't know, Mrs Whitenow. I can only say that time may bring about change. He certainly seems better when he is here.'

'True, my dear. I can't help wishing you did not have to leave us. I do think you have had a very good influence on him. He does seem at ease with you. Still, I'm not going to press you. You have your own life to lead.'

And I shall lead it away from here, Catherine thought as she walked down the track. She stopped at the gate and looked up to the fell behind the farmhouse, where she saw a figure walking up the path. Bennet Lestrange. She recognised his height, the black hat, the long tweed cape, and the shepherd's crook he carried on long walks. Had he been to Starvecrow? Surely not. He never mentioned Annot Syke. He had called the inhabitants of Starvecrow wretched people, but Annot had said that he had tried to buy Starvecrow. Why, she couldn't imagine. It was such a poor place. He wanted to be master of all. That would be it. Odd, though, to see him at the back of Starvecrow. Perhaps there was a way to Raven's Gaze over the fell.

It was odder still to see Annot's flushed face when she answered Catherine's knock.

'Oh, I didn't expect you. I'm that busy wi t'washin'.' Annot didn't open the door wide.

'I don't want to disturb you, Annot. I came to say goodbye. I may not have another chance to see you, and I wanted to give you something for the children.' Catherine handed her the

envelope which contained a pound note. 'I wanted to say —'
She broke off, seeing the deep crimson flood Annot's face. It
was so unlike her. 'I mean that I hope things will turn out all
right for you —'

Annot stepped outside and took the envelope. She knew it
was a banknote. 'I cannot tek this, Miss. It ain't right. Tha's
done enough.'

'No, please, it's for the children.'

They stood there awkwardly, as if something had broken
between them. Catherine was sorry. She liked Annot and felt as
if she had blundered somehow by offering money.

Catherine spoke first. 'Is there anything wrong, Annot? I
haven't offended you?'

'I'm sorry. It's right good of you. I'll put it away for Joe —
for when —'

'Well, I'll say goodbye, and I wish you well.'

'Same to you, miss… I'm sorry…'

Annot looked away towards the hills. There was nothing
more to say, so Catherine went through the yard gate and onto
the rutted path. She turned and saw that Annot was still at the
door, watching. She waved and Annot waved back, and then
she went inside the house.

Depressed, Catherine turned up her collar against the sudden
rain squall and hurried back up to Raven's Gaze, wondering
what had gone so wrong. Annot had looked upset. Perhaps
Bennet Lestrange had been there, but Annot had said she was
sorry. What for? Perhaps Annot had agreed to sell — but she
couldn't take Ted Syke anywhere. It was a puzzle. She couldn't
help hoping that Annot would get the chance to leave soon.
Death would be a release for Ted — for them all. And she
would be glad to be released from Raven's Gaze. That thought
spurred her up the drive, where she was stopped suddenly by

the sight of something dead and bloody on the path — a rabbit, she thought. Poor thing preyed upon by some carrion crow — or raven. She looked up at the tower, where a great black bird perched on the battlement above the lancet window where the light burned, and Bennet Lestrange was no doubt watching her. The raven's gaze, she thought. He was the raven.

She was startled to see him waiting in the hall when she went in. Mrs Whitenow was there, too, leaning on her stick. They both looked dreadfully serious. For a fleeting moment, she thought she had offended them because she had been to Starvecrow, but Mrs Whitenow stepped forward and said, 'My dear, a telegram has come for you.'

Her heart turned over as Bennet Lestrange handed her the flimsy paper, which she opened with trembling hands. The words swam before her eyes. She couldn't make sense of them. They seemed to say that Marjorie was ill and that she should come at once.

She stared and stared. The words were true. Cousin Marjorie's solicitor had sent them. Marjorie was in hospital, gravely ill after an accident.

Catherine hardly remembered the bustle of departure, blindly packing her case, drinking tea, Mrs Whitenow pressing her to eat a sandwich, the rain lashing down as Bennet Lestrange drove her to the station for the London train, which seemed agonisingly slow. But she had been grateful that Bennet Lestrange had put her in a first-class carriage. She was surprised to see John Lestrange waiting for her at Euston. His father had telegraphed to his friend, Freddie Hunter, he told her. He was here to see that she caught the Bournemouth train and had a cup of tea, at least, while she waited.

A taxi took them to Waterloo, where she sat at a table in the buffet while John went to get the tea. She thought of the first time they had met here after she had seen Pat Sinclair, who had spoken of Leo, and the discomfort she had felt in John's company. That meeting that had taken her to Raven's Gaze and kept her there while Marjorie... Her eyes filled. She wanted to rush to the platform, as if that would make the train come quicker. And now John was sitting down with the teas and offering to go with her to Bournemouth — only if she wanted him to. He could whistle up a taxi at Bournemouth to take her to the hospital — take her anywhere she wanted to go. But he would push off if she preferred. Whatever he could do to help.

'You're very kind,' she managed, 'but I couldn't put you to so much trouble.'

'No trouble at all. I can take you down at least and come back — honestly, I'm glad to do it. You've had such a shock. You shouldn't be on your own. I'll get the tickets.'

She found herself in another first-class carriage, with John Lestrange seated opposite her. She hadn't agreed but she felt glad that he had taken the decision out of her hands. A taxi to the hospital would save so much time.

She closed her eyes when the train started. She was so exhausted she couldn't speak. She couldn't tell if she were awake or sleeping, if the images that flickered under her closed eyes were real or a dream. John's face was watching, his dark brows knitted together, frowning as if he didn't know her, but when he leant forward, his face turned into the face of Lieutenant Adams, his eyes wide with terror and his mouth opening in a scream. She started from her doze as the train entered a tunnel, its whistle sounding a warning. Confused, her heart beating too fast, she looked at John, but his eyes were closed, the newspaper on his lap. She shook herself awake, remembering Lieutenant Adams's agonised face, and then she remembered Marjorie. What time was it? She had been asleep for about an hour, she thought. Another hour and a half, perhaps. Oh, God, so long. She dared not close her eyes again. The thought of Adams's poor face was as bad as imagining what had happened to Marjorie.

John opened his eyes and smiled at her. 'When did you last eat?'

'I had a sandwich, I think, with Mrs Whitenow — in another life.'

'Let's go to the dining car. It'll help pass the time, and you ought to try something, even if it's just bread and butter.'

Catherine looked down at the figure in the bed, the pale face, the head swathed in bandages, the white hands crossed over the breast. She was too late. Marjorie was gone. She felt entirely bereft, realising how much she had depended on coming back, how much she had wanted to leave Raven's Gaze and all the unspoken things that went on there, how she had looked forward to Marjorie's comforting embrace, her warmth, her love. And all the memories of their life together flooded back. She had been five years old, bewildered, shocked, wounded. She felt that way again, but there was no Marjorie to heal her. She wished now that she had told Marjorie about Leo. It should not have been a secret. There was no need. Marjorie would not have judged her.

She felt angry with Leo for the first time. The secrecy seemed like a betrayal now. If he had truly loved her, he would have declared it. She had been deceiving herself. She understood the truth now. He had been pledged to Lucy, and whether he had intended to break that pledge she would never know.

And if she had trusted Marjorie and told her, then she might not have gone to Raven's Gaze, for Marjorie would have understood. And she would have counselled Catherine to stay at home until she recovered. They would have talked. They would have walked. She would have been with Marjorie in the pretty street of Rodden Row. Marjorie wouldn't have fallen.

She stood holding the dead hand, whispering, 'I'm sorry. I loved you and I didn't know how much.'

John was waiting when she came from the ward to tell him that she had been too late. He took her arm and led her to another taxi which, he said, would take her to Marjorie's cottage or to a hotel if she wished. He would stay at The Grand Hotel for the night and if she needed help, she was to come to him or telephone, if that were possible.

She was grateful for his tact and promised that she would get a message to him the next day. She would have to see Marjorie's solicitor in Abbotsbury.

'It is very late. May I suggest that you stay in the hotel tonight? I can get them to send up some supper for you and perhaps tomorrow, you can take the taxi to Abbotsbury. You could telephone the solicitor from the hotel.'

She noticed for the first time that it was dark. The thought of the empty cottage appalled her. She thought of Marjorie having left everything as it was before she went out on her walk, before she had stumbled off the pavement in the street where her friend, Violet, lived, before the blood had streamed from her head. A simple accident and it had killed her.

'I'll leave you to collect your things and I'll take you to the train. The jewellery is in this bag here. I am sorry, of course, but you couldn't expect…'

Cousin Henry Fowell, Marjorie's brother, swallowed and blinked, his pale blue eyes disappearing into his round, red-veined cheeks. He looked uncomfortable rather than sorry. Catherine couldn't answer. She was too numb with shock. She hadn't ever thought about what would happen in the event of Marjorie's death. Henry walked out. She heard the front door close. *Her things*, she thought. Her life to be collected in a couple of suitcases and then what? Where should she go?

She sat down on the faded chintz-covered sofa. Marjorie's slippers were by her fireside chair, where she'd left them before. Catherine couldn't bear to look at them. She looked round the room at all the familiar things: the little gate-legged table with the red-shaded lamp; the abandoned knitting; and the oak bureau, where Marjorie had sighed over her accounts, and where Catherine found the letters that she had written about Butterbeck and the amusing Gawklands, and the letter in which she had told her she was coming home. She looked the picture of Abbotsbury church over the fireplace, the church where the funeral had taken place, the burn mark on the rug where a log had spat out a cinder, the brass coal scuttle — full, because Marjorie would have lit the fire when she came back. She imagined her in her slippers, seated by the fire, the evening shadows darkening outside the cosy room, waiting, thinking about Catherine's coming. Too late, too late…

None of it was hers. It all belonged to Cousin Henry. The solicitor had explained. The cottage had never been Marjorie's. It was family property. Marjorie's brother Henry owned everything, including the fine Queen Anne House in the countryside beyond the village. He was a wealthy man, and an avaricious one. Marjorie and he had never got on. They met from time to time, but Marjorie never spoke about who owned the cottage. It hadn't mattered, Catherine supposed now, for Marjorie had always believed Catherine would marry, just as Marjorie's father had supposed she would and so had left her very little.

Catherine had been left a hundred pounds and Marjorie's little collection of jewels — the little sapphire ring, the cameo brooch, and the gold bracelet which Marjorie had been given for her twenty-first birthday. She looked at the little worn velvet bag which Henry had so thoughtfully left for her — in case she was tempted to take anything that didn't belong to her, no doubt. He would have taken them if they had not been itemised in the will, she thought bitterly. Marjorie had had very little to live on, but she had taken in the grieving child. Catherine realised now what those sighs over the accounts had meant, and she had never thought to ask.

She hadn't even been allowed to stay here to wait for the funeral. Her home. Henry had wanted her out. Was he afraid she would refuse to go?

She went into what had been her bedroom and took the two suitcases from the top of the wardrobe. She packed everything that would fit in — her clothes, her shoes, the photographs of her parents, the Bible and books that had been her mother's. There were the poems of Keats and Tennyson. She didn't open them. Tennyson reminded her of all that she had lost, but her mother's name was written there, and she did not want to lose that, too.

She was ready when Henry came back. Had she not had the two suitcases, she would have walked across the fields to the little Abbotsbury Station, the way that she and Marjorie had walked for the last time, only three months ago, with her one suitcase. Marjorie had stood on the platform and waved until the train disappeared.

Cousin Henry manoeuvred the cases into his car, his face red with annoyance. She had a feeling that he thought she was probably stealing the silver teapot, the cream jug and sugar bowl, but even he didn't have the nerve to ask what she had got in the heavy cases. Catherine sat next to him but didn't speak. She walked into the station, leaving him to bring the cases and dump them at her feet. He was sweating, she noticed. Well, his ordeal was nearly over, but she wasn't going to make it easy for him. She simply looked at him without speaking.

He cleared his throat. 'Well, this is goodbye then.'

'So, it is. I don't suppose we'll meet again.'

'No — er — I daresay not. I hope —'

'I'll be all right. I daresay I will. I survived the war,' Catherine said coolly. Cousin Henry had been a magistrate during the war — prosecuting deserters and conscientious objectors, and farmers' sons who pleaded that they were needed to work the land, though he kept what men he wanted.

His face was the colour of beetroot now. 'Yes, well done and all that.'

She was suddenly tired of him. He didn't matter now — he was just a petty, grasping tyrant. 'Goodbye,' she said and turned away.

When he was gone, she realised that he had never even asked where she was going. To Bournemouth, she supposed. She would have to find lodgings in a place she hardly knew and apply for that post at the hospital. And if she didn't get it, what then? A hopeless blank. Perhaps, she ought to go elsewhere. To London and Pat? What did it matter?

But she must see John first to say goodbye. She thought of his kindness, his discreet helpfulness. He had booked her room for more nights in the hotel but had left her alone for the few days before the funeral, to which he had organised a car for her. The funeral had been arranged by Cousin Henry. The only mourners were Henry and his wife, the solicitor, Catherine, Marjorie's friend, Violet, and some neighbours. The young vicar spoke kindly of Marjorie as a good neighbour and of her contributions to the life of the church. Nothing was said about her taking in a little girl and being a mother to her in everything but name. The church fete-loving, cake-making, flower-arranging spinster was not Marjorie at all — as colourless and meaningless as a faded photograph about which some later grandchild or great-grandchild of Henry's would ask, 'Who was she?' The answer would be that no one could remember.

She had been tempted to rise from the pew and cry out, 'I loved her. She was the kindest, truest soul I ever knew.' But she didn't, of course. It would have done no good. No one would have understood. There was some balm in the kind words of Violet, who would miss her, and the neighbours who sought her out after the service, but she felt only loss and desolation as she watched Marjorie's coffin being lowered into the grave. Sherry and sandwiches were to be served at the Queen Anne house, but Catherine simply slipped away to find John, who was waiting with the hired car.

He didn't ask how the funeral had gone; he simply drove her back to the hotel and left her, only saying that if he wished her to do anything else, he would be on hand. Her sole relative, Henry Fowell, had just wanted rid of her. Blood was not thicker than water. Alone in her hotel room, she thought of her time at Raven's Gaze, where Bennet Lestrange, Mrs Whitenow, and John had welcomed her, and how they had been so kind about Marjorie. She could not have managed alone. Such kindness — to a stranger.

8

Catherine had gone to Bournemouth on the train, wounded by Henry Fowell's grasping selfishness, the emptiness of the funeral, and even the sound of a voice at the railway station announcing that the Bournemouth to Honiton train would be departing from platform two in five minutes. She was exhausted and completely incapable of making any plans about her future, so that when John Lestrange had suggested she return to Yorkshire with him until she was fit to make decisions, she had accepted and was touched and comforted by the warmth of Bennet Lestrange's welcome. To her surprise, he had met them at the station and had told her how sorry he was about Marjorie and how glad he was that she had decided to come back. The sentiment was echoed by Mrs Whitenow, who added that Catherine must stay as long as she liked — as their friend and guest.

She had been back for three weeks, and she hadn't given a thought to Annot Syke, Catherine reflected guiltily, as she walked past the gate of Starvecrow farm. She had been so wrapped up in her own grief and loss. She ought to see how Annot was getting on. No one at Raven's Gaze had mentioned her or Ted.

There was no familiar smoke curling from the chimney, and Catherine saw that the wooden sign bearing the name of the farm had gone. She walked down the path to the yard. No hens pecked in the sparse grass and the rubbish had been removed. The window shutters and the front door were firmly closed.

Ted Syke must have died, she thought, *and Annot gone to Leeds.* Well, it would be a relief to her and Ted — he had had no life at all, and the children would be better off. Annot would work at anything for them. It made her think. Whether a death was a relief or not, you had to pick up the burden and carry on. She had learned that in the war. A hard lesson but a true one, and she must learn it again. She imagined Annot, head held high and blue eyes flaming, with Clemmie in her arms, carrying her meagre possessions to the railway station, and Joe with a suitcase banging at his knees. Annot had gone to meet her future with courage after all she had endured.

At dinner that night, she mentioned the deserted farmhouse. She felt a stiffening in the atmosphere. Bennet Lestrange took a sip of his wine before he told her that Ted had died.

'When?' she asked.

'Oh, not long after you — I am so sorry, my dear, that was clumsy of me. I did not mean —'

'Yes,' interrupted Mrs Whitenow, 'a blessed relief, I think, that poor man's going. Annot has gone to Leeds with the children.'

'A widowed sister,' Bennet Lestrange said. 'Annot will have a better life away from here.'

John didn't speak. Catherine thought he looked uncomfortable and remembered their words about Ted Syke. She was sorry she had brought up the subject, but the silence was now awkward. 'What will happen to the farm?' she asked — an innocent question, she hoped.

'Annot sold it — to me. I gave her a fair price, knowing her difficulties, even though the place isn't much good for anything. And the money will help Annot to make a new life. She will be better suited to a town.'

Catherine agreed and the conversation turned to other things. Bennet Lestrange talked of his friend, Archie Bell, who was up at his lodge at Grouse Hall for a few days. Sir Archie would be holding a shoot in August, to which Bennet Lestrange looked forward every year. John didn't shoot. She knew that and understood. She remembered that John had pointed out the gun cupboard in the boot room beyond the kitchen when they had returned from a walk.

'I'm a disappointment to him in that matter, as well as everything else,' he had told her. 'But I've had enough of guns. He takes great pride in his skill, but he'd feel differently if he'd ever had to shoot someone. I hate the sight of his handgun — it's supposed to be something he was given at Oxford.'

Bennet Lestrange was still talking about Sir Archie and the other wealthy guests and how the autumn table at Raven's Gaze would be richer for the pheasant. He hoped Catherine liked the meat. Even John had a taste for pheasant, if not for shooting them.

'I had a taste for bully beef, but no one expected me to shoot the cow.' John's tone was light, but Catherine saw that Bennet Lestrange's answering smile did not reach his eyes. It was John's subtle reference to the war that annoyed him. Catherine thought that Bennet Lestrange resented that area of John's life which he could not control. The war and his injury would always place John just out of reach. She wondered when he might go away again. She thought of empty Starvecrow and Annot. It was certainly time she plucked up her courage and thought about her own future.

After dinner, when she and John walked along the terrace, she asked him if he were thinking of going to London.

'You mean now Sir Archie's here? I'm not expected to mix with the great and good — thank goodness. Bell's not a friend of mine. Too fond of killing things — like father,' he answered bitterly.

'No, I didn't mean that. Your last trip was interrupted — I felt sorry for that.'

'Don't, please. I wanted to help. Good Lord, Catherine, when I think what you did for me and what you've done for my grandmother, it was the least I could do. I hope you'll stay for the whole summer. You've only been here a few weeks, and the weather is so fine. It will be good for you — and me. We can escape together — I mean, you know, take a few trips. When he's busy, we could go to Manchester, Leeds — wherever you'd like.'

'Thank you, but I really must think about my future eventually. I cannot stay here forever. I must work for my living.'

He stopped and took her hands. 'Of course you must, but I think it's too soon after what you have been through.'

They walked on in the moonlight. The air was warm, and Catherine felt the peace of the night. It was so still that she could hear the sound of the brook gurgling down below. It was very tempting. She could stay a while longer. After a few minutes, she said, 'Annot told me she planned to go to Leeds, when the time came. What happened to Ted?'

She asked because she didn't want the subject of Ted to be a source of tension between them. John had been so good, and his words about Ted had been understandable. She should not have judged him so harshly.

He stopped and looked out towards the silvered hills. 'I don't know — Grandmother said that he just died while we were in Bournemouth. Just faded away, I suppose. Poor devil — what was the point of his living in that state? Just a shell. My God, I'd rather have been —'

Catherine touched his arm. 'I know, I know. I'm sorry, I didn't want to upset you. I know it's better for him and for her.'

'I'm still sorry I went on about him, Catherine. It was damned insensitive of me.'

'Don't be sorry. It's over now. I liked Annot, and I just wanted to know what happened. It was good of your father to buy the farm.'

'It suits him to have things in his possession. And people — oh, let's not talk about sad things. We'll do something to cheer us up. We'll go to that pub in Kirkby Stephen tomorrow. He'll be down at Grouse Hall, taking sherry with Sir Archie and polishing the guns, so we can go by ourselves.'

Catherine walked on her own past Starvecrow Farm and was surprised to see Mrs Slee and her red-haired niece coming along the track. Of course, now the farm belonged to Bennet Lestrange, Mrs Slee would be cleaning it out. She waved and hurried on, having no desire to discuss Annot with Mrs Slee, who would no doubt have something unkind to say about Annot's housekeeping.

She took the path which ran by bubbling Rowantree Gill and thought of Marjorie's delight in the names on the map, and grief swept over her. Grief ambushed her often when a chance remark brought Marjorie's death back to her, and with it that sense of being untethered that had begun the moment she had looked down at the hospital bed. She looked up to the fells. Where did she belong now? Not here, she thought, though she had enjoyed the outing to Kirkby Stephen where she and John had visited the church and laughed together, remembering Bennet Lestrange's relish in telling them about the stone Saxon figure of the Devil in chains — bound for a thousand years, he had told them, but only by day, because he walked by night, of course. They had been glad that he wasn't able to go with them.

Bennet Lestrange wasn't exactly the enemy, but laughing about him brought her and John into an unspoken alliance against a rather dominating parent — it was natural, somehow, and she was glad to hear John's laugh rather than his bitterness. He was complicated. He took things hard, yet he could be so kind and sensitive, as he had been in Dorset. Of course, he was not perfect, but she felt protective of him because she wondered if Bennet Lestrange disliked the fact that his son was maimed — flawed in some way. Bennet Lestrange cared for perfect things. He clearly felt nothing about John's courage in the war. Maybe, the other, absent son had been perfect. He could not have been braver than John, surely. John had said he was the favourite, yet no one spoke of him. But then, grief was strange and a lonely business, and each person grieved in his or her own way, as she was doing here by the stream. It bubbled on, careless of human feelings, making its way to the wide river and then the sea, the sea which licked the Dorset shore and would do so forever, knowing nothing of Marjorie Fowell or the millions of dead who had gone before into that darkness from which there was no return.

Catherine took a deep breath of the fresh, windy air and walked on quickly. It was no use brooding over such unfathomable matters. She had no idea where she was going, but she must compose herself before returning to Raven's Gaze. Where the stream met another footpath, she came across a farmhouse — Rowantree, where Grizel Knipe lived. Now, here was something she could do. Grizel Knipe might be able to give Catherine news of Annot. The farmhouse looked very like Starvecrow, but it was much better kept with an intact roof, a horse and cows grazing peacefully in the field, what looked like a dairy, and a tidy yard where a woman was hanging out her washing.

Catherine called out, introducing herself to the sturdy woman with grey hair tucked under an old straw hat, weather-beaten cheeks reddened by the winter winds, and grey eyes as clear as water, suggesting that Grizel Knipe could see further than most people. She gave Catherine a very kindly smile as she invited her in, saying, 'I know of thee from Annot, my dear — she liked thee, an' tha was kind to help her out. 'T'weren't no life for her an' them bairns.'

The kitchen was spotless with a scrubbed pine table, shining copper pans, a kettle bubbling on the range where the wood glowed red, and the smell of newly baked bread. Grizel Knipe poured her a cup of tea from a homely brown pot.

'I wondered about Annot, Mrs Knipe, and what happened to Ted.'

Grizel Knipe looked out of the window before she replied, 'Aye, a bad business. Poor lad. Nobbut skin an' bone at the end. He weren't fit for a soldier, nor a farmer. He couldn't stand the place, nor could he stand Annot — a mistake, that marriage. Annot were a bit dazzled by him — a gentleman, she thought, a way out of drudgery. She were a servant up at Hawes an' when their Joe were comin', Annot's father insisted... Not a man you'd cross, Dick Thwaite. He saw to it that they was wed. Annot were too much for Ted — too lively, too strong. See, he were weak an' he came to resent her because she were the doer an' he were the dreamer.'

'Poor Annot. She seems to have had no luck.'

'Tha means Clementine?'

'No, no, I admired Annot. She didn't care what people said about her.'

'No more she did, an' she loves that little girl. She's no regrets about her an' she weren't for tellin' who the father was.'

'Mrs Whitenow said it was a labourer who worked for them — a red-haired man.'

'She'll mean Carver Slee. Could have been, I suppose, an' I can see why Annot wouldn't say. A bad lot, he were. All them Slees is rotten. Esther Slee's husband was known for grazin' his sheep on other people's bit o' the fell — always gettin' into fights. Died in a ditch after fightin' in Hawes. No one knew owt about it, o' course, an' no one missed him.'

'Mrs Slee obviously doesn't like Annot — because of Carver Slee, I suppose.'

'That'll be it. The Slees all stick together, but whatever happened, it'd be his doin' an' poor Annot — she was that lonely. He'd take advantage. She shouldn't have, I know, but —'

'I understand, Mrs Knipe, I do.' *More than you know*, Catherine thought. 'I don't judge her. I saw what it was like at Starvecrow.'

'Well, Carver's long gone, and good riddance. Annot doesn't need him.'

'I hope Annot and the children will be better off in Leeds.'

Grizel Knipe turned her eyes to the window again before she said, 'Aye, 'tis to be hoped... I don't know where she's gone.'

'Mrs Whitenow said Leeds — to her sister.'

'I wonder how she knew that?'

'Annot told me that's what she'd do if — I mean when — where else could she go?'

'I took the bairns when she came an' said Ted was badly. My Dandy offered to go down, but she said not. Ted were dyin' an' she didn't want them to see, an' it were her to do for Ted on her own. I understood. That little lad, Joe, had seen enough.

An' then in the mornin' she came up to tell me he'd gone. When I went to t' farm to lay him out, Annot were all packed up. She asked me to see to everythin' — funeral an' that. Couldn't stand no more, she said. It seemed hard an' I were that sorry, but I sort of understood. He hadn't been any sort of husband to her, an' she wanted out of it all. There was money on the table for me to see to the burial. An' Mr Lestrange came to tell me t' farm was bought an' paid for. I don't know when that came about.'

I do, thought Catherine, remembering Bennet Lestrange walking up the fell behind the house and Annot red-faced and flustered. Annot had sold the farm because she knew that Ted was going to die. She thought of the second bottle of laudanum.

'When did all this happen?'

'Ted died a month ago. I remember because when she came up with the bairns, it were pourin' rain. Next mornin' he were gone.'

'Better for him, I think. A release.'

'Aye, 'twere no life for any of 'em — I couldn't blame Annot for wantin'…'

They sat in silence for a while. Catherine could hear the shush of the coals on the fire and the old clock ticking. A peaceful room, she thought, a room in which good people had lived for generations, a room where the shadows were benevolent ghosts. Those who were gone were memorialised in the scent of lavender and rosemary in the jar on the windowsill, in the battered chair by the range, in the clogs on the hearth, in the old bread knife on the table, its handle smoothed by many hands, and in the stitching on the sampler on the wall, the date of which was 1720. A long-ago Agnes Knipe had stitched it, and she was not forgotten. Yet

Catherine's mind couldn't be still. She couldn't help wondering at the coincidence of Bennet Lestrange's appearance behind Starvecrow Farm and Ted Syke's death, but it didn't make sense. She could not believe that Annot would have brought about Ted's death for money. Bennet Lestrange had had no reason to wish for Ted Syke's death, aside from his desire to take possession of the farm. She thought of Annot's fierce pride. Perhaps he had angered Annot that day by offering to buy the farm, but Annot would have had no choice if she wanted a better life for Joe and Clemmie.

Grizel spoke again. 'Dost tha know anything about this?'

Catherine saw an empty bottle of laudanum in Grizel's hand. Grizel had wondered about Ted's death, then. She looked directly at her. 'I gave it to Annot to help ease Ted's pain — she knew not to give him too much —'

The clear grey eyes looked back into Catherine's. 'Would'st tha blame her?'

Catherine held that honest, compassionate gaze. 'No, never. I gave her a second one and I didn't repeat the warning. I saw what a dreadful state he was in.'

Grizel nodded. 'Then we'll let it be. T''isn't for us to judge.'

There was no need for more words. Catherine let the peace of the room wash over her before she stood up. Grizel took her to the farm gate, where they stood, Grizel looking up to the hills with that far-seeing gaze.

'It's a hard life an' no mistake. A lonely one, too. Tha's to be used to it.' She looked back at Catherine. 'Tha's been through it, I can tell, but tha mun think o' the life to come, however hard it seems now. Lovely eyes, tha has, my dear, hazel eyes with that bit o' green. Tha should'st look a long way, see what's over that horizon, if tha can'st.'

Catherine walked back and stood at Starvecrow for a few moments. *Could it be?* she asked herself. Perhaps she had put temptation in Annot's way by giving her the second vial of laudanum. Perhaps Bennet Lestrange had put temptation in Annot's way by offering her money to buy the farm. She thought of Grizel, who said her mind was at rest. She accepted what had happened, had seen into the heart of the matter. Catherine thought of that maimed young man and Annot's vitality, and of Joe and little Clemmie. She could not blame her. If it had been so, then let it be, she thought, and hoped that Annot was thriving wherever she was.

She walked on, her eyes on the hills, but she could not see over the horizon, where dark clouds massed in the purpling sky. A storm was on its way, she thought, quickening her pace. She ought to hurry home. And then she stopped again, feeling the first icy drops. Home? Where was home? A tide of loneliness and grief swept over her again, and she wept for Marjorie and for the first time in months, for Leo.

9

On a warm afternoon at the beginning of June, Catherine and John sat in the little wood where the brook bubbled over the stones and the thrush sang in sunlight and shadow. It was there that he asked her to stay with him at Raven's Gaze.

She had come across him again sitting on the fallen tree in the despondent way he had sat when she'd seen him there first. He looked so forlorn that she didn't hesitate this time, stepping forward to say, 'Oh, John, is there something wrong? Can I do anything?'

He stood up. 'I was thinking about you. I don't want you to go. Stay, Catherine and marry me.' She was too astonished to speak. He came over and took her hands. 'These last weeks, they've been — the best. I've come to care for you. I think you know that. I wonder if you can feel the same... I...'

Then he turned away from her. She did care. She had come to care very much what happened to him. Yes, he was damaged, moody at times, but what might Leo have been after the war? She would not have turned from him. Perhaps she and John could... They could ... find peace together. She looked at his bowed head, and pity wrung her heart. He was lonely and he needed her. She was lonely, too, and whatever she told herself about courage and duty, deep down, she was afraid of the future. Marjorie was gone. Leo was gone, and she did not know whether he had loved her as she had loved him. She had never heard from Cousin Henry Fowell. Pat Sinclair was preparing for her wedding — she would spend her honeymoon in Devon, visiting friends such as the Beauforts. How Pat harped on them in her letters. Even her friend in

Manchester was now engaged to be married and was giving up nursing. There was no one who needed her. No one who wanted her. Only John.

Bennet Lestrange and Mrs Whitenow were delighted. They quite understood that she preferred a quiet wedding. John felt the same, so the ceremony took place in a little, gloomy church on the road between Garsdale and Hawes, in which they shivered as they repeated the vows spoken by an elderly clergyman with nervous, watery blue eyes. John had looked nervous, too, as he placed the ring on her finger, but it went on smoothly. The weather was gloomy, too, so they did not linger outside the church where the clergyman shook their hands, but spoke only to Bennet Lestrange. In any case, there were no friends or neighbours to throw rice, nor anyone to catch Catherine's bouquet. Bennet Lestrange took one photograph at Raven's Gaze. Catherine thought that it would not show them at their best — it was too cold for them to stand and smile. When she saw it, she noted how she had looked down and how cold and strained John had looked. He hadn't said he was in pain.

Mrs Slee prepared a simple lunch, after which Catherine went to her own room. There were spare rooms next to John's along the right-hand corridor at the top of the first landing. She had thought...

Now, sitting on her bed in her new creamy lace dress, she didn't quite know what she had thought — or rather, she had assumed vaguely that she and John would have a bedroom and a sitting room to themselves. She hadn't dared put her thoughts into words, not even to John, and certainly not to Mrs Whitenow. She was conscious that a bride ought not to ask such things, and she was painfully aware that she was not what a bride ought to be. She had had a lover. She had no idea if John had had any previous love affairs. They hadn't spoken of their former lives, except about the war.

She went to the mirror to take off her hat. *John doesn't know me*, she thought, looking at the woman who had lain in Leo Beaufort's arms and who had felt the rightness of it. John had not said he loved her, but what did she really feel for John? She had pitied him in that moment under the trees, when she had said she would marry him. After that they had gone on as before, though she had found something touching in his eagerness to be married as soon as possible. She had thought that he held back from embracing her because he was a gentleman, and she had made no move because she was conscious that she was not what John believed her to be. And another thought came to her, as if something icy had touched the back of her neck. *I don't know John Lestrange.* They were strangers. In separate rooms.

She looked down at the rings on her left hand, the ruby set in diamonds, which Bennet Lestrange had told her was a family heirloom — from the Lestrange family. It had belonged to his great-grandmother of Rosemount, the country house in Ireland. He had saved it for just such an occasion as the marriage of his son and heir. John had taken the ring from his father and placed it on her third finger. Mrs Whitenow had been present, too. A curiously public occasion for an engagement, Catherine had thought, but their pleasure was so apparent that she had accepted it. Of John, she was not sure. He had fumbled with the ring and had not joined in with the laughter. Perhaps he would have preferred to give it to her in private after the celebratory dinner. However, he had taken her hand and said he hoped she liked the ring.

Bennet Lestrange had laughed and said that she must — it was a precious thing, and the fact that it fitted surely showed that the young couple were meant to be together. A toast to that, he had said. Champagne was poured, but Catherine noticed Mrs Whitenow's glance at Bennet Lestrange, a glance she couldn't quite read — something ironic, she thought, but it was gone in a second, and Mrs Whitenow was clinking her glass with Catherine's and saying how glad she was that Catherine was to be part of the family. John had not looked at her when she held her glass to his.

After he had placed the wedding ring on her finger, he had kissed her. Not passionately — more in a shy way, as if he did not know what she might feel. Now she waited for him. Now they might cease to be strangers.

But they did not. Not in their deepest selves. Catherine knew that on the first night when he came to her room and when he went away again. Their lives split into two parts. By day, he was exactly the same John with whom she went for walks and on picnics and drives without Bennet Lestrange who was much occupied with the shooting season. They went to country towns and visited bookshops. He gave her a lovely suede-bound copy of Tennyson's poems to remind her of the woods, he told her, and she was touched and hopeful. But at night, when he came to her, he might have been the stranger she had thought of on her wedding day.

In September, Mrs Whitenow suggested that they take a holiday by the sea. She thought the sea air would do them good. She thought John did not look as well as he might. She looked at John and suggested that Grange-over-Sands, a quiet little town, would suit them. John looked away, merely saying that if his grandmother believed that Grange would suit, then he would write to one of the hotels immediately.

'The Grand Hotel has a good reputation,' Mrs Whitenow said, smiling at Catherine. 'There is golf, I believe, and good walks.'

'As you wish,' John said and left the room.

'You will enjoy it, I'm sure, my dear Catherine,' Mrs Whitenow said, as if she had not noticed the coldness in John's tone.

'Yes — I hope so. John is —'

'In need of a change, I think. You are both too much with us. Young people ought to have time for themselves. Go and keep him company while he makes the arrangements. Tell him that you are looking forward to the holiday.'

Catherine went to her own room. She knew that John did not want her company, and Mrs Whitenow must be blind not to see that. But she was right in saying that John did not look well. Was the strain of being that divided self taking its toll on him? Though he behaved as if they were good companions, she would sometimes see that absent look on his face, even by day. There might have been a wall of glass between them, and she looking through it to see a man she did not know, performing the life expected of him.

They took the train from Oxenholme, where John told her that he had booked them into The Grosvenor Hotel at Morecambe. He said he did not care for Grange-over-Sands, a rather dull place. Morecambe was livelier, and the sands very fine for long walks. Catherine didn't mind where they went — she simply hoped that if they were alone for a few days, away from Raven's Gaze, she might be able to reach him, at least talk to him about what was wrong between them. However, she was surprised that he left her alone on the first afternoon

— he had some business to attend to in Lancaster on behalf of his father. She did not ask but went down to what turned out to be very fine sands and walked a long way, happy to feel the wind on her face, and, she admitted to herself, the freedom to do as she pleased. She took an early dinner in the room and was in bed, pretending to be asleep, when John came back. She heard the sound of glass breaking in the bathroom and then he came into the room. The bedside table rattled as he got into the other single bed. As soon as she had seen the two beds, she had known that the holiday would not bring them together. The whiff of alcohol told her that he had been drinking.

After a silent breakfast the next morning, they walked along the sands in bright sunshine and bracing wind. A man in an army greatcoat slept under the pier. He lay on his back, his eyes closed and his open hands on the wet sand. She thought he was dead until she discerned the slight rise and fall of his chest. She was horrified that the man looked so filthy and unshaven, for he had his service ribbons pinned to his ragged coat. He looked like a pauper. When Catherine made to go nearer, John pulled her back, telling her there was nothing they could do.

'But he might be ill,' she protested, pulling away from him. 'Surely, we should —'

John followed and the man's eyes opened as Catherine looked down at him. She had seen that look many times before, blank and staring. The eyes, a strange pale green, fixed on John. Lieutenant Adams's eyes, she thought, her heart lurching suddenly. Poor, mad, Christopher Adams. But he wasn't Adams. The long black hair and coarse features belied that. Still, what a dreadful state this ex-soldier was in.

She looked at John, who seemed to recoil from the stare. His anger shocked her. 'I can smell the drink on him. Leave it, I tell you. The police will find him and clean him up. A hopeless case, I should think. Leave it.'

She felt for some coins in her pocket and put them in the man's hand. 'At least we can give him something.'

But John was already walking away. He didn't speak when she caught up with him, and as they walked away, she looked at the grey heave and roll of the sea and felt an empty sickness. That sea circled the world; it had taken that poor wretched man to France and brought him back again to lie forgotten on the sands. *Oh, John*, she thought, *where is your pity?*

At dinner, John was mostly silent. It was to do with the man on the beach, she guessed, and was reminded of his words about Ted Syke. She had forgiven him for that, but now she thought that any ex-soldier, injured or damaged in some way seemed to bring out contempt, even fear in him rather than compassion. She had mentioned a story from the newspaper about an ex-soldier in Kendal who had been arrested for fighting and who had been discharged from the army with shellshock. When she had expressed the opinion that such a man ought to be in hospital, not prison, he simply said, 'And a fat lot of good that will do.' It was another breach between them, and she didn't know what to do about it.

After dinner, he said he fancied a breath of fresh air. The truth was that he did not want to spend a whole night in her company. He never did. She knew that her idea of trying to reach him was a hopeless cause. After his walk, he came back at about two o'clock in the morning. She could smell the drink, not that he had taken any at dinner. Again, she pretended to be asleep. And so the next few days passed, John disappearing on business in Lancaster and Catherine taking her long, solitary walks along the promenade. She did not see the ragged ex-soldier again, but she didn't forget him.

*

When Mrs Whitenow asked how they had enjoyed Grange, John answered that they had found it very pleasant. Catherine felt obliged to agree, though he did not explain why he had lied to his grandmother. How sick she was of their secrets. Not that she was able to ask him what he meant. He did not come to her room after they returned from the hopeless trip to Morecambe. It had driven them further apart, but she was relieved, too, because she was certain she was expecting a child. When she told John, he appeared to be pleased, but it was hard to tell by his restraint which was so marked in contrast to the fulsome delight of Bennet Lestrange, who treated her as if she were made of fine porcelain.

Then one morning in October, John was gone without a word to her. On business, Bennet Lestrange told her. Raised voices after breakfast in the dining room told her a different story. She stood on the stairs and heard Bennet Lestrange say, 'No, I say. The matter is closed. There is no point in your going there. You can do nothing without my permission —'

She heard the door slam and heavy footsteps in the hall, and she darted back upstairs. When she peeped into his room before going down again, she saw that John had gone.

'He seems to be taking an interest at last,' Mrs Whitenow said during lunch, keeping up the fiction. 'He will be back in a few days, so you mustn't worry. It's time you took a nap, I think. You must rest as much as you can.'

But Catherine insisted on taking a walk on finer afternoons. She found that she preferred to be alone. The fuss made of her was stifling sometimes and she felt sure that when she did go out, Bennet Lestrange watched her. Not that she could do anything about that.

When she came back one afternoon, she was surprised to see him outside, looking up at the porch. He turned to her and quoted the words on the stone roundel: "'Afterwards I know not whom.'" Then he smiled and went on, 'Well, I do now, thanks to you, my dear Catherine. To my grandson.'

Afterwards, she thought about that satisfied smile and wondered what he would say if her child were a girl.

December brought fierce gales. The cloud-tossed sky was dark grey, looming over the house and tower; rain spilled down the high walls turned black in the tempest. Day and night seemed the same. The wind battered at the house, where the fires sizzled when rain came down the chimneys.

Catherine was comfortable enough in her new room. She had John's bedroom, where she slept alone in another, bigger four-poster bed around which she would pull the curtains closed at night, when the wind seemed to shriek at the windows so that she felt as if she were out on a stormy sea. She had a comfortable sitting room, too, and there was a nursery set up in an adjoining room, where there were an old-fashioned cradle and the wickerwork perambulator she had seen in the old nursery. She didn't like it but dared not say, for she did not want to admit that she had seen it before, but she did ask Mrs Whitenow if it had been John's, to which the answer was that it had been. No fond reminiscence of John's mother or when she had pushed her baby in it.

Catherine had only one thing on her mind: her baby must be safely born, for then she must decide once more what her future should be. John did not matter. He had gone away again, and she was glad. She could not bear his watchfulness. At first, she was moved by his solicitousness when he had returned, but one afternoon in late November she had woken from her nap with a sense of foreboding. John was standing by the window of her room. The afternoon was dark grey, and she could see John's outline against the dying light in the window. He was looking out and something about the set of his head and shoulders and his clenched hand suggested tension. She didn't move but watched him from under her half-closed eyelids. When he turned, she saw the brooding expression in his dark eyes. And she was reminded of that time on the train to Bournemouth, when she thought she was dreaming his face looking at her as if she were a stranger. He looked the same now. She did not know who he was.

Under the covers, her hands crept to cradle her swelling stomach. The baby had kicked before she went to sleep and she had felt a surge of joy. She was going to tell John when he came up, but she didn't move. He left the room quietly and she heard the click of the door closing. He had gone away again the next day.

The baby continued its flutterings, as if a butterfly were dancing in her stomach. Oh, the joy of this new life. The quickening, they called it. The baby was alive, but whatever she had felt for John Lestrange was dead.

10

The story was that John had left for Ireland to administer the property there. Catherine didn't know if it were true or not, and she brooded over his strange behaviour in her room on that gloomy November afternoon. Why had he looked at her so darkly? The answer came to her swiftly: because he did not love her. She dreaded the thought of seeing him again. The breach between them was irreparable, and there was nothing she could do until her child was born.

So, she kept up the pretence with Bennet Lestrange and Mrs Whitenow that he would be back soon — certainly before the birth of his first child. *Oh, there were to be others*, she thought — a nursery full of heirs, in case the first one was not suitable. John was to come back and expect to resume what passed for their marriage. It could not be. She had made a terrible mistake.

John must be in London, she believed, enjoying himself with his friends, and with that image came a chilling thought. Perhaps John had someone else, a mistress whom he could not marry for some reason. She remembered Sabine and Raoul, Sabine who had looked up at John with such fondness, and John whose face was transformed when he saw her. It had been joy, Catherine thought. She had never again seen that light in John's face.

And Sabine had taken John's arm and had sat in the back seat of the car with him when he had left the CCS. Sabine had said that she would look after him. Not "they". John had been surprised when Catherine had referred to Sabine and Raoul as a couple, and had changed the subject. There were such obviously close friends of his, and yet he hadn't referred to them again. He'd only mentioned his friends in London, Freddie Hunter and his fiancée, Alice.

The truth came to her in a moment of absolute clarity. She had been blind. How Bennet Lestrange had enjoyed teaching her the origin of her name, Sisley. Caecilius meant "blind", and he had said that she would be able to find her way in the dark, knowing that she could not see what he meant to do. He was always looking at her in that assessing way, testing her, teasing her. And she had been blinded — by grief and loss. Loneliness, too, but how could she have known? Yes, she had not felt entirely comfortable at Raven's Gaze, and she had sometimes wondered in the early days if Bennet Lestrange and Mrs Whitenow had hoped for a match between her and John, but she had never imagined that there could be such cold calculation. Enemies in most things, they had been allies in that one purpose: John must marry and provide an heir to Raven's Gaze Hall. Of course, John had told them about his meeting with her at Waterloo, and he had complied with their plan in exchange for his freedom and no doubt a substantial income from Bennet Lestrange. John had married her to get a child for Bennet Lestrange and Mrs Whitenow.

Catherine had been determined to leave Raven's Gaze. She didn't know what plans they had devised to make her accept John's proposal before she left for good. She remembered wondering at Bennet Lestrange's insistence that John return before her departure, and John's ironic agreement — he had known what he was supposed to do. But she would have refused him. She would have gone. Only Marjorie's death had brought about her return. And now they meant to keep her here because of the heir.

That thought made her sit up in bed. She felt a sudden sense of claustrophobia and wrenched back the bed curtain, feeling her heart beating too fast. She watched the dying fire and listened to the rain lashing and the intermittent gusts of wind which sounded like the rumble of gunfire. The windows shuddered under the impact. She thought the shutters might burst open. The baby kicked. He had woken, too. Or she. A girl. Let the baby be a girl. They — they, as in Bennet Lestrange and Mrs Whitenow — might not care if she had a girl; they might leave her alone. She could pretend all was well for a few weeks, even if John came back. Of course, he would not come to her. The memory of his brooding eyes told her that. There would be no second child. She had time to plan her escape. She could not stay here, but to whom could she turn?

Grizel Knipe, perhaps. Grizel knew everyone in the dale, and she'd know who might take Catherine and the baby to a railway station. She could wait at Rowantree farm. Grizel wouldn't tell, but Oxenholme was safer, perhaps, rather than Hawes Junction. If her child was a boy, Bennet Lestrange might pursue her. Yes, she would go to London from Oxenholme. To Pat Sinclair — Pat wouldn't turn her away, but it didn't matter; she had money, and there were lodgings. She thought of the tents and huts she had lived in during the war — she had endured privation. She could endure lodgings as long as the baby was safe.

The thought of leaving comforted her; she burrowed into the bedclothes, feeling for the stone hot water bottle and slept at last, only to be woken by a noise which sounded like a pistol shot. *Bennet Lestrange*, she thought madly, but the sound came again. It was the sound of a door banging and then the sound of glass breaking. The wind outside was furious. She waited and listened to the repeating sounds, but there were no voices or hurried footsteps. Bennet Lestrange would be in his tower and Mrs Whitenow asleep along the other corridor. Mrs Slee would be in her cottage.

Catherine couldn't bear the sound. It set her teeth on edge. She found herself listening for the next explosion of noise. It reminded her of the war — those sleepless nights when every nerve strained as she had waited for the next boom of guns or shell burst. She'd not sleep again. *The old nursery*, she thought. Could the noise be coming from upstairs? She slipped on her dressing gown, reached for the lamp, which was still burning on the bedside table, and thought to put a log on the embers of the fire before she crept into the freezing corridor. The thought of the nursery chilled her, but the repeated slamming noise went on. No one would come.

She hesitated at the door to the spiral staircase; the lifting of the latch sounded like another pistol shot in the silence. She stood, shuddering in the icy draught. The first stone steps of the spiral staircase chilled her feet. She was a fool not to have put on her slippers. She gripped the iron rail with one hand and held up the lamp with the other. Shadows unfolded, rising and falling up and down the walls, seeming to reach out to her so that she shrank back instinctively, lowering one foot to the step below, half turning to go down, but the noise continued as if someone were hammering to get in. She couldn't stand it, so she hauled herself up, counting each perilous step. Thirteen steps led her to the landing. The doors to the maids' rooms and the nursery door were closed. The noise seemed to be coming from further down the corridor, from the room Mrs Slee had said wasn't safe. *Oh, God.* She thought of her baby. He — she — must never know this place, but she must stop that noise.

The door was at the end of the corridor, a huge oak door thickly studded with iron and fastened with a massive oak bar fitted into iron slots. *A prison*, she thought. A place to lock someone in. She put down the lamp and lifted the bar with both hands, then pushed at the door with her foot. It opened silently and she secured the bar by its iron hook. It made no sound. The room was supposed to be dangerous, but someone must come up here. Probably Mrs Slee. The door hadn't creaked, and though the bar was heavy, it was not stiff with disuse.

She felt the rush of bitter chill air. A window must be open. Her heart leapt as another bang broke the silence. Raising the lamp, she saw that a shutter was hanging open and darted across to fasten it, feeling broken glass pierce her foot as she reached the window. She grasped the shutter with her free hand, noting the iron-barred window and the broken pane. She fastened the shutter to its neighbour, slipping down the wooden catch. The noise ceased and that was all that mattered. She exhaled, realising that she had been holding her breath and that her heart was racing. She stood still to calm herself and to make sure her child was quiet.

When she felt steady enough, she raised the lamp to look round the room. A gasp of fright escaped her. There was a horrible shadow on the wall opposite — something hanging by a rope, something turning slowly in the draught. She looked up and saw the stone hammer which Bennet Lestrange had called a dobbie stone, supposed to ward off evil spirits. *Nothing to be afraid of*, she thought, lowering the lamp, *a silly superstition*. Then her heart jumped again as she saw tucked against the wall to her left, an iron-framed hospital bed on which the metal side bars were raised, bars meant to stop the patient from falling out. It was then that she noticed the leather straps dangling from the metal frame at the bed head and the ones looped round the end of the bed. It was the kind of bed that was used to restrain a patient, a patient who must be kept prisoner — a patient dangerous to himself — or herself, and others — a mad patient.

She could smell them. Taste them. Sickness and terror and despair. It was as if they cried out from the very walls of this icy cold room, filled the frozen air into which her breath congealed, mingled with the shadows created by her lamp. She hardly dared to move or breathe, but she could not help looking at the bare boards, the chipped table by the bed, the single glass placed there, the burnt-down candle in its tarnished brass holder, and most terrible of all, the mattress with its dark stains and the leather straps.

She must not stay. She must never say what she had seen. She forced herself to be calm, to walk carefully to the door, to close it quietly, to lower the heavy bar back into place. And as she turned, that dreadful sound came again. She had not closed the shutter tightly enough, but she dared not go back in. The horror of that room was worse than anything. She forced herself to walk slowly back past the silent nursery, past the maids' rooms, down the spiral staircase. She slipped into her own room, where she sat by the fire and listened until the cold, grey dawn light crept in when the wind died down and the frightful banging stopped at last.

'You look rather tired, Catherine. Did you have a bad night?' asked Mrs Whitenow solicitously.

Catherine knew she must look dreadful. She had not slept at all. Her mind was full of terrible images. If she dozed, it was Lieutenant Adams's haunted face that she saw, or the man under the pier, or Ted Syke. She had seen his face just the once, but it had been enough. She remembered his gauntness, his hairless skull like a death's head, the mouth fallen in, the eyes completely blank. And all those faces turned into John's face. John lying on his bed at the CCS, his eyes absent, his eyes afraid of Lieutenant Adams, his eyes afraid of the man under the pier. Not John. Surely not. She could not believe that John had been the patient in that room. But who?

Mrs Whitenow was gazing at her, all concern, but Catherine had acquired some heightened perception in the night. Mrs Whitenow's ivory face now seemed like a mask, her silvery grey eyes too penetrating.

'Take some tea, my dear, and a little toast, and then I think you must go back to bed. Did the storm keep you awake?'

'I was restless. I couldn't get comfortable, and it was rather noisy.'

Mrs Slee came in with hot water and fresh toast, which she placed before Catherine, who felt a sudden sickness at the sight of the cook's large, scarred hands. It looked as though someone had slashed at them with a knife. Someone mad. Catherine felt that she could never take food from those hands again. She picked up her teacup to cover her revulsion.

'Mrs John has had a bad night, Mrs Slee, so please see to the fire in her room and make up some hot water bottles.'

'Yes, ma'am.' Mrs Slee looked at Catherine. 'I'm that sorry, miss. It was a terrible night. Lot o' bangin' an' crashin' at my place. Thought the chimney were comin' down. No damage here, ma'am?'

'I don't think so,' Mrs Whitenow said. 'I didn't hear anything but the wind.'

'There's a window broken on the top floor an' one o' the shutters is open. Saw it as I came across. Might have been the storm. Tha didn't hear nothin', Mrs John?'

Catherine felt Mrs Slee's steel eyes upon her, but she looked straight at her. 'I don't know, Mrs Slee. The night seemed all noise to me.'

'I'd best go up an' see. The old nursery, I think.'

Mrs Whitenow looked up from her tea. 'Yes, it might well be — yes, you should go up. See that the shutters are securely fastened, too.'

Catherine felt very glad that she had not gone into that room to refasten the shutter — Mrs Slee might have realised that someone had been up there. She might guess it had been her. Catherine had no intention of telling anyone that she had seen the room. It was clear that she was not supposed to know.

'Mrs John and I will wait here by the fire while you see to her room and the hot water bottles.'

Catherine was dismayed to see that Mrs Slee was still lighting the fire when she went back upstairs.

'I've put the bottles in thy bed, Mrs John, and there'll be a good blaze in a minute or two. Shall I help thee undress?'

Those hands, Catherine thought, *must not touch me or my child.* She thought of her bloodied foot — Mrs Slee must not see that. In any case, she had no wish to be helped, nor to be betrayed into any admission that she had heard the shutter banging in the night. 'No, thank you, Mrs Slee. I shall just sit by the fire for a while.'

'Is there anything I can get thee? More tea? Some warm milk?'

'No, thank you again, but I shall be all right if I sit quietly.'

Still the wretched woman lingered, watching the fire, fiddling with the poker and the logs until Catherine felt she wanted to shout at her to just go away, but she merely said, 'That fire is burning well now. I'll just go to the bathroom and wash my face.'

'Yes, well, if that's all, I'll be getting on. I ought to fix that shutter in the nursery. I'm surprised it didn't keep thee awake. It must have been banging half the night.'

'The wind gusted so hard — that was enough noise,' Catherine said as she went out to the bathroom. She looked in the mirror at the dark circles under her eyes and her white face. She felt angry. She had been well so far in her pregnancy. *Damn them*, she thought, *for their secrets*. She must not let them make her ill. She must be strong for her baby's sake. That room was unused now. Whoever had been the patient was gone now. No madman would come down the thirteen steps to haunt her.

But as she lay on her bed, watching the swirling rain and heavy clouds lour down on Raven's Gaze, her restless mind returned to that iron bed, and again to John. Could she really be sure that he had not been the patient in that room? She went back in time to France, where he had recuperated after his discharge from the CCS in November 1917. He had been wounded at Estaires in April 1918, and he had almost lost his leg in September 1918 at Arras, where there had been thousands of casualties — the wounded, the gassed and the dead. No doubt torn between fear and duty as they all had been, he had pretended that all was well, dismissing his injury as bad luck. Outwardly coping, inside he was a divided man. She had met him again at Waterloo Station in the winter of 1919 after that painful meeting with Pat. He had told her that he had been staying in France again, but anything could have happened in the eighteen months between their meetings. She had no proof that John had been in France all that time. Then there were his absences from Raven's Gaze, his visits to a doctor in London — a specialist doctor? She remembered Mrs Whitenow's concern, her suggestion that Catherine might help him, and that moment in her bedroom, when he had seemed a perfect stranger.

What if her theory that he loved elsewhere was just her imagination? What if his absence in their most intimate moments was evidence of something broken in him — something that she could not mend? Not that there had been many intimate moments. He could pretend by day, when she made no demands on him other than the friendly companionship they had enjoyed. Now he was supposed to be in Ireland. Letters came to her enclosed in letters to his grandmother. She never saw the envelopes. Was he in France with Sabine? Or was he somewhere else — somewhere worse? She thought of his fear of Lieutenant Adams, of Ted Syke, of the man under the pier — his horror of madness. Could that mean...?

And she remembered what Annot had said: *They've got their secrets at Raven's Gaze an' I'll keep mine.* Annot had cleaned for Mrs Whitenow at Raven's Gaze. What had Annot known?

It was too late. Annot was gone, taking her secrets with her, and there was nothing she could do except keep her own secrets and pretend that all was well — as all at Raven's Gaze pretended.

And that was how Catherine coped the next few months, eating lunch as often as seemed politic with Mrs Whitenow, typing for Bennet Lestrange, whose book was nearing completion, and even going with him in the car to Crosby Ravensworth. 'Ravens again?' she asked politely. No, the name was from Old Norse, he told her, and he lectured on about the old house there which had a spiral staircase leading to a sealed room in the attics in which a woman had been imprisoned — only her bones remained. 'Like Poe's story,' he said, '"The Fall of the House of Usher". You know it, of course.' She knew he was taunting her, but she only smiled back. She didn't want to know about abandoned sisters or wives. He knew that she was one of them, but he never talked of John. She was often tempted to ask him where exactly his son was, but she let the matter rest. If he thought she were stupid, let him. He would learn.

She still insisted on taking her walks, telling Mrs Whitenow that she must keep fit and healthy for her baby's sake. Mrs Whitenow had to agree, as did Bennet, whom she knew watched her from his tower. Though they told her not to go too far, sometimes on a fine day she would call on Grizel Knipe, whom she came to like and trust, but to whom she said nothing of her plan to leave Raven's Gaze as soon as she could. That must be her secret until the time was right. Grizel Knipe said that she would come to Raven's Gaze if Catherine needed her. She'd brought many a child of the dale into the world, but if Mrs Lestrange wanted the doctor from Hawes, she understood.

Catherine thought she would like Grizel Knipe, but she said nothing to Mrs Whitenow or John when he made his infrequent visits. She did not resist the ministrations of Doctor Hall, who assured her that she was well and that her child would be a healthy one. He asked John one day in February if he hoped for a son, and she held her breath, waiting for his reply. He didn't mind, he said at last, as long as the child was well, and his wife, of course. He didn't look at her, and she knew that he lied. His duty would be done if a son came. Perhaps he would be happy if her son lived, and she died. That would be convenient for everyone at Raven's Gaze.

She felt a determination to take matters into her own hands and asked what would happen if Doctor Hall could not come for some reason. She knew Mrs Grizel Knipe from Rowantree. Could she be recruited in case of emergency?

'Indeed, yes,' Doctor Hall assured her. 'I have every faith in Mrs Knipe. I shall speak to her. And, of course, you have Mrs Slee, who is no stranger to nursing and childbirth. A most competent woman.'

She didn't look at John, but she heard his intake of breath. He was nervous, but she was determined. *Never Mrs Slee.* 'I'm sure she is, but from what I know of Mrs Knipe, I think I should trust her more.' She felt John's eyes on her. He didn't know about her friendship with Grizel Knipe. Perhaps her reference to Grizel worried him. He must know of the connection between Annot Syke and Grizel. And Annot Syke knew that there were secrets at Raven's Gaze.

John went out of the room with Doctor Hall, and she did not see him again that day or for another month. But it was interesting how, as her time came closer, Bennet Lestrange would accompany her on her walks, which must be short, he said, for she must not overdo it, a sentiment echoed by Mrs Whitenow. She did not want Bennet Lestrange's company, but she put up with him, determined that she would give no sign that she was anything but the compliant daughter-in-law he pretended to cherish.

But she did not forget the room upstairs. She didn't need to see it again. The image of that bed was imprinted on her mind, especially when the cold wind rattled the windows and rain poured in torrents. These were times when she sought refuge in her room and thought about John and whether he had been the patient. Or his mother of whom nothing was ever said, or the son of whom Mrs Whitenow had spoken with such regret and longing. It was a mystery to which she would probably never know the answer, but it was such a dark secret that it seemed to her now like an almost palpable presence. She sometimes caught a shadow on the wall by the door which led to the spiral staircase, as if someone hovered there, someone who had come down or was about to go up. Once she turned to look before she went to her own room and caught a glimpse of the open door and felt the icy draught coming down the stairs. She was sure she heard the sound of a foot on the stone — Mrs Slee, perhaps, checking on the windows in that room.

She never closed the bed curtains now. She couldn't bear the thought of someone coming secretly into her room and she not knowing that someone watched. Very often sleepless, she imagined someone in the old nursery, or in the room at the end of the corridor, watching, waiting. She felt it at night, when she made her weary way past those mute armorial figures to go upstairs after some interminable supper with Bennet Lestrange and Mrs Whitenow, at which she ate only to preserve the health of her baby. Sometimes there would be a curtain rippling at her window, swelling out for a moment so that she looked down, breathless, expecting to see a pair of feet revealed by the draught.

That dark secret was not the ghost on the stairs, not some seduced serving maid; it was the darkness at the place of skulls, the dark thing in that massive oak chest, the darkness at the heart of Raven's Gaze. It was in Bennet Lestrange's unfathomable eyes; it lay behind the glitter of Mrs Whitenow's pale gaze, and in the hands of Mrs Slee. And in John. Those thoughts made her more determined than ever to leave Raven's Gaze as soon as she could. Her child would not be brought up in this house and with these people.

She thought of the men she had watched returning to the Front, heaving on their packs, squaring their shoulders, their eyes on the horizon, knowing what was to come, marching away, whistling and singing. And her colleagues, the doctors, the nurses, the orderlies, the stretcher-bearers, resolute under fire and storm. *Courage*, she thought. *Muster it now.*

11

Catherine did not know if she were awake or dreaming. She thought the fire glowed in the darkness, and that she heard voices. She thought she heard the word, "Raven", whispered somewhere in the shadows, and the word, "Never", whispered back. She tried to speak but no sound came; she tried to sit up, but her limbs were leaden. She could not open her eyes; then there was only blackness, as if she were sinking into some dark place where there was no light or sound.

When she woke again, it was daylight and the grey eyes of Grizel Knipe were looking down at her, eyes which seemed anxious, but then cleared. Grizel smiled and helped her to sit up, and then Catherine remembered.

'My baby?'

'As right as rain and waitin' to see his ma. He's here. An' tha'll be right as rain when tha's seen him.'

Grizel reached into the cradle by the bed and the bundle was placed into her waiting arms. Catherine looked down at the little solemn face, and she knew him more fully than she had ever known anyone. He knew her, too, his wise eyes taking in her face. Their recognition lasted but a few moments, but it was real and unbreakable. He was hers and she his, and nothing else mattered. Not John, not Bennet, not Mrs Whitenow. She would keep him safe and close, and when the time came, she would take him away.

'How long have I been asleep?'

'Eight hours. Baby came last night, Mrs John, but I was here with Doctor Hall. It were hard, I know, but tha was a brave lass through it all. Doctor thought tha should rest. The chloroform, scc. He had to use it. Young master there was wrong way round, but he's here now, safe and sound, and tha looks like a young lass again.'

Catherine remembered then. How her waters had broken, and Mrs Whitenow had sent for Mrs Slee, who had helped get her into bed and how she had put those scarred hands on her belly. The baby was coming, Mrs Slee had told Mrs Whitenow. She remembered Mrs Slee's worried look and the urgent whispers between the two women. Mrs Slee had hurried out and Mrs Whitenow told her that Betty had been sent to get Grizel Knipe, and Mr Lestrange was to take the car to Hawes for the doctor. She remembered the pain and Mrs Whitenow bathing her face with a cool face cloth, and how she had striven not to cry out, and how then there had only been Grizel who had comforted her. Grizel's gentle hands had soothed her as she'd told her that Doctor Hall was on his way. Grizel and he had delivered many a babe. There was naught to worry about — she was to breathe... And she remembered Doctor Hall with his sleeves rolled up and Grizel holding her hand in a warm grip as the pain nearly tore her in two. And she remembered the piercing cry of the baby, and Grizel telling her that he was a fine boy with a fine pair of lungs.

'There's naught to worry about now,' Grizel said when the baby let out a cry. 'He's hungry. Now, I've given him a bottle, but it's thy milk as he'll want, an' I can help thee with that.'

And Grizel taught her what to do, and the next few days were the most peaceful she had ever known. Grizel was to stay for as long as Catherine wanted her. And she did. Grizel meant safety for her and her child.

Mrs Whitenow came to look at her great grandson and Bennet Lestrange came to look at his grandson. 'Perfect in wind and limb, I'm told,' he said. 'I congratulate you.'

Perfect as a Georgian pounce pot, she thought. Bennet Lestrange did not refer to his son, who had not come, and she did not ask why. She didn't want to know anything about John Lestrange.

'My father's name was Thomas,' she replied in answer to Mrs Whitenow's question about the baby's name. 'He shall be called Thomas.'

'A very good name,' Mrs Whitenow said. 'A new life and a new start. I wonder if you would add the name James, after my husband. I can see that he is a Whitenow. It would please me to know that the name will carry on.'

Catherine agreed. It was part of her act. James might be a Whitenow name, but she'd had an Uncle James, and Thomas would be named in her heart after the two Sisley brothers.

Bennet Lestrange did not look pleased. No doubt he wanted a name of his own choosing, his own, perhaps, but he only said, 'As you wish.'

'We do,' Mrs Whitenow said firmly, but Bennet Lestrange had turned his back and was leaving the room. 'He cannot have all his own way,' she continued. 'Thomas James will be more a Whitenow than a Lestrange, just as my — just as it should be.'

Catherine smiled, but she was thinking that he would be neither. He would be hers. And when Mrs Whitenow was gone, she looked down at the sleeping child. *Not John's*, she thought. She could see nothing of John in him. Perhaps Thomas would resemble her or his namesake, though she could hardly remember her father. Majorie had said that he was tall with brown curling hair and hazel eyes, which Catherine had apparently inherited. But she remembered her mother with fair hair and grey eyes. Thomas would be a Sisley, she was sure.

*

A bitterly cold May brought snow to the dale. Catherine watched the whirling flakes obscuring the view of the sky and the fells at which she looked so often, imagining herself making her way down the road to freedom as she imagined Annot Syke had done. She remembered Bennet Lestrange saying that they had been trapped in for six weeks. She looked at the curtain of mist and snow and felt trapped, too, though she knew that it would be folly to try to leave now with a baby of two months, and she didn't feel strong enough. Grizel, who still came to see her, urged her to rest, to eat well and build up her strength. She would be able to spend time outside when the better weather came.

'But when, Grizel? When?'

'In God's own time, my dear. And tha's safe here, and little Thomas. Up the dale, there's them as can't hardly manage. Mr Harper's grocery cart can't get through an' neither can Doctor Hall. Owd Jane Parr's that sick with a bad chest — she's eighty years old an' not like to live. But change'll come, tha can be sure o' that.'

Catherine dozed, listening to the contented snufflings of the baby and the soothing click of Grizel's knitting needles. She was never without her knitting — all the daleswomen knitted as they worked, and Grizel was one of the fastest. Grizel's company was the most welcome to Catherine, a comforting presence in the house, but she was afraid that there must come a time when Grizel would stop coming. She had her farm and her husband to look after, and her grandchildren.

Mrs Slee was always about, changing the bed, collecting the laundry, bringing trays, though sometimes Betty came. Once or twice, Catherine had woken from a sleep to find Mrs Slee bending over the cradle. She had felt revulsion to see her there, her scarred hands large in the dim light and her face intent on the sleeping child, and she hated even more to see those hands pick up the baby to bring him to Catherine, but she thanked her and was glad to hear the door close on that malign presence.

One afternoon after a particularly windy night during which she had lain awake, unable to stop thinking about the rooms upstairs, she was glad to see Grizel come in.

'Just a fleetin' visit, my dear. I'm on my way to see owd Jane Parr. She's not got long an' I'm needed, but I've brought the shawl. See, it's finished. Blue for thy boy.'

The shawl was pale blue and as a slight as gossamer. Catherine felt tears spring to her eyes. Such beautiful work. Such kindness.

Grizel saw. 'There now. 'T'weren't meant to make thee cry, lovey.'

'I'm sorry, Grizel. Sometimes, I feel so weak and it's this house. I don't belong here.'

'It happens, lass, after a birth — tha feels downhearted. My lass, Janet, she was just the same. Cried at the least thing, but she picked up, an' tha will, too. Mr John'll come back, I'll be bound, an' then tha'll not feel so lonely.'

Catherine couldn't say anything about John. 'It's this house — it's full of secrets. Dark things. Annot knew. I'm afraid sometimes…'

Grizel patted her hand. 'There now, don't take on, my dear. Things'll come right. Don't be thinkin' about such things. That babby needs his ma to be strong.'

'Annot said that Raven's Gaze has secrets. What are they? What do you know about the house?'

'I only knew it in the old days, when Mrs Whitenow's husband were here. I did a bit o' work when I were but a lass, an' my Dandy worked at one o' the farms they owned afore we came into Rowantree from Dandy's uncle.'

'Mrs Whitenow never talks of her children. I know her son died. I saw the old nursery. It was so sad. What happened?'

'Poor young James — named for his father. He were away at the school an' 't'were there he died... I don't think Mrs Whitenow ever got over it. She doted on that boy, but no one could spoil him. He were the sort of lad that had a grace about him — goodness, you know. Always smiling. A tragedy, it were — things might have been so different here, or if Mr John's brother had not been killed out there in France. That were dreadful news. To think he were never found. That's a hard thing to know, but it happened a lot, they say. He were a nice young man, too, favoured Master James in looks.'

'They never speak of him, either.'

'Some folk can't speak o' the dead, my dear, though 'tis better they do, for then the dead rest easy in their graves an' the livin' rest easy in their beds.'

Catherine thought of that room upstairs. 'And what if they don't rest easy in their graves?'

'Ah, well, there are them as have seen —'

'Not here?' Catherine felt a shudder of fear.

'Nay, lass, don't be worryin' about that. I'm talkin' about the dale. Nay one's afraid of such things, just sorry that they can't rest in peace. For folks in the dale, death and its mysteries are to be accepted, never feared. 'Tis the cycle of life and death. The hills and the valleys, the trees, the rivers, they last forever, but we don't, an' we know it as well as we know the spring will come, however long the winter is. But grand folks in grand houses, they think different. They don't belong to the land, but tha needn't be afraid. Yon babby'll grow up to be a fine lad, and tha'll be with him to see him grow.'

'You are very wise, Grizel, but I should like to know what happened to Mr John's mother — my baby's grandmother.'

'She were an odd child, Louisa, that I do remember. High-strung, they said. A temper, she had. You never knew what she would do. Wanted her own way — she and Mrs Whitenow at it hammer and tongs. She went to school in London, and there she stayed until she came back, married to Mr Lestrange. They wasn't an ideal couple. Miss Louisa were never —' Grizel stopped, her face flushed — 'well, 'tis their business, an' it's not for me to talk, an' I ought to be gettin' on my way.'

'Just one more question. There's a room upstairs — the one with a big oak door. Did you ever see what was in there?'

Before Grizel could answer, the door opened, and Mrs Slee came in with a tray. 'I thought I'd bring some tea, now, as Mrs Knipe's here. Tha'd like a cup, I daresay, Grizel.'

'Nay, lass, I've to get on to see Jane Parr. Not long, I think.'

When Grizel had gone and Mrs Slee had taken away the tray, Catherine thought about what she had learned. No wonder Mrs Whitenow never spoke of her son, James, or her lost grandson. It was in her character, she thought, remembering her stoicism about her leg. She was ashamed to reveal her pain. Catherine could understand Mrs Whitenow's feelings now that she had a child of her own. She could pity her, but it was too late. Mrs Whitenow wanted Thomas to be another James, and she had used Catherine to get what she wanted. She must know where John really was. She was prepared to lie and lie again.

And that other child, Louisa. . Highly strung. Ill-tempered. An unhappy marriage. She was never spoken of — was it because she had been the patient in the upstairs room? Oh, if only Mrs Slee had not come in, she might have learned something from Grizel. There would be another time, though. Grizel might know the secret that Annot Syke had known.

It wasn't just Jane Parr who fell sick and died. The snow was followed by rain and a bitter wind, even though it was May, and on that wind, sickness came to the dale. Joe Atkinson of Lunds died of typhoid. And the people of the dale and those at Raven's Gaze held their breath, for Mrs Slee remembered her sister who'd died of typhoid twenty years back, she told Catherine. Her sister's baby had died of the same disease. Typhoid had been a killer in them days, too. Rife it were.

'Mind,' she continued, 'things was very bad then. We only had an earth closet up at Black Tarn an' death came callin' all the time. Babbies — well, we was used to it. My sister's babby were but three month old when the typhoid took her — near age as thine — and there were a three-week-old at the same time, as I recall. Terrible death, is the typhoid. Still an' all, young Thomas there's got it easy compared to most.' She glanced at the cradle. 'God willin', he'll likely be spared.'

Catherine felt bereft when Grizel stopped coming. A note came to tell her that owd Dandy had been taken badly with bronchitis. Grizel didn't want to bring infection to Raven's Gaze. But it was too late. Mrs Whitenow succumbed and was forced to her bed, even her determination undermined by a hacking cough and a high temperature, so weak that Catherine, despite her terror for the baby, tended to her until Doctor Hall came. Only time, he told Catherine, would tell. Mrs Whitenow was strong — but whether she was strong enough at her age, he could not say. If Mrs John could continue to look after her, then all might be well. He could not spare a nurse, but Mrs John would know what to do for the patient. Catherine did know that Mrs Whitenow should be kept warm and should be

nursed upright in a sitting position, supported by pillows —
just as the soldiers with pneumonia or tuberculosis had been at
the Front. Doctor Hall left her a Nelson's inhaler with
instructions to mix some Friar's Balsam and hot water so that
the patient could inhale through the glass mouthpiece.
Catherine had used the inhaler before.

Mrs Slee could not take on nursing, she declared. She'd
enough to do in the kitchen, though Betty wouldn't mind
tending to the babby. It was the last thing Catherine wanted,
but when she saw Mrs Whitenow shrunken in her huge bed,
struggling for breath, her eyes dark with pain, her instinct was
to do whatever she could to alleviate the old lady's suffering.
She thought of Mrs Slee's great hands attending to Mrs
Whitenow's personal needs and knew that she would hate the
indignity. Catherine would have to be her nurse; she would
wash her and turn her to prevent bed sores, even though she
longed to be back in the nursery. She did not trust the sullen
Betty at all. She made sure that she hurried back to the nursery
as often as she could just to open the door so that Betty would
never know when she was coming. Even so, when she saw
Betty with Thomas in her arms, it was all she could do not to
rush in and snatch him away.

Mrs Slee was prevailed upon to watch in the sick room when
Catherine could take a few hours' rest. She bathed and
disinfected herself before she nursed Thomas. It was the best
she could do, and he still seemed to thrive. Betty slept in a
truckle bed in Catherine's bedroom at night, for Catherine
slept in Mrs Whitenow's room. She did not dare leave her
alone. She hardly dared to think what would happen if the old
lady died in the night — to be at Raven's Gaze alone with
Bennet Lestrange and Mrs Slee was hideous to contemplate.

She imagined his eyes upon her, watching day and night from his tower. How would she escape then?

For now, Bennet Lestrange kept to his tower rooms, though sometimes she saw him walking away from the house with his shepherd's crook and long tweed cape. As she turned to look at her restless patient, she thought of Annot and the death of Ted Syke, and wondered about the day she had seen him behind Starvecrow. She was haunted, too, by the memory of that room above, and who had been strapped to that iron bed. And once after yet another sleepless night, listening to the wheezing breath of Mrs Whitenow and the midnight noises of the house, she saw Bennet Lestrange depart, and was tempted just to go to her room, pack her things, take her child and leave. She could order Betty to sit with Mrs Whitenow while she made her preparations. It would be easy. Then she heard again the bubbling liquid in the old lady's lungs and saw the thin hands work on the counterpane and found she could not do it. Bennet Lestrange wouldn't care about Mrs Whitenow, and nor would Mrs Slee or Betty. Mrs Whitenow would die, and it would be on her conscience.

In the lonely wastes of one long night, Catherine woke in her chair. Mrs Whitenow had seemed peculiarly restless, so Catherine had not undressed, but she had dozed off when she sensed that Mrs Whitenow slept. She had no idea of the time or what had woken her until she heard a noise, as if someone were whimpering in the darkness. She realised that the noise came from the bed. Mrs Whitenow's eyes were open. Catherine took her hand, which felt deadly cold, and the ivory face turned to her, but Catherine knew that she didn't see her. Then Mrs Whitenow spoke.

'James, James, where is James?' The words were a hoarse whisper.

'Hush,' Catherine whispered back, stroking the thin hand, 'try to sleep.'

Mrs Whitenow's head turned on the pillows and she murmured again, though Catherine couldn't catch the words. Then she held her breath. Mrs Whitenow seemed to be mumbling, 'Louisa … won't come… Louisa…' Catherine tried to soothe her by moistening her dry lips with glycerine and Mrs Whitenow's eyes closed, but her hand was still cold in Catherine's clasp. Then her eyes opened again, and looking beyond Catherine, she said quite clearly, 'Raven,' and closed her eyes, muttering, 'Raven … here … up … up…'

Catherine did not move from the bedside. She waited until Mrs Whitenow slept. Was this a turning point? Was the restless muttering some kind of crisis which would mean recovery or death? The words about the raven almost seemed like a premonition. She remembered the talk of ravens at her first dinner when Bennet Lestrange had told her how the sighting of a raven meant death, and Mrs Whitenow had scoffed. But Catherine had seen a raven on the roof of Starvecrow Farm and a dead rabbit pecked to death. And Ted Syke had died. She had seen a raven on the tower and Marjorie had died. Yet she thought Mrs Whitenow's breathing seemed easier, almost like someone letting out a long sigh of relief. Or was it grief?

She would send for Doctor Hall tomorrow, though what he might do, she had no idea, except she thought that Mrs Whitenow ought to be in hospital.

The night seemed as interminable as the night she had spent listening to that dreadful slamming of the shutter. James and Louisa, she thought. The names of her dead children on Mrs Whitenow's lips. Was she thinking of them because she was dying?

Catherine turned up the oil lamp and took Mrs Whitenow's hand again. It was colder than before, and she saw a bluish tinge on the back. Her question was answered. Death had stolen into the room, was waiting in the shadows beyond the ancient bed in which so many Clayburns and Whitenows had died. Catherine sensed that dark presence as she had done before, so many times. Mrs Whitenow would not live through the night and there was nothing that she could do.

She sat on in the deepening shadows, her eyes closing, then opening again suddenly, for she heard something. It was the sound of a footfall at the door. *Bennet Lestrange?* she wondered, sitting bolt upright in her chair, waiting for the door to open. No one came in, though she thought she heard something like a sigh breathed into the empty air, but she heard no footsteps going away.

In the cold and weighted silence that followed, she became aware that Mrs Whitenow's breathing had changed. She went to the bedside and watched. The rattle came and then the long sigh which told her that Mrs Whitenow had breathed her last. Catherine closed the pale eyes of the woman she had never really known, who was taking her secrets with her. She crossed the still hands and sat down again to wait for dawn.

And just as a line of grey light crept in through the gap in the heavy curtains, she heard from above a great crash, as though something heavy had fallen. Then there were hurried footsteps — someone coming up the stairs. She opened the door and looked down the corridor. Bennet was opening the door to the spiral staircase. She heard his feet on the stones as he passed the nursery. He was making for the room at the end of the passage.

She closed the door. Mrs Whitenow lay as she had left her, as still as a marble effigy. Then she heard the footsteps again. He was coming. She sat down to wait.

He came in to tell her, 'The dobbie stone has fallen.' He looked at her and laughed. 'The curse has come upon us as Mr Tennyson —' He faltered as he saw Catherine pointing to the bed.

'Mrs Whitenow is dead.'

She watched him as he stood quite still by the bed. She couldn't see his face, but she knew that he would be gazing steadily from under his dark lids.

He turned to her, the usual sardonic smile at his lips. 'Her last message. Did she think that Raven's Gaze Hall would fall at her passing? It will not, I can assure you of that.'

12

The mournful tolling of the passing bell accompanied them to the funeral of Mrs Whitenow in the gloomy little church where Catherine and John had married. The weather wasn't any better than it had been on that day. An icy wind swept down the fell, spitting rain mingled with hail, and leaden cloud loured over the graveyard with its green-stained gravestones, its grim monuments, the stone-blind angels and cracked urns, and the rain-blackened vault in which, according to Bennet Lestrange, Mrs Whitenow's husband and children were buried. He had not mentioned John's brother, who was lost in France. Catherine did not even know his name. There was no one left who would speak his name with love. That seemed to her sadder than the macabre scene before her now: the vault, the undertakers in their black top hats, the streamers blowing in the wind. Beyond the graveyard wall were the carriages and the black horses with their black plumes and the mute boy in deepest black, his hat too big for him. The white, pinched faces of neighbours or strangers looked on. It was a grotesque pantomime, she thought, staged by Bennet for his own dark purpose.

There were four mourners, including Mrs Whitenow's solicitor, Mr Huggon, who looked as cold as Catherine felt and as uncomfortable in the silence that accompanied them to the graveside. Catherine had not wanted to go because she didn't want to leave Thomas with Mrs Slee and Betty, but she couldn't say so, and she did not want to make any fuss. *Keep quiet*, she kept telling herself, *the time will come*. So, she stood, mute and frozen, as the door to the vault was opened to reveal the darkness inside. She did not know if she imagined the gust of wind or the faint smell of corruption that seemed to blow from within. The coffin was placed in the vault where Mrs Whitenow's dead son and daughter lay. She couldn't bear to look. Not that she felt much for that austere old woman who had deceived and manipulated her.

When she wasn't assailed by grief for Marjorie of whose funeral she was reminded, she felt an icy rage against the two mourners flanking her. She didn't look at them, but she sensed Bennet Lestrange's dark gaze upon her. Was he thinking about how he could keep her and John in his power? John had returned for the funeral. Surely, he could not disappear again, leaving her alone with Bennet Lestrange — that would not be proper. Not that she imagined Bennet Lestrange would pay attention to propriety. If it suited him, John would be allowed to go; if not, then John would have to stay. What mattered to Bennet Lestrange was the baby — the heir to Raven's Gaze Hall. But if John stayed, then how was she to deal with that?

They returned to the house in an equally frozen silence, carrying their secret plans in their hearts. Catherine was determined not to speak and was glad of the veil which hid her face.

'Do take off your coat, my dear.' Bennet Lestrange's cutting voice broke the silence as they went into the hall. 'And that veil. A little too depressing, I think. It is all very sad, of course, but there is no need to overdo it. She was hardly the friend of your bosom.'

Cruel, Catherine thought. Mr Huggon paled, and John looked away, but she did as she was told. No point in antagonising him. She followed them into the drawing room.

'A warming sherry is what is needed,' Bennet Lestrange said, rubbing his hands and pretending all was well. 'And some of

Mrs Slee's sandwiches before Mr Huggon sets about the business for which we all wait.'

'A sherry would be most welcome.' Mr Huggon looked glad of something to do with his hands. Catherine felt the same. They drank their sherry, but no one touched the sandwiches. Catherine saw that John didn't even acknowledge the plate offered by his father. The decanter passed him by, too, but she noticed how he clenched and unclenched one hand and looked nervously at the black document case on the table. Mrs Whitenow's will was in there. John must be wondering whether she had left him enough to buy his freedom — from his father and from Raven's Gaze. And from his wife, no doubt. A glance at Bennet Lestrange showed that he must know what was about to be revealed. His face was eager, the glint of malice visible under his dark eyelids as he sipped his sherry.

Mr Huggon put down his glass and cleared his throat nervously as he unlocked the case and took out the papers, which rustled ominously in the silence. Catherine kept her head down, but she could see John's hand making that convulsive movement.

Mr Huggon began with the small legacies that were left to Mrs Slee, to Betty, and to the gardener, all of whom Mrs Whitenow hoped would stay in the service of Mr Bennet Lestrange. Silence greeted the preliminary announcements and Mr Huggon coughed again before he continued reading. 'The residue of my estate which includes the property Ashes Farm by the town of Hawes, six cottages known as Salt Row in the same town, and the sum of five thousand pounds, I leave to my great-grandson, Thomas James Lestrange, provided he remains in the care of his grandfather, Bennet Lestrange, who will be his legal guardian, and in the care of his mother,

171

Catherine Lestrange, at Raven's Gaze Hall in Ravendale in the county of Yorkshire. At the age of twenty-one, Thomas James Lestrange will have the use of the property and money for himself and his heirs, should he have such. Mr Bennet Lestrange will, unto the date of Thomas James Lestrange's majority, administer the properties and money on the boy's behalf. Bennet Lestrange will have responsibility for the comfort and support of Mrs Catherine Lestrange and her son. From the money provided for the care of Thomas and his mother, sums may be withdrawn to provide a suitable education for the boy at a nearby school of good reputation, which must not be Sedgehill School where my son, James Arthur Whitenow, lost his life.'

Catherine saw John turn on his heel. His footsteps were loud on the stone floor, as was the sound of his tapping stick. The door creaked and was firmly shut. There was silence as the footsteps died away. Mr Huggon's hand trembled and the papers crackled as he put them down. She heard him let out a tremulous breath.

'Ashes to ashes,' Bennet said with a sardonic laugh, as he lifted the sherry decanter again. 'And an interesting old place, as I recall — once a parcel of a tenement called "le Eshes" back in 1582,' he continued as he poured more sherry for Mr Huggon, who appeared too astonished to demur. 'A Clayburn property and nearly a ruin. Haunted, naturally — a Clayburn drowned his wife in the pool there. She walks at night, dripping water on the stairs. That's how they know. The wild Clayburns and their unwanted wives, eh? More sherry, Mrs John?' He didn't wait for a reply. 'Ashes Farm — an interesting inscription above the door: "*Non mihi sed successoribus.*" You have the Latin, Mr Huggon?'

'Not for me but for my successors,' Mr Huggon translated faintly.

Bennet raised his glass. 'To my ward and grandson, Master Thomas James Lestrange, then — the successor. Just as it should be. And I shall be here to ensure that Mrs John and her boy are very well looked after — until my heir is twenty-one. To a long and happy partnership.' His dark gaze lingered on Catherine, who saw that same satisfied smile he had given her when he had shown her that other inscription above the porch at Raven's Gaze.

'There is the other matter which Mrs Whitenow wished me to discuss with you. Ought we to —'

'Certainly not, Mr Huggon,' Bennet Lestrange cut in. 'That is private to me. I will take care of it, of course. We shall find a more suitable time. And now —'

Mr Huggon took the hint of his dismissal and gulped down his sherry. He bade Catherine a hasty farewell and Bennet went to see him off. When she had met Mr Huggon earlier in the day, he had spoken to her kindly and congratulated her on the birth of her child, who would, he was sure, be a worthy heir to Raven's Gaze Hall. Looking at his mild face and kindly eyes, she had briefly thought he might be an ally. His nervousness and hurried departure dispelled that hope. He was a functionary, in thrall to Bennet Lestrange; he would do his duty to the law, and Mrs Whitenow's will was the law.

She watched Mrs Slee come in with her tray. She wore a satisfied smile, too. She'd be pleased with her legacy. A very nice bribe to ensure her loyalty. Betty had received twenty pounds in the will. She thought of Betty's sly eyes, Betty who was upstairs with Tom in the nursery. A feeling of dread possessed her. They were all in on it, and the dead hand of Mrs Whitenow was meant to put the seal on Catherine's imprisonment. Bennet Lestrange thought he had won. No. She did not want the money. Her Thomas did not want the money. He had her. She would be better for him than any five thousand pounds. Bennet Lestrange believed that she could be bought. That she could be kept here for twenty years — an unwanted wife. That would not happen.

And her husband? John was clearly angry about the legacy. He must have expected that, having done his duty, he would be rewarded with the price of freedom, but his name had not been mentioned in the will, which meant that he was still dependent on his father. Would Bennet Lestrange let him go? Would John have the courage to go without the money?

The rattling of the teacups on the tray as Mrs Slee went out jerked her from her reverie. She must get upstairs before Bennet Lestrange came back to taunt her.

She was surprised to find John in the nursery, and even more surprised to see Betty with him, holding out the gurgling baby to his father. John was smiling. She couldn't stop herself exclaiming, 'John.'

He turned. 'Catherine, my dear.' And then he said to Betty. 'I'll take him. Mrs Slee will want you downstairs.'

Betty handed him over with a smile, though she never smiled at anyone. 'Yes, sir,' she said. As she passed Catherine, she was certain that Betty smirked. *Conspiracy*, she thought, and another thought came unbidden. A conspiracy of ravens. Bennet Lestrange had told her that. She looked at John holding the baby and smiling down at him. What did this mean?

'He's a fine boy,' John said, as if he were suddenly the proud father.

Confusion and fear made her reckless. 'Yes, he is. A pity you have not seen more of him.'

'You know very well that I have to earn my crust. Even more so now.'

She wanted to strike him. She could hardly believe that he could keep up the fiction that he was always absent on his father's business matters, but she mastered herself. She had made one mistake already. 'So, you will be going away again soon, I suppose.'

'I must.'

But he did not go. She guessed that for some pleasure of his own, Bennet Lestrange kept him at Raven's Gaze. Catherine did not now think that John had been the patient in the room, nor did she believe that his absences signified that he was mentally ill. He loved someone else, she was sure of that, and he was waiting for his chance to go back to his lover. She wished he would go and there would be an end to the black comedy in which they all acted the parts written by Bennet Lestrange. Bennet Lestrange, the jovial father and grandfather; John, the doting husband and father; Catherine, the submissive wife and mother; even Mrs Slee, the loyal servant. Only Betty broke the rules, for out of her sly eyes, there peeped malice and such loathing for Thomas that Catherine began to be frightened of ever leaving her child with her.

And it seemed impossible to escape. They were always about her. Whenever she ventured into the gardens with the perambulator, the gardener was tending the bushes or the flowerbeds, or John accompanied her, or she felt Bennet Lestrange watching from the tower. When she left her room or the nursery, either Mrs Slee or Betty would be in the corridor, dusting or sweeping. Even at night, she thought she heard footsteps in the corridor as though someone were pacing up and down. One of her jailers? For that was how she came to view them all. Even if she managed to evade them, there was Thomas to think of. She could leave everything behind, simply put on her coat and go, but where would she take him?

She had hoped that Grizel might come and that she might ask for her help. It was impossible for her to go to see her. She could not leave Thomas in their hands, and someone would be sure to come with her. But Grizel did not come. Catherine had wondered if Grizel had been told that she was not needed, that Catherine did not want her. Grizel would hardly be able to come without invitation.

And even if she escaped, suppose Bennet Lestrange and John caught up with her. Bennet Lestrange was Thomas's legal guardian. She thought of his smile and the triumph in his eyes when he had shown her the papers which Mr Huggon had drawn up and he had said, 'You really should see these, my dear. It is well you understand the legal status of Thomas's guardian.' She had read them without comment, feeling that predatory gaze on her and inwardly shuddering. It was as if he could read her mind.

Of course, John had signed the papers. He had hoped for his reward, she guessed. Well, he had been disappointed. Not that she felt sorry for him. It had all been done without her knowledge because she was only a woman with no power at all. Bennet Lestrange could take her son back at any time. She knew that she would have no chance of keeping her boy — a wife who had deserted her husband, a mother who intended to deprive her child of his inheritance. Mrs Whitenow had trapped her, and the ropes were bound by Bennet Lestrange, and John, whose intentions she could not fathom at all. Every morning, she expected him to have gone.

But she could tell that as time passed, he was feeling the strain. He barely spoke at mealtimes, and he hardly looked at her, but she knew he was torn, for she watched him with the baby and saw that he was enchanted by the way the little hand wound round his finger, and the way Thomas gurgled and blew bubbles. Once or twice, John had forgotten the truth, for he smiled at her over the baby's head, and once she had seen tears in his eyes. She pitied him then and wondered for a moment whether their marriage might be saved, but the moment passed when Bennet Lestrange came in and took the baby from him, declaring that the little boy was a Lestrange through and through who would turn into a fine young man. His grandfather would see to that.

John went out without a word. It was impossible, she thought, watching Bennet Lestrange with his grandson. She couldn't stay here with or without John. She could not live with Bennet Lestrange and watch him take over her child, corrupt him and destroy her. She would have to find a way.

13

Time ticked on, each day closing like the locking of a door. Catherine listened to the hall clock, its inexorable strokes reminding her, every hour, every half hour, every minute, that she was waiting. The days were darkening, twilight coming in on stealthy feet, closer and closer, slipping into the corridors and corners. Summer had come and was waning. When it had come, there had been fine days when she could wheel the perambulator about the garden. Bennet Lestrange had taken photographs of Catherine with the baby, of her leaning over the perambulator, of John with Thomas on his knee, of the three of them together, posed as a happy family. And they all knew it was a lie.

Catherine in the nursery with Thomas. John in his room. Bennet Lestrange in his tower. Mrs Slee and Betty in the kitchen. All of them waiting, it seemed. Even the house, so still and quiet at dusk, seemed to be holding its breath. Waiting for something to break. Waiting for John to go. Waiting for her to break cover, to run screaming from the house with Thomas in her arms.

She listened at night to the footsteps outside her room. She listened for any other human sound, a breath, a whisper, a word spoken, but there was never anything but that slow pacing up and down. Sometimes she thought she would go mad with listening. Grizel's words about the unquiet dead came back to her. Those of whom no one spoke did not rest easy in their graves. Who was there? Louisa? Mrs Whitenow? They had died in this house, in that ancient bed. So many births and deaths. And what of those who had died elsewhere?

James Whitenow and John's brother. Did they return to listen, to hope that a voice would speak their names in loving memory?

Sometimes Catherine had wild imaginings of footsteps coming down from the top floor, a featureless face at the keyhole of the door to her room, some ragged thing coming in. Something mad which would seize her and carry her up to that room, where she would be strapped into the bed, and they would say she was mad. And she would go and sit by Thomas's cot and stay there throughout the impenetrable night, waiting. In the morning, she despised herself for her weakness — how could it be that she, Nurse Catherine Sisley, who had endured the rigours or war, was frightened of shadows?

In the mornings, she would be hollow-eyed and exhausted, too weary to take more than a piece of dry toast and a cup of tea, ignoring the eggs and bacon that Mrs Slee or Betty brought up and took away again, Mrs Slee clicking her tongue in disapproval and Betty smirking as if she hoped Catherine would starve to death. One morning, when Mrs Slee was leaving with the untouched food, she heard her mutter to someone outside — probably Betty — 'She can suit herself, the crackpot piece o' nothin'.' A snigger answered the muttering. And then Catherine thought to herself that she was playing into their hands. They would say she was ill, too sick to tend to Thomas. Doctor Hall would be sent for. She would be sent to hospital — never to return.

The next morning, she determined to go downstairs before Mrs Slee came up. She rose early, bathed and washed her hair, dressed it carefully, and pinched her cheeks to bring some colour to them. She would show them that she was not defeated. She played with Thomas for a while and looking at his innocent smile, felt that she was ready to face them down.

Later, she could not say how she fell down that first flight of stairs which ended at the place of skulls. She could not say that in the morning gloom she had felt a rush of cold air; she could not say that a shadow had moved in the darkness near the spiral staircase; she could not say she was sure that she had felt a hand on her back because when she looked up, there was no one there. John came up the stairs and found her, and she saw Mrs Slee at the bottom of the second staircase, holding her tray. She was not badly hurt, only very shaken, but when John helped her up, she found that she could only stand on one foot.

John and Mrs Slee helped her back to her room and examined her ankle. The pain was intense, yet she felt sick at the sight of Mrs Slee's scarred hands touching and pressing.

'Badly sprained,' she said. 'It needs strapping up and then tha'll have to rest it.'

Catherine fought back the impulse to say that she knew, but asked, 'Have you any ice?'

'Oh, aye, if tha thinks it'll do any good.'

'I do. It'll reduce any swelling and then it can be strapped up.'

Mrs Slee went out and Catherine asked John to fetch a bandage from Mrs Whitenow's room. 'The top drawer of the chest.'

He went without a word. Mrs Slee came back with the ice in a bowl and the bandage.

'I'll manage now, thank you.'

'Have it thy own way. Am I to bring the tea and toast? And milk for little 'un.'

'Thank you, and please bring me a walking stick so that I can get to the bathroom.'

'No need for that, Mrs John. Me or Betty can help tha get about.'

'No, thank you. However, you can bring Thomas's cot here and he can sleep by my bed.'

When Mrs Slee had finally left her alone, and the cot was safely installed, Catherine went over the fall in her mind. She thought about that sensation of a hand on her back. Had she imagined it? She had been terribly keyed up as she went along the corridor, her mind on the way in which she was going to behave in front of Bennet Lestrange and John, how she was going to be perfectly cheerful and show them that she wasn't afraid of any of them. She had turned onto the first step, one foot poised to go down, and had hesitated, feeling the cold air rush at her, aware of a shadow moving, and then she was tumbling down the stairs. She felt again the hand on her back. She had not imagined it. Someone had been there.

It couldn't have been John or Mrs Slee who had come up the stairs to help her. Surely not Bennet Lestrange, she thought. Unless… Did he want to be rid of her? No, not yet. Not yet, for the baby's sake. Thomas was too young to lose his mother, and, in any case, when she thought rationally, he would know that a fall down that short flight of stairs would be unlikely to kill her —

Kill her — she shook herself. Ridiculous. That way madness did lie. *Use your common sense*, she told herself. *Think*. That rush of cold air meant the door to the staircase was open. The shadow — someone coming down. There was one other person who was spiteful enough to do such a thing: smirking Betty Slee, who was always where she shouldn't be, sneaking up the backstairs, hanging about in the corridors, pretending to be doing her work. A stupid girl, but capable of malice. She wouldn't think of the damage that might be done, but she'd enjoy playing a trick on Catherine, whom she obviously disliked. A little push to give her a fright.

Catherine was angry then. But the cold truth was that she couldn't do a thing about it. Whom could she tell? She had no proof, and it would seem another example of her deterioration. Perhaps Bennet Lestrange or Mrs Slee had put Betty up to it, or perhaps Mrs Slee had managed it herself. She could have slipped down those back stairs and reappeared at the bottom of the main staircase with the tray. She was capable of any kind of malice, too.

But whoever had pushed her or orchestrated it had trapped her more than ever. She could not even walk downstairs. However, her ankle would heal, and then she would find a way to get out of here. There was always a time early in the morning when the footsteps ceased, and before she heard Mrs Slee or Betty come with her tray. In that gap of time, they were in the kitchen, John was in his room, and Bennet Lestrange in his tower. She would go then with nothing for herself, only whatever the baby would need. She would go to Grizel at Rowantree and ask if Owd Dandy could take her away in his trap — to the railway station at Oxenholme. She would disappear to London. She would ask Pat and her colonel for help. They were well-connected people who might be able to find her employment as a nurse — a private post again in a household which would take Mrs Sisley, a war widow, and her child.

Eventually the swelling on her ankle went down with the continued application of ice. She could bear to put her foot down without too much pain and got about her rooms with the help of her stick, but she was careful to conceal the improvement from Mrs Slee and Betty, who carried in the trays, changed the bed linen, and brought clean laundry. She laughed secretly at Betty's huffing and puffing and obvious resentment of being a maidservant to Mrs John. She barely concealed her dislike now, but Catherine didn't care. Let them think that she couldn't walk anywhere. Interestingly, the footsteps at night ceased, and she no longer lay awake listening and imagining that mad thing pacing outside her room. The watchmen or the ghosts — if that was what they were — were quiet. She slept more easily, knowing that she had a plan.

She hardly saw Bennet Lestrange. He came in occasionally to look at the baby, and Catherine loathed the way he observed Thomas as if he were assessing what he was worth — as much as a silver pounce pot, she wondered? But she was amused to see the equally assessing look that Thomas gave his grandfather, as if he knew exactly what the man was. At least John had looked at his child with tenderness and got smiles in return. But John was no longer at Raven's Gaze.

Catherine had known that he was leaving when one morning he had come to ask how her ankle was progressing. She had told him that it would take time. He had lifted Thomas from the cradle and carried him to the window, where he had stood looking out. Then he put the baby gently back into his cot, picked up his stick, and turned to look again for what seemed a long time. Then he looked at her. His face was very white, and his mouth twisted as if he were about to say something. She noticed how his hand clenched the stick so hard that the knuckles turned white. She waited, unable to speak. He turned and walked away. The door closed and he was gone. She knew by that long, agonised look that she would never see him again.

It was Betty who brought the news. Her usually sullen face was lit up with excitement, the excitement of one who brings bad news and enjoys the importance of knowing what someone else does not, and that it will hurt them. Catherine knew that something dreadful had happened, and her arms tightened round her baby.

'Police 'as been, an' Mr Lestrange says tha's to go downstairs t'drawing room. Straightaway, 'e says. I've to stay with t'babby an' Mrs Slee'll come up to tek you down.'

Catherine didn't ask why. It was to do with John. She just knew. She stood up. 'There's no need to fetch Mrs Slee. I can manage.' Catherine limped to the cot to put the baby down and reached for her stick. 'Leave him where he is, please. There's no need to pick him up.'

The sulky eyes flared at her. 'Weren't goin' to.'

Catherine struggled down the stairs to the drawing room, where she found Bennet Lestrange drinking brandy. He pointed to the decanter, but she shook her head. 'Just tell me.'

'John is dead.'

She sat down. 'How? When?'

His face was an unreadable mask. The crystal glass in his hand glittered like ice. 'He has killed himself and his mistress.'

'The French woman? Sabine?'

'So you knew?'

'I guessed. I know why he married me. I am not the fool you think me.'

'I never thought you a fool. You had much to gain from the — er — arrangement.'

She ignored the jibe. Of course, he chose to believe she had married for what she could gain, but that wasn't important. 'But why — why has he done such a thing? Both dead. It's horrifying. Why?'

'Money, I imagine. He hoped for something from his grandmother, a vain hope, as it turned out, and then he thought I would provide for him. I gave him a choice: he could either stay with his son or throw in his lot with Madame Dupont and live on the scraps she might cast his way. You will have guessed that she was married — no divorce for a Catholic. He chose the coward's way out.' He handed her a newspaper. 'Read all about it.'

Catherine couldn't speak. She stared down at the headline, which shouted in large black letters: *Double tragedy at a London Hotel.*

She could hardly believe what she was reading. The gist of the story seemed to be that John and Sabine had taken a room at the Somerset Hotel, and the following morning the chambermaid had found them dead — both poisoned with prussic acid. The gentleman had entered their names in the register as Monsieur and Madame Arras of Paris.

'How did the police come here if —'

'The name of his tailor was stamped on the buttons of his trousers — he did not think of that, of course. My tailors, forsooth, Dixon and Hatton of Hanover Street, whither the police went and found out the name John Walter Lestrange of Raven's Gaze Hall. Mr Dixon, enjoying the drama, no doubt, helpfully pointed out the label concealed in the waistband of the trousers, which bore the Dixon name and address, and the date on which the clothes were sent to John Lestrange, and he provided the address to which he had recently sent some shirts. Freddie Hunter —'

Catherine remembered. 'His London friend.'

'Indeed. Mr Hunter identified John and the lady — he knew all about them, of course.'

'A suicide pact?'

'So the police tell me. There will be an inquest, but I cannot go.'

'Why not?'

He raised his glass to her. 'And leave his grieving widow and infant child without protection? Besides, I have nothing to tell a court that his friend, Mr Hunter, has not already revealed — that John Lestrange married a charming young woman of whom I am very fond. But he, my son, betrayed her from the very beginning, leading a double and secret life.'

She stared at him, aghast. 'You have told the police this.'

'Mr Hunter told them enough. Of course, I told them I knew nothing of John's sordid secrets. How could I have known that my son was a liar and a —'

Stung, she interrupted. John was dead. 'War hero — do not forget that. He —'

'Oh, it will be mentioned in court. War neurosis will be the reason for his temporary — insanity. Cowardice, some call it.'

'You know nothing about the war, what it did to fine young men, to their bodies and their minds. You weren't there. He was at Arras — in the thick of it.'

She saw his hand whiten round the glass. He looked at her with such naked hostility that she almost gasped.

'I know enough. I knew my son,' he said, ice in his tone.

You did not, she thought, but an argument with Bennet Lestrange was pointless. 'And what about Sabine?'

'Blinded by desperation — they could not be together in life, so they died together.'

She heard the bitter sarcasm in his voice. He felt nothing for his son. She thought of John's face as she had last seen it. There had been a kind of agony in it. Had he known then what he would do? She remembered Sabine's cap of shining hair and humorous eyes, and the smile she had exchanged with John. Oh, the pity of it. For John to end their lives in an anonymous hotel room — after all he had endured. Monsieur Arras — Arras, where he had nearly lost his leg. And what other damage had he suffered? Tears sprang to her eyes. She could not hate them now.

She stood up and put down the newspaper on a side table. Bennet Lestrange sipped his brandy. His face was unchanged. This was his doing and that dead old woman who had wanted her son alive again in Catherine's baby and cared nothing for her grandson.

She turned and looked at his contemptuous face. 'Poor John,' she said, 'and poor Sabine.'

She left the room, leaning on her stick. She felt so exhausted by the horror of it and Bennet Lestrange's callousness that she could hardly get up the stairs. Poor, poor John. Perhaps the verdict of insanity of which Bennet was so sure was true. The two of them so hopeless and desperate that they... And they planned it. Bennet Lestrange had said it was sordid. But she could only think that it was a tragedy.

She stopped on the landing and looked up at the door to the spiral staircase from where the cold draught always blew. That dreadful nursery and that more dreadful room where a mad patient had been strapped to the bed. Had it been John whose death would be attributed to war neurosis? It would be true. The war had damaged John. Add to that the damage done by his father and his grandmother because of the loss of his brother. She remembered the odd pause before Mrs Whitenow had said, "Ah, John, yes, John, my grandson," as if she had meant someone else. There was something about his son that Bennet Lestrange simply did not like. And John had been damaged by his grandmother because he was not the grandson who had been killed in the war, John's brother, who perhaps would have become the true heir to Raven's Gaze. Mrs Whitenow had said that John was like his father — a Lestrange. Or perhaps she couldn't love John because he was not her own son, James, who was a Whitenow, the truest heir, not a Lestrange — not a stranger. And it had been the name of her son James on her lips when she died.

But she could do nothing for John now. She could not say that she was sorry, too, for the dreadful mistake she had made. She had played her part in this tragedy, but it was too late to weep for them. It was John's son she must think of now. What did John's death mean for his son and his widow?

Catherine hardly saw Bennet Lestrange in the months after the dreadful news had come, though she found a newspaper left in her room in which there was a grainy photograph of the Somerset Hotel and an account of the inquest, which she could not bear to read. What was the point? She felt only anguish at the thought of those deaths, and she wept over the two photographs the newspaper had published, one of John in his uniform as she remembered him at CCS 17, his face solemn and unreadable. Presumably Freddie Hunter had provided that, and there was a photograph of Sabine, Madame Dupont. She looked, too, as she had looked when she had come to collect John, with that wide, engaging smile and neat cap of hair. They looked young, she thought. Such waste — as if there had not been enough waste in the war. She would never know their story, only that they had loved each other, and that John had not had the courage to stand up to his father and fight for that love because the war had ruined him. She was tempted to throw the newspaper on the fire, but she could not. She put it away in a drawer.

When she did see Bennet Lestrange, he did not refer to the newspaper, nor, indeed to John's death. He behaved as if nothing had been changed. He continued with his work, though he did not ask her to do any typing. His book was nearly finished; it would be privately published for those who were interested in the history and legends of the Dales country, and those friends and neighbours who could appreciate the scholarship. All this he told her when he came to see his grandson, for whom he would keep a copy. No doubt Thomas would be proud to see his grandfather's name on the cover, which would be of the finest tooled leather. Thomas, Bennet Lestrange called the baby, lingering on the second syllable as if the name were unfamiliar — certainly not the name he would have chosen. Catherine was sure of that, but she pretended not to notice. The name "John" was never mentioned.

Catherine observed him covertly when he was watching Thomas, who was now able to roll when she put him down on the rug. He spoke in his usual pedantic way, but there was something subtly different about him. The bruised eyelids seemed darker and the skin beneath his eyes was dark, too. His face seemed darker, as if it were stained in parts. Did he have a conscience, she wondered? But his eyes still lingered on her when he talked, as if he were calculating what to do with her or perhaps when he might do without her and claim the boy for his own. That would not happen.

She made no move to leave, though her ankle was healed. Thomas was thriving at eight months. He was a big boy. He would be tall, she thought, and when he was older and sturdier, that would be the time. For now, she would be patient and watchful. No harm must come to him. She wrote to Pat Sinclair to tell her she was a widow now and that she thought of coming to London when her son was a little older. She asked Pat if she would enquire about nursing posts in private houses. Pat replied that she would ask for her, and Catherine only had to let her know when she was coming, and she could stay with them until she was settled — two more in the house would be welcome. Pat had a daughter now and another on the way — son or daughter, George didn't mind. Catherine smiled when she read the letter. So like Pat, cheerful and practical. And optimistic. There was real hope of escape now.

One afternoon, after Bennet had gone, taking his long, dark look with him, she studied her child, who smiled back at her, all dimples. His eyes were still blue, his hair fair. She thought she could discern her father in him, and she stared for ages at the photographs she had taken from Marjorie's cottage. One showed two young women in white dresses with impossibly narrow waists and their hair piled up, looking too heavy for their delicate heads. She turned it over: *Diana and Sylvia, summer 1892.* Catherine had no idea who Diana was, but Sylvia was her mother. She'd have been twenty then, younger than Catherine was now, and innocent — just a girl on the threshold of life as Catherine had been when the war began, and before innocence was destroyed in the mud of France and Flanders. There was another photograph of a young couple, he, young and solemn, in a dark suit with a spray of white flowers in his lapel, carrying a pair of white gloves; the bride in her flounced wedding dress, the veil cascading to the ground. *Sylvia and Thomas, married 1893.* How sad, she thought, that she could not really remember them. She scrutinised the young man. Her father. A stranger. The black and white photograph showed darkish hair, but the eyes? Had they really been hazel like hers? Had Marjorie wanted her to have something of her father's, and did she just wish for it now so that Thomas would be a Sisley, not a Lestrange?

Thomas was not at all like John or Bennet Lestrange. But was he like John's mother? She often thought of what Grizel had told her about Louisa Whitenow, and it worried her. She remembered the photograph she had seen on Mrs Whitenow's mantelpiece. She had not seen it clearly that first night, and she couldn't remember having seen it again. She had never been alone in that bedroom, and when Mrs Whitenow had been ill, she had been too busy with her patient to think about the photograph. She thought about it now. Louisa had died of a fever after her child was born. The child in the photograph was not a newborn, so she must have died soon after John's birth. Then the child in the photograph must be John's brother, whom Grizel had said looked like Mrs Whitenow's dead son, James. Not a Lestrange. Would it be possible to see Thomas in the child in the photograph or in his mother, Louisa?

It was that silent time between lunch and tea when Mrs Slee would be in the kitchen, preparing supper. Catherine had no idea where Betty might be. She might be sneaking about anywhere. Catherine often thought she could sense her. Betty left behind her scent — an unpleasant mingling of stale food and sweat, and the same breath of hostility that Catherine felt in Mrs Slee. She was convinced that it had been Betty who had pushed her, but she knew it was hopeless to accuse her. She made up her mind to risk going to Mrs Whitenow's bedroom. She could leave Thomas in his cot for a few minutes while she went to have a look for that photograph. She wanted to know what Louisa Lestrange had looked like, and that baby in her arms.

The corridor outside her room was empty, so she slipped along the room where she had not been since the old lady's death. There was no trace of her now. The curtains of the four-poster bed in which her son had been born had been taken down and the bedding removed. The tables were bare, as was the top of the chest of drawers, where Mrs Whitenow had kept her jewels in a rosewood box. She opened the drawers; they were empty. The silver candlesticks and the porcelain figures had gone from the mantelpiece, and the photograph. She opened the wardrobe door. All her clothes were gone. All that was left was the faint scent of lavender.

Mrs Whitenow had been erased, as had her son, daughter and grandsons. Bennet Lestrange was in sole possession now. She imagined for a moment her own room empty. That was what he would like. Only his grandson left — until he killed him with cruelty disguised as kindness.

Catherine closed the door and slipped back to her room. It was maddening to think that she might never know if Thomas looked like his dead grandmother or John's brother. She looked at her son, who was peacefully asleep, and thought of the old nursery where all those unused things were stored. Might Mrs Whitenow's possessions have been put up there to moulder away? The photograph in an old suitcase, with the porcelain figures and other trinkets? Bennet Lestrange would not want a photograph of his dead wife. She couldn't recall any photographs in his tower room — not even of the owner of the silver pounce pot, the kindly grandfather. No wedding photographs, no photograph of his sons. Because he had no feeling for anyone but himself. She looked at the sleeping child again. A few minutes, perhaps — that would be all it took, and then she might know.

The door to the staircase was ajar, which made her stop and strain her ears to listen. She felt the cold draught, but there was no sound, so she crept up, step by step, listening for any sound. Mrs Slee and Betty must be in the kitchen. When she stepped into that miserably dark corridor, she felt the cold draught again. She didn't look in the old nursery but felt her way along to the room at the end, where she saw that the door was open. She stood motionless, listening. Was someone in there? Mrs Slee? She crept closer, but there was no sound. She held her breath and listened again. There was no one there, unless it was someone who did not breathe at all. Her hand shook at the thought, but she pushed at the open door and stepped into darkness. The shutters were closed — made fast, perhaps, by Mrs Slee after the storm. And that was not all. As Catherine's eyes adjusted to the dark, she realised that the room was empty, apart from the fallen dobbie stone and its frayed rope, the stone which had fallen on the night of Mrs Whitenow's death. But there was no hospital bed, no straps, no mattress, no chipped table, no burnt-down candle. Her heart jolted and seemed to stop for a moment. Had she imagined all that? Had she been mad herself?

And then she knew. She had not imagined those things, for as she stood there, she could smell them. Taste them. Sickness and terror and despair. It was as if they still cried out from the very walls of the icy cold room. They had known she had been here. Bennet Lestrange or Mrs Slee might have taken away the physical evidence, but they could not erase the horror that had happened here.

Mrs Slee had warned her not to go near the room upstairs, so she must have known who had been strapped in that bed. Mrs Slee, who went about the house as silently as a spectre and listened at doors. Mrs Slee, whose insolence was always there, half-hidden in her sly eyes, knew the secret of Raven's Gaze.

14

Catherine waited for a fine afternoon. She was determined to visit Rowantree farm. Grizel must tell her what she knew of Louisa Lestrange. Catherine had to know if she had been the patient in the room. There had been one. She had not imagined it. The idea of Louisa strapped in that bed haunted her, and she fretted constantly about her lovely, smiling boy. Would he be like his grandmother — that wilful, unstable child who became a woman of whom no one spoke? Not even Mrs Whitenow, her mother, talked of her, except to say that her daughter had married a stranger.

Rowantree was not far away — a mile, perhaps, beyond Starvecrow, up the narrow path that ran by the brook, but that rough and steep way was impossible for the perambulator. There was another way. She would go down the road which led out of the valley and turn up the hill, the way the carts went. It was longer but easier.

She passed the gate to Starvecrow. As far as she knew, the farm was still empty. She wondered if Bennet Lestrange intended to leave it to decay into a ruin. Annot had said that nothing thrived there. Catherine supposed that no one would want to live there. Annot's life must be better in Leeds. What a life she had led at Starvecrow, yet she had had the courage to leave and take her two children to a new life. Perhaps Grizel had news of Annot.

She turned up the hill onto the wider track — still rough, but there was smooth grass on the sides, and it was not as steep as the path by the stream. Thomas looked round in astonishment, and she reflected that he had hardly seen anything of the world. His wide eyes looked up at the hills and the sky above, and he chuckled with delight. He was a placid baby who rarely cried, though his coming teeth made him feverish at night so that she watched him by candlelight, ever fearful, and the teething ring soothed him. She liked to watch his wonder at the candlelight, and she would wait until he slept, and she heard his contented breathing. He knew she was there.

He loved her. She loved him. There was nothing wrong with him. Yes, it was true that madness could be hereditary, but why should Thomas not take after her and her parents and grandparents? But she had to know about Louisa — it was better to know the truth than to be haunted by uncertainty, and when she knew, she would say so to Bennet Lestrange. She would face him. She would show him that she was not afraid of him or of the secrets of Raven's Gaze. Yes, she would stay. She could not get round the fact that Bennet Lestrange was Thomas's legal guardian, but she would stay as a free woman who had the right to go wherever she wanted.

There was no smoke curling from the chimneys of Rowantree Farm. The gate was closed. There was no washing on the line, no horses or cows in the field. The front door was firmly shut and the shutters fastened across the darkened windows. Owd Dandy and Grizel were gone.

Mrs Slee was sweeping the porch when she got back to Raven's Gaze — waiting for her, Catherine thought. She must have watched her go and probably guessed where she had been, and deliberately not told her that the farm was empty. Mrs Slee must know that Grizel had gone. However, Catherine did not care. On her way back, she had thought about what she must do. Grizel could not help her. Even if she found Louisa's photograph, it would tell her nothing about what had happened to Louisa. She must ask Bennet Lestrange about his wife and that room. Now she saw Mrs Slee coming down the steps with her broom. No such thing as witches — just a sour woman with an overweening idea of her power, which Catherine was ready to challenge.

'I've been to Rowantree. What has happened to Grizel?'

Mrs Slee blinked in surprise at Catherine's firm tone. 'Owd Dandy's dead an' Grizel's gone to bide with her daughter in Hawes. Not that it's any of —'

'My business? Why should it not be? I liked her.'

'Aye, well, now tha knows.'

'So I do. I shall go to see her in Hawes.'

At that moment she heard a car and was surprised to see Bennet Lestrange driving up. The car, she thought. That was another thing she would ask about. Why should she not have use of it? She had learned to drive in the war. She could take it and drive to London.

He came up with a box in his hands and stopped to look at Thomas in the perambulator. 'It is good to see you outside,' he said. It was extraordinary how he could act the part of the concerned father-in-law, as if he cared tuppence whether she was inside the house or out.

'Yes, I felt like a walk and went up to Rowantree to see Grizel Knipe. I thought she might have news of Annot Syke and her children.'

It was his turn to blink now. 'Andrew Knipe died.'

'Dandy?'

His lip curled. 'If you will have it so. I bought the farm from Grizel Knipe.'

'What will you do with it?'

'I shall decide in my own time, though to whomever I let it, I hope you will not be taking my grandson to mix with the tenants. It would hardly be suitable.'

He stalked past her into the house, and she turned to see Mrs Slee smirking. Catherine picked up Thomas to carry him inside. 'Would you bring in the pram, please, Mrs Slee?'

Mrs Slee looked at Thomas. 'Ain't like Mr John, is 'e?'

'He is like my father, after whom he is named.'

'If tha says so. I'm thinking 'e's a look of his grandma, Miss Louisa, as was.'

'You knew her.'

'Oh, yes. A fine-looking girl, with lovely brown hair. Lighter eyes than Mr John. Never a strong lass, though. I 'ope yon lad don't 'ave that weak side.'

'I'm certain he will be a fine, strong boy, thank you, and take after my family. And as far as Louisa is concerned, Mrs Whitenow told me she died very soon after John's birth.'

'So she did, poor lass.'

'A fever, I suppose — it is not uncommon after childbirth.'

'Aye, that's what they called it, childbed fever. Tha was lucky to 'scape that.'

'Thanks to Grizel. I will be very pleased to see her again.'

Catherine went up the steps before Mrs Slee could answer, but she couldn't help wondering if Mrs Slee were lying about Louisa. What did that sarcastic "that's what they called it" mean? That Mrs Whitenow had lied about her daughter's death? It was hard to tell. Mrs Slee's hard eyes gave nothing away, except the usual hostility. She took Thomas upstairs and put him in his cot with his teething ring. The little silver bells would distract him while she sat and thought. Perhaps Mrs Whitenow and Mrs Slee had told the truth — in a way. It was possible that poor Louisa Lestrange had suffered from puerperal insanity. Catherine knew about that from her training. Its symptoms were hallucinations, delusions, mania, even violence done to themselves and others — in short, a kind of madness. Neither Bennet Lestrange nor Mrs Whitenow would wish for madness to be talked of in the dale.

She thought of that terrible room. Women who suffered from such a condition were often kept at home, looked after by a nurse. Doctor Hall had said Mrs Slee was used to nursing. Perhaps those scarred hands had held down the violent, raving patient to administer the sedative which Doctor Hall had provided. Doctor Hall must know, but would he tell? Would Bennet Lestrange tell? It was time to ask him.

Bennet Lestrange called out his pretentious, 'Come,' when Catherine knocked and entered his tower room to find him at his desk, gazing at his book. On a side table she saw the box he had been carrying earlier. There were other copies of the gold-tooled, leather-bound volume in it — for the deservingly learned recipients, and his grandson, of course.

'Ah, my dear, just the person I need. You can assist me in parcelling up the books. I should like to send them out as soon as I can.'

So, she was to be his assistant again. It was as if the scene outside had never taken place, as if John's death had never taken place, as if time had collapsed and she had left the room minutes earlier, having delivered some typed-up pages. As if Mrs Whitenow were still in her room upstairs and Thomas never born.

She must not hesitate. 'I came to ask you something about John's mother. Mrs Whitenow told me she died after John's birth. I wondered if she had suffered —'

Smooth as a serpent, he cut across her words. 'Oh, yes, a fever took her — too soon, but there was nothing to be done. A sad time in our lives.' He looked down at his book again, his long fingers stroking the leather, the mark on his hand darker now, and rippling as if it were a live thing. The wing of the raven. He turned back to her. 'Now, I'm sure Mrs Slee will look after the child while you assist me.'

She wasn't going to give in. 'How did the fever affect her?'

The black eyes gave her a familiar appraising look, and there was a deliberate pause before he answered, 'By death.'

'What symptoms did she exhibit before she died?'

'Ah, Nurse Sisley is back. Professional interest or just morbid curiosity?'

She ignored the jibe. 'Did she exhibit symptoms of mania?'

'You mean, was she mad? Is that what is worrying you? Madness in the Whitenow family that could infect the descendants? My dear Catherine, my wife, very tragically, died from fever and blood loss after the birth of her child. Doctor Hall and Mrs Slee assisted at the birth, but nothing could be done. I do not wish to discuss it further. Do you understand that it is a painful memory which I would rather not revisit?'

She felt inept and insensitive, as he had intended. 'Of course, I'm sorry.'

'Now, as to my book, surely you are willing to help me?'

She couldn't bear the thought of being alone with him. 'Surely Mrs Slee can help with the books.'

He shuddered. 'Hardly — those clumsy hands on my book! Think of the grease of a thousand meals.'

'What happened to her hands? The scars, I mean.'

'Scars? How should I know? She was brought up on a farm — it is a rough life.'

But the scars are not old, Catherine thought, opening her mouth to speak, but he was already standing up and handing her another book from the box. 'It is very fine, don't you think? Are you not proud to think that you played a small part in its production and may now play another?'

'Yes, it is very fine, and I will help, but I must do it in my own room. I cannot leave Thomas.'

He looked at her coldly. 'Surely, Mrs Slee can help with the boy.'

She served him back. 'The grease of a thousand meals.'

'Touché, my dear. Very well, take the box. There are brown paper and string here, and the list of addresses. Now, you must excuse me. I am busy.'

Busy with your own pride and pomp, she thought as she gathered up the box and papers and made for the door, but he hadn't finished with her yet.

'A moment,' he said. She looked back to see the sardonic smile. 'Just one more thing, my dear Catherine. If you were thinking you might go visiting any more neighbours or —' A long glittering look rested on her. She felt the box shake in her arms. He was going to say something dreadful. 'Or, perhaps, of taking the boy over the hills and far away — to the south, perhaps, do remember that I am his legal guardian.'

She stood outside the door, weak at the knees, his words clear as ice in her mind. *The south, perhaps.* He said nothing without deliberation. Oh, God, she had talked of Pat Sinclair who lived in Kensington and who was to marry a colonel, and Bennet Lestrange had no doubt seen the letters she had written to Pat and placed in the box in the hall. Of course, he had. The watcher. He would know the addressee of every letter that left Raven's Gaze Hall. He had probably read her letters. He knew what she had planned to do, and he would never consent to her leaving Raven's Gaze, even for a few days. He would do everything in his power to stop her.

*

200

'What are you doing in here?'

Catherine, who had heard Tom crying as she came down the corridor, was shaken to find Betty holding the little boy in her arms, his mouth open in distress.

''Eard 'im skrikin' and as tha wasn't in 'ere, I thought I'd see what were wrong. Only tryin' to 'elp. Teethin' ain't e?'

Catherine took a deep breath and stopped herself from rushing over to snatch Tom from Betty's arms. 'Yes, he is. I'll take him now.'

Betty passed Tom to Catherine. Her hands were hot, and she noticed the girl's flushed face and feverish eyes. What had she been up to? 'Thank you anyway. You can go now.'

After the girl had flounced away, Catherine nursed Tom and wondered what Betty had been up to. It could be true that Tom had cried if he had woken up to find she was gone. After all, she was always there. She didn't know how long Betty had been in the room. And why was she so red in the face? And those glittering eyes, malicious as the eyes of Bennet Lestrange. Something inhuman about both of them.

When Tom had calmed down, Catherine undressed him. She didn't know what she was looking for. Some sign of harm, but there was nothing. His cheeks were red, and his forehead felt hot but that was the teething. He fell asleep eventually, so she put him in his cot and watched for a while until the redness faded, and his forehead felt cool.

She looked at the box she had brought from the tower. She'd better complete her appointed task. The sooner it was done, the sooner she could send them back to Bennet Lestrange. Mrs Slee could take them after she had been in with the lunch tray. And then she could think about what Bennet Lestrange's knowledge about Pat Sinclair meant for her and Thomas. There had to be another way.

Mrs Slee didn't come. Nor did Betty. She went out to the top of the stairs, but there was no sign of them. If she wanted any lunch, she would have to go down and get it.

Mrs Slee was in the kitchen, setting a tray. She looked up when Catherine came in. 'Oh, it's thee. Tha can tek thy own tray. Save my legs for once. I'm a bit behind. I had to take Mr Lestrange's first.'

'Where's Betty?'

'She ain't feelin' too good — sent 'er 'ome.'

Catherine's heart gave a leap. That red face and those feverish eyes. 'What's wrong with her?'

'Monthly trouble, I'm guessin'. Says her stomach 'urts.'

Two weeks later, Betty still had not returned to Raven's Gaze. It was a long time, Catherine thought, for monthly troubles. Mrs Slee tutted at Betty's fecklessness. Mrs John would have to fetch her own trays for now. Mrs Slee couldn't be up and down a dozen times a day for them what had younger legs than hers. She'd be sendin' a message to her sister-in-law over at Hag End to find out what the young baggage was up to. Hag End, one of Bennet Lestrange's places. Catherine shuddered at the thought. It was an ill-omened name.

On a rainy morning about ten days later, a message came back in the person of Mrs Slee's sister-in-law, a faded woman in a shabby black coat who sat at the kitchen table while Mrs Slee looked down at her with expressionless eyes. The woman's red-rimmed eyes told Catherine the story she had been dreading before Mrs Slee spoke.

'Yon Betty's passed. Nowt to do for 'er. Measles done for 'er.'

The words dropped like stones on Catherine's ears. She turned her back on the shabby woman's wracking sobs and fled back to her room. Thomas had been feverish on and off for days. His temperature was high. She had thought his runny nose was a cold caught on the day she had taken him out for the first time up to Rowantree, the day she had found Betty with Thomas in her arms. Betty with her red face and hot hands.

The rash appeared a few days later, but Thomas was too young to fight the disease. Nurse Catherine Sisley, who had fought against every kind of filth, gas, gangrene, trench foot, sepsis, haemorrhage, and pneumonia, could not prevail against the pneumonia that developed in one small boy who had caught measles from Betty Slee. And Doctor Hall came too late.

15

1932

A young man — not Mrs Slee's brother — waited for Catherine at Garsdale station and led her to a car. It was twilight, just as it had been twelve years ago. Nothing had changed. She remembered the steep descent down a bumpy lane, onto a main road where she made out the cottages, the sudden right turn into a narrower road, and the wall by which the fingerpost indicated 'Ravendale 2'. She took in the great hills as the car rattled up the rutted road and stopped suddenly, so the driver could get out and open a gate. The hills were now closer, sweeping down to the very edge of the road, and she could see the glint of water tumbling down, distant lights, and the track which led to Starvecrow where Annot Syke had once lived.

Annot, who had sent the news of the death of Bennet Lestrange, had urged her to come back to Raven's Gaze because she ought to know the truth about what had happened there. What was Annot doing at Raven's Gaze? The letter did not carry the address of Starvecrow, so she could not have returned to her old home. In any case, Bennet Lestrange had bought Starvecrow. Had Annot's life in Leeds been a failure so that she had sought employment at Raven's Gaze? Catherine remembered Annot's contempt for Bennet Lestrange and Mrs Whitenow, and her and Mrs Slee's mutual dislike. She could not imagine her returning to Raven's Gaze as a supplicant.

Setting aside the letter, she had looked at the photographs and remembered everything. And she had wept for her boy, whose death had almost destroyed her. All those years ago, she had lain unresisting and mute in her bed while Bennet Lestrange had enacted his final cruelties. She'd had no nurse to tend her, only Mrs Slee, whose hard-eyed, tight-lipped ministrations were part of that cruelty. She had witnessed the burial of her child in that gloomy vault where Mrs Whitenow lay with her son and daughter. There was nothing to mark the existence of the great-grandson for whom she had schemed.

And when Catherine had come to herself again, Bennet Lestrange had been waiting in his tower room, his hands caressing the silver pounce pot. He had told her that Mrs Whitenow's will was now irrelevant. There was nothing for her now that she had failed in the purpose for which she had been brought to Raven's Gaze. The sooner she left, the better.

She turned away to the open door, but he spoke again to deliver the last thrust of the dagger. 'Unless, of course, you wish to stay and beget me another heir. A second wife for me, a second husband for you. A business arrangement, of course, like your first one.'

Catherine walked out, shaking with rage. How dared he? But, of course, he dared. He had no more idea of her feelings or anyone else's than that stone block in the hall. Her darling child was no more precious to him than a silver pot. She went back to her room and packed one suitcase with her books and her photographs, the jewellery Marjorie had left her, and a few clothes, hardly knowing what she was doing, but knowing enough to leave the ruby set in diamonds which Bennet Lestrange had told her was a family heirloom — from the Lestrange family — and her wedding ring, which she replaced with Marjorie's little sapphire ring. She left the silver and ivory teething ring which had been Thomas's — given by Mrs Whitenow. She wanted nothing that belonged to Raven's Gaze.

She had gone into her future. She had taken the train from Waterloo to Bournemouth, where she had taken a post at the hospital and eventually become Sister Catherine Sisley, whom everyone respected and no one really knew. She dedicated her life to the patients in her care, including the ex-soldiers, like the mute young man whose frozen features had reminded her of Lieutenant Adams. The young man's mother had wept as she'd consented to his transfer to a private asylum. She had already lost one son at the Front. Catherine and the doctors could treat his chest infection but not the sickness in his mind. There were those who were brought in suffering from malaria, trench fever and dysentery. And those who suffered from neglect and poverty, because the "Land fit for Heroes" had not a place for them. She often thought of the man under the pier at Morecambe and of how John had recoiled from the sight. It had marked the beginning of the end of their marriage, the night she knew that the breach between them could never be repaired.

The car stopped and she looked up at the tower, enfolded in the descending darkness. The light was out. She would never have to see those dark-lidded eyes or sense that cold, predatory gaze again. She had once asked about the strange name, Raven's Gaze. It had been his gaze. Bennet Lestrange, the carrion bird, was dead, and she was glad.

Light spilled out from the porch and a tall figure came out and stood on the steps. For a moment, Catherine thought of Mrs Whitenow standing there on the night she had arrived, but this was a younger woman coming down the steps to greet the car. In the light from the headlamps Catherine picked out an elegant black dress, pearls at the neck, and shining brown hair swept up to reveal the face of Annot Syke, who opened the door.

Catherine got out to find two hands reaching out and Annot saying, 'I'm glad you came. I wasn't sure you would.'

'I wasn't sure myself, but he is dead, and I want to know what you have to tell me.'

'That's why I waited. I knew the time would come, and here it is. Come in.'

'You live here.' Catherine realised that by the way in which Annot walked ahead of her into the hall — as if she owned the place.

Everything seemed the same at first glance. She remembered the oil lamps and branched candlesticks from that first time, the shadows in the corners and on the stairs, and the smell of age and woodsmoke. The fire still burned in the huge fireplace and the clock still ticked. But somehow, the atmosphere was different, lighter. A coat had been flung carelessly on one of the armoured figures, which had a cap rakishly askew on its helmet. The other figure had a school scarf wound round its neck, and a school satchel lay on the bottom step. She couldn't help wondering what Bennet Lestrange would have made of such treatment — of course, she remembered, he had no sense of humour, except of that sardonic kind which enjoyed weakness in others.

On the huge oak table, there were bowls in which the green shoots of bulbs peeped out and newspapers and books were piled haphazardly. A fishing rod had been left there, and she noticed the fishing basket and waders. Joe, she thought, remembering him for the first time. He'd be twenty-two — a young man. She wondered if he were here. And Clementine, the red-haired baby, would be about fourteen. Gracious, where had the years gone?

Annot was looking at her. Catherine recognised the shrewd gaze. 'Yes, we're all here, me, our Joe and Clemmie.'

'I imagined you'd be in Leeds.'

'I didn't go to my sister's — she'd no room, really, what with her own children, but I did live in Leeds for a while, and then about seven years ago he sent for me.'

'Sent?'

'It's long story. Not to be told standing here. Come into the parlour. Janet'll bring tea.'

'Not Mrs Slee?'

Annot laughed. 'I sent her packing — back up to Black Tarn with the witches. I knew Janet would come — anyroad, we can shift for ourselves.'

Catherine couldn't help smiling. The old Annot was still there in that flash of defiance. 'I don't doubt that. And who is Janet?'

'Grizel's lass. She's here in the cottage with her children. Her husband died.'

'Grizel?'

'She's here too — just the same. You'll see her later.'

'Good — though, I confess it's all a bit bewildering —'

Catherine was interrupted by the sudden entrance of a girl with long red hair swept back from her white forehead and tied with a ribbon. She was wearing a school uniform. Clemmie, she realised, and when the girl moved into the light of one of the lamps, she realised something else. A silence ensued. Just like the awkward silence when she had first arrived, and Mrs Whitenow had stared at her with those oddly glittering eyes, assessing her suitability as the potential mother of the future heir of Raven's Gaze, a role for which Annot Syke could never be fit. Yet here Annot was, changed and not changed. A different voice, different clothes, but the same straight blue gaze. Annot would tell the truth about her daughter.

Annot spoke first, glancing at the girl. 'She's part of the story. I can see you recognise her. Clemmie, go and get Janet to bring some tea and stay in the kitchen. This is Mrs Lestrange — you'll get to talk to her later.'

'Secrets, I suppose.' Clemmie smiled and reminded Catherine of John — not that he had often smiled. She remembered him smiling down at Sabine. John, who looked so like his father, Bennet Lestrange. Which of them had given this child that mouth and that high, broad forehead from which the red hair swept back? Her eyes were dark, too. Catherine remembered John's rage at Annot for turning down their charity. Perhaps his anger had had another cause.

Clemmie was still smiling. 'Mum has often talked about you. It's nice to meet you at last.'

'You, too. You were only about two years old when I saw you last.'

'The tea, Clemmie,' Annot said, and Clemmie went across the hall and through the kitchen door. Tall, too, Catherine noted as she watched her go.

They went into the parlour in which she had taken her first solitary breakfast. It was the same, except with that sense that it was lived in. The tea table by the fire. A shawl on the back of a chair on which knitting had been left. Grizel, she thought, remembering the blue shawl she had knitted for Thomas and finding that she could not breathe. Loss and guilt swept through her like a tide, and she thought what she had thought thousands of times since then. She should not have left Thomas to cry alone while she was chasing shadows. She should not have left him to be picked up by Betty Slee, who'd had measles. And she should not have come back. It was too much to bear. She buried her face in her hands, then felt Annot touch her shoulder. Annot was steering her towards a chair by the table, making her sit down and taking the seat opposite. When Catherine had mastered herself enough to look up, she saw the sympathy in her face.

'I was so sorry —'

'Don't,' Catherine interrupted. 'I can't bear to speak of him yet. Nothing else matters — not even who Clemmie's father was. I don't care if it was John, though I feel for you. It must have been dreadful to see him marry me, and yet you were always —'

There was a knock on the door, and a young man put his head in, saying, 'I've taken Mrs Lestrange's things upstairs.' The young man was the driver of the car. The young man was Joe, whose blue eyes smiled at her. 'You didn't recognise me.'

Catherine looked up at the tall, brown-haired, open-faced young man and saw fleetingly the boy he had been. 'You were ten, I think, soaking wet and with a grazed knee.'

He laughed. 'Yan bletheren clumpet, Billy Moffat — I remember. Billy and I are still friends, though he has a laugh at my toff's voice, as he calls it. The old voice didn't suit Mr Lestrange. He sent me to school, and I learned fast and with my fists from time to time, though I can still do the "yans" over a pint with Billie. Oh, here's the tea. I'll leave you to talk.'

Annot went to the door and took the tray from an invisible Janet. 'You'll need this — what shall I call you, by the way? Mrs Lestrange sounds —'

'I use my maiden name. I'm Miss Sisley now, but call me Catherine, please.'

'I will. Now, drink some tea. No one will come in, and we can talk in peace. Some things I'd rather the children didn't hear.'

'About you and John?'

Annot didn't falter. 'It wasn't John. It was him — his father had red hair, apparently. Convenient that Carver Slee had red hair, too —'

'Bennet Lestrange? That's why you came back?'

'Not for him — for Clemmie and Joe. You see how they have grown up. They wouldn't be what they are if we'd stayed in Leeds. It was a struggle there, but we managed at first with the money from Starvecrow. He gave me fifty pounds for the place. It seemed a fortune to me, but it didn't last long. There was rent, clothes, food, and no work at first. And there was Joe — he had to take a factory job for us to make ends meet. He started work at thirteen — my Joe, bright as a button and nothing but drudgery for him, and Clemmie. I had to pay for the school, but she'd have had to leave eventually. I wasn't going to see her dreams smashed as well. She's clever.'

Catherine thought about the day she had seen Bennet Lestrange at the back of Starvecrow. 'Did Bennet Lestrange persuade you to go to Leeds?'

'He wanted me gone — he thought I might tell you about me and him, or you might guess about Clemmie eventually. Mrs Slee knew, and she hated me for it — and for the rumour that her nephew, Carver, was the father. Still, Bennet paid her well to keep her mouth shut.'

'Mrs Whitenow?'

'I don't think so, or perhaps she preferred to believe in Carver Slee. I don't think John knew, either. Bennet did slip me money from time to time. I hated taking it, but I needed it.'

'But how — I mean —'

Annot answered with a half-smile. 'You mean how did it happen that I got pregnant by Bennet Lestrange? I was fed up — and a fool. Ted had gone to war, it was a hard winter, and I couldn't manage the farm. He came down and said he'd buy me out. It wasn't mine to sell, but he said I should sell the livestock — we had some sheep on the fell, a few pigs and a cow. He said he'd arrange it all, that I'd be better off with the money, and I could do some work at Raven's Gaze. I thought he was being kind — I didn't realise, and then he kept coming. Ted had never — I'm sorry, you'll be shocked. I let him — because I wanted — something — I don't know what —'

'I'm not shocked. I understand very well. If you knew my life before Raven's Gaze, you might be shocked, but that story is for another time.'

It was Annot's turn to be surprised, but she went on, 'And I was angry. Angry about having nothing, angry at Ted for being so hopeless, angry because the farm was a failure and so was I. I thought — I don't know — I thought he wanted me. Someone wanted me for a change, but I was stupid as well. I didn't realise that he was using me because he could — just an ignorant servant. When I went up to Raven's Gaze, he liked to take me into the tower. Oh, he liked the secrecy, and so did I — one in the eye for Mrs Whitenow, and Slee, and the world, I suppose, but Esther Slee found out. She caught me coming out of his room. I looked guilty, I suppose. And then I was expecting Clemmie — I didn't tell him, but Slee knew, and she told him. When we thought Ted had been killed, Bennet offered me money to go away, but then I heard Ted was alive and wounded. He was in hospital for ages, and I had to bring him home. I couldn't abandon him. He didn't even notice I was pregnant — he was too far gone. Grizel came when Clemmie was comin' and we managed. John came down to ask if I needed anything. Wouldn't come in and see Ted, though. He was a coward about that. I hated the lot of them and sent him packing, too. That's it — I don't regret Clemmie.'

'How could you? She's lovely. You made a mistake, but she is not a mistake.' Catherine took a deep breath. 'My boy — Thomas — it didn't matter who his father was. I made a mistake in marrying John, but I didn't regret Thomas. I forgave John, but I could not forgive Bennet Lestrange or Mrs Whitenow. I understand that you came back for the sake of Joe and Clemmie, but how could you live here — with him?'

'He was ill. He wanted to see Clemmie — the only child he had left. He was her father, after all, and something had gone out of him — some strength. He seemed old suddenly. He could hardly get up and down the stairs. When I came to see him, I realised that Mrs Slee had the upper hand. He had to rely on her because she knew the truth about him and me. When I came for good, I told her to tell anyone she wanted — it'd make no difference to me. I packed her things, locked the cottage, and told her to sling her hook. I was stronger than her by then.'

Catherine couldn't help smiling. 'I can imagine.'

'I wasn't frightened of her. I threw a bundle of money at her as well — just to see her on her way, though I reckon she'd taken plenty over the years because she went without a fight. The place was filthy, the food was rotten, his clothes unwashed. He said he'd marry me if I'd come. I said I would — in name only, but I looked after him, and he was all right with Joe, and in his way, fond of Clemmie. She knows he was her father. I've been honest with them. Joe remembers Ted, and they didn't know Bennet at his worst. And they have all this. Everyone knows in the dale, but it's Joe that's put things right. He's taken to running everything and he sees the tenants are looked after, and the farms. He's Billie Moffat's friend. Not a snob. They like Joe. And they resented Bennet and Mrs Whitenow. They looked down on the dales folk, and he was a hard landlord. No one was sorry about his death. They thought he was a devil.'

'I thought so, too.'

'You had reason.'

'What was wrong with him?'

'Drink and kidney disease, the doctor said — you remember those dark patches on his eyes? Gave him that devilish look at times. That's a sign, apparently.'

'There was a mark on his right hand, too. I always thought it looked like a bird's wing — a raven's wing.'

'Oh, yes, he used to tell me the history of Raven's Gaze when we were in the tower. He liked the sound of his own voice. When I came here with Joe and Clemmie, he taught me to speak properly, though he still winced at my accent. If I was to have Raven's Gaze, then I had to be fit for it. I did it for the children and to prove to him that I could. He paid for the schools and read to them, and they had to read back to him. Not in the later years, though. He didn't speak much at all, but I kept my part of the bargain. When he became really ill, I nursed him.'

'Did he regret what he had done?'

'Hard to say, Catherine. I think he knew he was a failure. He had nothing but his property and no heir to carry on his name. I'd find him in that tower by that window, even though he could hardly stand. Always looking out, always a glass in his hand. Whisky, brandy, port — anything. He was never drunk, though, just silent as time went on. He lost interest in Clemmie and Joe, and me. I don't think he really saw me. Nothing came of that book, by the way. Folk sent notes to say thank you. It was reviewed in the newspaper — the *Gazette*. An interesting curiosity, I think it said, and that was it. He was just a shell of a man at the end, muttering about ravens.'

'How odd. I remember Mrs Whitenow doing the same thing just before she died.'

'This house, I suppose. It's as if they cared for it more than anything. Did she think Bennet had taken it from her?'

'I don't know, Annot. They didn't like each other. They were only bound together in wanting John to have an heir, which is why I came here — not that I knew it at the time. They created a disaster between them.'

'You didn't love John?'

'I was fond of him at first — before we married and it all went wrong. He was very kind to me when my cousin Marjorie died. She was the only mother I had ever known. I was lonely — as you were, and I was a fool, too.'

'Not in the same way. I wasn't fond of Bennet, and I betrayed Ted for a few stolen hours of excitement.'

'It was Bennet Lestrange's fault, all of it. He knew John was in love with someone else.'

'The French lady — Grizel told me about John's death. Bennet never mentioned him.'

'Nor me, I'll bet.'

'No, he didn't, and I had enough sense not to say anything, but I knew I'd try to find you after his death.'

'But you waited six months before you wrote. How did you find me?'

'I remembered you said you'd come from Dorset and that you were going to take a nursing job in a big hospital there, so Grizel and I looked on the map and thought we'd try Bournemouth, as it's a big town and there must be a hospital. We've a telephone now, so I asked the exchange for Bournemouth Hospital, and I rang and asked for Nurse Lestrange. Of course, there wasn't one, and Grizel rang and asked for Nurse Sisley, and when they asked who it was, she put the telephone down, she was that nervous. But we knew, so I wrote. I wanted to wait for a while, though. I wanted the children to get used to Bennet's death and used to the idea that I was going to invite you, and I needed to work out if it was the right thing to do. This would have been your boy's house. Grizel said that you had a right to know everything, and — most important, she said — to come back to where your Thomas is, if you wanted to.'

'I can't answer that now. I've kept him in my heart. I've tried not to think of where Bennet Lestrange put him. Is he with him?'

'No, Bennet has a grave in the churchyard. That was his wish — he didn't want to be buried in the Whitenow vault. Not with Mrs Whitenow. But we — Grizel and me — make sure the vault is tended to. We wanted to look after him for you.'

Tears welled in Catherine's eyes. 'Oh, you are so good — and I, his mother, left him. I have been so selfish.'

'No, no — we understood. We only felt sorry that we'd lost you.'

'I should like to see Grizel. She was so very good to me, and I hadn't the chance to go to Hawes after — I just wanted to get away.'

'I understand that. It was the same for me and Starvecrow. But what about you in the last twelve years? I've so often thought of you and hoped you would have a better life.'

'I'm a sister at the hospital now, in charge of a very busy ward. It's what I was meant to do — what I should have done after the war.'

'And you're alone — you haven't —'

'Not yet — I might. It's difficult to decide. It's partly why I came. Before I go forward, I need to go back and lay some things to rest — some unanswered questions, not just about what happened to Bennet Lestrange.'

'I know. Grizel said you'd talked about Ted's death. You can ask us anything, but not now. You're exhausted. I'll take you upstairs to your old room and you can wash and sit awhile before supper. I'll come and fetch you for that.'

They went upstairs, past the place of skulls and the door to the tower, which was ajar. 'Joe's rooms now. He's made them his own, and rightly so,' Annot said, leading the way. She turned back as they went up the next flight. 'Bennet has gone, you know.'

As she followed Annot past the spiral staircase, Catherine wondered if that were true. She glanced up at the door and thought she felt the icy draught. Here was the old Raven's Gaze. Secrets up there. She was glad to know that Annot, Joe and Clemmie had their home here. They deserved it, but she still wanted to know what had gone on in that room. It was the last piece of the jigsaw on which the lid of the box could be firmly closed. Thomas was safe — nothing could harm him now. She had almost told Annot about Doctor Sam Meadows. He was a widower, aged forty, with a thirteen-year-old son, William. She liked them — wanted to love them — and Sam had asked her to marry him. Sam knew all about her and John, and Leo, and had not judged, because he had lived through that war, too, out there as a doctor. He was haunted by what he had seen, but his memories had served to drive him on to care for the sick and the poor who still lived in the shadows cast by the war. She wanted to say yes, but she was afraid, and then Annot's letter had come and with it a chance to lay her ghosts to rest.

When Annot left her, she looked around her old room. *Ghosts*, she thought, remembering how she had grieved for Leo on that first night. But he belonged to another time — the time before Raven's Gaze. When she thought of him, she felt his loss as the loss of a young girl's dream of a hero. Another girl had slept in a young man's arms in a Kensington Hotel. Another girl had felt that joy and hope and had cared nothing for the risk, because time had no meaning and love was everything. John, Bennet Lestrange, and Mrs Whitenow were nearer. She closed her eyes and felt them in the silence. They were still here, the memories of them come as ghosts to haunt her.

She pulled back the heavy curtain and opened the iron-framed window as she had done that first time to look out at the night, and in the deep, dark silence, she thought of Thomas and wept. When the weeping abated, she went to the bathroom to bathe her face in icy water. Annot was waiting when she returned to her room.

'I'm that sorry,' Annot said, looking at the traces of grief.

'I know. I'm ready now, and —' she touched Annot's arm — 'I'm very glad to see you again.'

Annot tucked Catherine's arm under her own and they went downstairs.

16

Supper was in the kitchen and Grizel was there, passing round soup bowls and fresh bread. She stopped to look at Catherine and smiled. 'Mrs J——' Her smile wavered on the name.

'Catherine, please.'

'Well, Catherine, lass, I'm right glad to see thee. Now sit thee down. Tha'll be famished.'

Sausage and creamy mash were spooned out by Annot onto the plates with rich brown gravy poured by Grizel, and the talk was of the doings in the dale, the tenants at Rowantree where Grizel had lived with Owd Dandy, the families which had left the dale, the death of the owner of Grime Hall where Bennet Lestrange's shooting friend had lived, and who would buy it now. Joe and Clemmie had hearty appetites. They wolfed down Grizel's tansy pudding, laughed a lot and teased each other. Catherine didn't have to say much and was warmed by the subtle kindnesses of Annot and Grizel. It was all so different from those other days when she had dined so formally with Bennet Lestrange and Mrs Whitenow and witnessed the undercurrents of hostility. This was a family, an unconventional one, but they were at ease with each other. They were not haunted by the past. They'd accepted the trials and pains of it. Annot had come to terms with the decisions she had made for the sake of her children.

While Joe and Clemmie cleared the table, ready to wash up, Annot and Grizel took Catherine back to the parlour, where Grizel took up her knitting and Annot poured cups of coffee.

Then she sat down and said, 'You want to know about Ted.'

'Did Mr Lestrange have anything to do with his death? That last day I came, I saw him on the path behind your house and then you were so — odd. I thought I'd offended you and I was sorry for it. I wondered if he had been at Starvecrow, and then when I came back from Dorset you were gone and Grizel said that Ted had died, and you had the money to go.'

'Grizel knows it was for Joe and Clemmie. She told me she had spoken to you about the laudanum. I was that ashamed when it happened — I couldn't even tell her where I was going.'

Catherine looked at Grizel. 'Grizel wouldn't have blamed you, and neither would I. It was afterwards that I wondered about Bennet Lestrange.'

'He said he'd do it. I admit I was tempted. He counted out fifty pounds in new five-pound notes on the table. He did it on purpose, because he knew I'd never seen that much money all at once. As I looked at it, I thought of the future, of years living as we were, and I thought of the last four years of hopeless misery, so I stretched out my hand. And then he said there was no point in keeping the wretched creature alive — if you'd seen the way he looked at Ted, as if he was an animal to be put down for his convenience... And then I heard Clemmie crying upstairs and I came to my senses. He wanted rid of her, too. I was that furious and I told him to get out, but he left the money on the table, as if he knew I'd... When you came, I was still furious and guilty. I was as bad as him, because I might have let him —'

'But tha didn't do it, lass. No one could blame thee for wishing — only a saint would never think of it,' Grizel said.

'And I'm not one of those, but I did help Ted on his way by giving him more of the laudanum. Not for the money, but for him. I just wanted him to be asleep — out of it. Sometimes his eyes would change and there'd be such a look of anguish, as if he realised what was happening to him. I couldn't bear to see it. And it was for me and the children. Our Joe — he saw too much. He was only six when Ted came back — his childhood blighted.'

'I thought of all that when I found the empty bottle,' said Grizel. 'I think I knew, Catherine, when tha came to see me an' I told thee what had happened. The tellin' out loud made it clear, but Annot knows that I thought about poor Ted an' that I thought it better for all of 'em. It's a long time ago. We can't change aught. We've to accept what's happened and them that's gone are in the Lord's hands now, whether they be good or bad. It's the living we've to think on.'

They sat quietly for a while, listening to the crackling of the fire and the click of Grizel's knitting needles. She was right, Catherine thought, but she had to ask about the last ghost of Raven's Gaze, Louisa Whitenow, Bennet Lestrange's wife, and whether it was she who had been the last inhabitant of that room. She wanted the dreams of what Thomas might have become, the dreams that had made her ache and yet feel comforted, to be true. She wanted no taint of madness to mar those images she had conjured. Her son would have been a fine boy and man.

'I want to ask you something, Grizel,' she began. 'I want to know about John's mother. I asked you once about the room upstairs —'

'What room?' Annot asked. 'The old nursery?'

'No, the room at the end of the corridor.'

'It's empty — well, except for Bennet's stuff. We put all his books and papers up there. We'd no use for them. No one used the room. The servants slept up there in the old days.'

'That's right,' Grizel agreed, 'an' in Bennet Lestrange's time, no one wanted to live in — folk didn't like him or the place, 'cept Esther Slee, and she only stayed for the money. No one liked the Slees.'

'It wasn't empty the first time I saw it.'

'But what's the room got to do with Miss Louisa?'

'I went in there one night when there was a storm. There was a window shutter banging. I couldn't sleep, so I went up to the attics. The door was barred, but I got in and I saw something — a hospital bed with leather restraints hanging from the bars of the bedhead and foot. Someone had been kept there — someone mad. It was a comfortless place, a prison — just the bed, a chipped table, a tarnished candlestick and a bare floor.'

Grizel and Annot stared at her in baffled astonishment. Grizel spoke first. 'And tha thought it was Miss Louisa?'

'You told me she was unstable, and Mrs Slee said she had died of childbed fever, and I know that the effects can be a kind of madness, hallucinations, delirium, even violence — I wondered about Mrs Slee's scars. They weren't old ones. Did she look after Louisa?'

'Aye, she did, but Doctor Hall was there when she died, too, an' he told my ma all about it. Yes, Miss Louisa had the childbed fever an' she lost a lot of blood — that's what killed her. It wasn't unusual, an' Miss Louisa wasn't what you'd call strong an' her nerves was always bad. But she wasn't mad in that room, Catherine, never that.'

Annot looked at Catherine. 'You're sure, that you — no, of course you are. You couldn't imagine a thing like that, but who? I can't understand it. That room was empty when I came back.'

'It was empty when I went up there a second time, but the smell was still there —'

'Smell?' asked Annot.

'Yes.' Catherine looked at Grizel, whose eyes had always seemed to see further than anyone else she knew. 'It smelt of sickness and terror and despair — of terrible suffering.' She turned back to Annot. 'Did it smell of anything when you went up there?'

Annot looked thoughtful. 'I could smell damp. I didn't feel anything, except that the room was stale, but … well, Clemmie said the room made her feel sick. She never liked that part of the house. I thought she might like your old rooms — for a bedroom and study, but she didn't want them. She doesn't like that staircase. Says it's always cold, even when the door's shut. I just thought — well, it is a bit creepy up there, so I didn't make a to do about it.'

Grizel looked at Catherine, her clear grey eyes troubled. 'Then, lass, there was something. Maybe not an actual smell, more a memory in the room that somehow stayed there, as if the suffering couldn't be got rid of. And Clemmie felt it, but I cannot think who might have been up there.'

'Mrs Slee knew. She caught me coming down the spiral steps and warned me away from the attics, and she and Mrs Whitenow suspected I'd been in there during that storm, so they had it cleared it out, and — I've realised something —'

'What?' Annot and Grizel asked together.

'I saw someone at the entrance to the spiral staircase. It was the day I fell down the first flight of stairs one morning. I could swear someone pushed me. I think it was Betty Slee up to mischief. It wasn't serious, just a badly sprained ankle. I couldn't walk for weeks, but how convenient for them. They could clear out the room without any chance of my knowing about it, and if I went up there again, all the evidence would be gone. I did go, and it was empty.'

'But what evidence?' Annot asked. 'What were they hiding or who? You don't think John Lestrange — after the war?'

'No, I worked out that it wasn't him. He wasn't mad — just deeply damaged by the war and by his father. Bennet Lestrange had no time for him. John told me that his brother had been the favourite — he should have been the heir.'

'I remember him,' Grizel said, 'a nice lad. Mrs Whitenow were fond of him. I think he reminded her of her son, James. They were alike, as I remember — not dark like Mr John. He looked like his father, o' course.'

'Mrs Whitenow spoke of James once when I first came here, but never again.'

'Tha asked me about that once before, my dear, an' I said then that Mrs Whitenow never gave aught away about anythin'. Too proud, I reckon.'

'Bennet Lestrange never mentioned his dead son — never even spoke his —' Catherine paused — 'name. Grizel, what was his name?'

'Bennet, after his father, but his second name was —'

'Raven,' Annot said. 'I thought it was that daft. Some crackpot idea of Bennet's.'

'His father called him Raven,' Grizel said.

'There was a Raven Clayburn in the mists of time, Bennet Lestrange told me when I first came, and he said the name was sometimes used until the end of the century. I think he brought up the name deliberately to needle Mrs Whitenow. I remember that Mrs Whitenow said it would never be used again. He enjoyed taunting her and he did it to me, too. It was as if he were always trying to find out one's weaknesses. He was a cruel man. But "Raven" was the word on their lips when they died.'

'Raven Lestrange died in France,' Annot said.

'Aye, I mind it. There were a telegram — Esther Slee told me. It weren't long after the news came about Will Bents. That were at the end of July in 1916. Tha remembers, Annot, the Bentses from over at Nouse Bottom? They had a telegram, too. Never had such a thing before.'

'I remember,' Annot said. 'It was September when I got the news that Ted was missing, presumed dead.'

'Poor Will was the Bentses' only son. He didn't have to go because o' the farm. Harry Bents would have stopped him, but his ma, Sarah, encouraged him. She were proud to have a son fightin' for the country. I went up there after the news came but Sarah Bents wouldn't see me, but I saw her once on the road. Like a ghost, she were, an' she didn't speak. They said she never spoke again. An' she lived another fifteen years.'

'Bennet and Mrs Whitenow couldn't speak of Raven. I never spoke of Ted after we left. Then Joe asked me when he was about thirteen and said he was a working man now and had a right. I didn't talk about Ted because I felt guilty. I thought it was all about me, but I had to remember that Ted was Joe's father, and I told him. Not everything, only that Ted had fought in the war, and given his life for his country —' Annot stopped and when Catherine looked up, she saw the tears running from her eyes. 'I couldn't tell him the truth — that they said he was a coward — and that I helped — I couldn't cry then — nor after. But now… I was a liar as well as —'

Grizel took Annot's hand. 'Your Joe's a fine lad, and he'll be a good man because of you. He don't need to know any truth about poor Ted to spoil him.'

'I never spoke of Thomas to anyone,' Catherine said. 'I felt guilty, too. I left him alone to cry, and Betty Slee had measles. My boy died because I was too busy asking Bennet Lestrange about Louisa. Because I wanted to know the secret — and I didn't think —'

A silence followed as Catherine and Annot wiped their eyes. Then Grizel said, 'Tha's to let go, my dears. 'Tis done and tha's paid for all of it. Tha's to forgive thyselves. Sarah Bents never forgave herself, and her daughters paid a heavy price for that. She'd nothing to spare for them. Let be.'

'Brandy,' Annot said as she went to the decanters on the side table. 'We need warming up.'

Catherine remembered Bennet Lestrange cradling his crystal glass of brandy when he told her about John and Sabine. It wasn't grief that had stopped him talking about his sons. It was because he had cared only for his house and his land, his silver and himself. And John was not what his father wanted him to be. And his other son had failed him. Raven Lestrange could not give his father the heir he wanted because he had died in France — or so she had assumed, but...

'A telegram,' she said when Annot had given them their drinks. 'Grizel, Mrs Slee told you about the telegram. Did she tell you anything after that?'

'Only that his body were never found.'

'Is there a memorial to Will Bents anywhere?'

Grizel looked surprised at the question. 'A plaque with his name and Ted's, tellin' that they served in the war.'

'Even though some said that Ted was no good as a soldier, he got that. And rightly so,' Annot said.

'It's in the church — where the Whitenows and thy boy are buried.'

'No plaque or tablet for Raven Lestrange. No prayers, no bells. No holy glimmers of goodbyes —' Catherine stopped, seeing Annot and Grizel gazing at her. 'That's from a poem by Wilfred Owen, who was killed in the war. I just remembered those words. And they are true for Raven Lestrange. Nothing about him at all.'

Annot spoke first. 'Are you — are you saying that Raven isn't lost in France?'

'If he is, then why isn't his death recorded with Ted's and Will Bents's? They are commemorated for their service in the war — remembered as heroes.'

'Maybe Raven wasn't a hero and that's why his father — I mean, we know more about it now. They said they were cowards. Some were shot for it, but now they say it was shellshock. Their nerves couldn't stand it. When I think of what Ted went through... Are you thinking that Raven Lestrange was one of those — that he lost his mind?' Annot asked.

'You and Bennet Lestrange are not the secret of Raven's Gaze Hall. Nor is Louisa. Raven is the secret. I think he went mad because of the war. I saw it when I was a nurse out there — so many of them — young men entirely broken, sometimes mute as marble, sometimes raving. They were sent on to special hospitals.'

'Aye,' Grizel agreed, 'they wouldn't want anyone to know — the heir to Raven's Gaze Hall, possibly regarded as a coward. And Will Bents, a farm labourer, called a hero. That's what folk said, not that it mattered to his mother.'

'Mrs Whitenow wouldn't have liked it either,' Annot added, 'and to be linked with Ted. I knew what folk said about him... I knew he couldn't stand it out there.'

'John only spoke about his brother once. We were in that little wood, and he said he used to go there with his brother. They decided to join up, but John said — I remember his exact words — he said, "He was never to come here again." I assumed he meant that his brother was dead, and he told me I mustn't speak of him to Bennet Lestrange or Mrs Whitenow. John knew. He couldn't cope with any kind of mental suffering.'

'That's why he wouldn't come in to see Ted — he was frightened.'

'I think so.'

'And you think Raven was in one of those special hospitals and they didn't tell anyone?'

'I think so but...' Catherine began slowly, unsure of her listeners' response to the idea that had flashed into her mind when she had asked about the memorial to Will Bents. 'Suppose they brought him back here. And he was the patient in that room.'

Annot and Grizel looked even more astonished this time. Grizel shook her head. 'I can't hardly think... Nay, lass, it's too dreadful. Someone would have known, or — think on't — they'd have to keep him a secret until —'

'Until he died.'

'And then what?' Annot put in. 'They can't have covered that up — they can't have buried him in —'

They looked at each other's white, horrified faces, knowing that each of them thought of Bennet Lestrange in the dead of night, and imagined Mrs Whitenow's ivory mask of a face, illuminated by a lantern, and something wrapped in sacking.

'Mrs Whitenow's last words were about Raven. She said, "Raven is here — up, up, up." She thought he was there when she was dying.'

'Bennet spoke of ravens at the end. I just thought that he was rambling, but now —'

'Uneasy in his grave. Grizel, when I talked to you about them never talking about their dead, you said that the unloved were unable to rest. That room was haunted by something — or someone. I used to hear footsteps outside my room at night. I saw movement on the spiral staircase and sometimes that door was open, but there was no one up there. Raven Lestrange was there — or the memory of him. They couldn't forget. He came back to them as they were dying. I heard something the night that Mrs Whitenow died — someone outside the room, but no one came in. Grizel, you told me that such things do happen.'

'Aye, I admit, it's true. Up there at Rowantree, my Dandy's auntie always said that her mother walked. Her last and third child died at three months an' she went out into the night. She never came back, but Dandy's auntie said she saw her in the bedroom where the child had passed. And Annot, tha knows it, too. All about here, folk have tales to tell.'

'I know, I know, but this — no, no, Catherine, I can't believe it.' Annot frowned. 'Not even of him. No, no — keeping his own son a prisoner, digging a grave with her standing there... Raven can't be here.'

Catherine remembered accompanying Bennet Lestrange up into the fells to the Devil's Pot, where he had speculated on the bones buried deep there. She remembered the smell of decay, and Black Tarn where Mrs Slee lived. The tarn, a bottomless pool. Nothing would ever be found there. And he had relished the phrase, *a conspiracy of ravens*. And a murder of crows. Murder.

Her thoughts were interrupted by Grizel who said, echoing her idea, 'Esther Slee would have known, and her brother knew every inch of Raven's Gaze.'

'But he's dead now,' Annot said, 'and he wouldn't have said anything. Too frightened of his sister.'

'Then we'll have to ask her. Think about Black Tarn — the bottomless pool — and think about those hands of hers. How did she get those scars?'

'I never asked,' said Grizel

'Doctor Hall told me that Esther Slee was used to nursing. I can imagine what kind — what she might have done to her patient.'

'I still can't believe it —' Annot began.

'I can believe anythin' of Esther Slee,' Grizel said.

Catherine thought about that, and she thought about Mrs Slee's words when the news came about Betty's death. *Measles done for her.* As if she had been glad. She had known all along that Betty's illness was not her monthly trouble. She had known about the measles, and she had not told Catherine. She thought about her years of grief and guilt, but Mrs Slee had killed her boy. 'So can I,' she said. 'She knew that Betty Slee had measles, and she didn't warn me.'

'Downright wicked,' Grizel said.

'And Bennet Lestrange. He would have killed Ted. What did he say about him, Annot?'

Annot's eyes widened as she remembered. 'He said there was no point in keeping the wretched creature alive.'

'Perhaps he thought that about his own son who would never get better.'

'Esther Slee won't tell,' Grizel said, breaking the frozen silence which followed Catherine's words.

'It's a crime. She was involved. She must tell,' Catherine said. 'She must.'

'Stop a minute,' Annot said. 'We're getting ahead of ourselves. I know you believe it, Catherine, but we've no proof that Raven was even here. It seems so — outlandish. Grizel, you can't think it's true that Bennet would have killed his own son?'

'I don't know. I don't want to think it of him — or Mrs Whitenow, but 'tis a mystery. What Catherine says about them memorials makes me wonder why Raven isn't remembered, and he, Bennet Lestrange, was a man with no right feelings. Esther Slee would have lied for them, if there were money in it... Still, I reckon we need to sleep on it. It's late. We're tired an' we're mebbe imaginin' things. We'll think clearer in the mornin'.'

Catherine was thinking. She understood Annot's doubts, but she was still sure that Raven had been in that room. However, she ought to suggest something practical. 'Annot, maybe there's something in Bennet's papers. There must be some record of Raven's life.'

'We'll look tomorrow when it's light before we go tearing up to Esther Slee's place. She'll shut the door in our faces unless we have some proof.'

In her room, Catherine watched the fire die down and thought about the night of the storm and the hideous banging of the shutter, her icy climb up the spiral staircase, and the room itself. If the patient had not been Louisa, and she believed Grizel was right about that, then Raven was the only answer. However far-fetched it might seem, and however unsure Annot and Grizel were, she was sure that Raven Lestrange had been the patient in that bed, even if he had not died there. Perhaps John had not known he had been brought home, but he had known his brother had gone mad. It explained his horror of Lieutenant Adams, and the man under the pier, and Ted Syke, and his own suicide, maybe. Perhaps he had been overwhelmed by the burden of guilt and shame if he had believed that his brother had been confined to an asylum, and he had not had the courage to see him. He had never had the courage to stand up to his father.

And she saw again Mrs Whitenow's shrunken face on the pillow and her shrivelled fingers plucking at the counterpane. And she heard those last words: *Raven is here ... up ... up...* Up in that room. The living ghost.

17

Catherine sat up after a fitful night of fragmented dreams, in which faces rose from dark water — the horrible grinning faces of Bennet Lestrange and Mrs Slee, and an unknown face, the water streaming like unstoppable tears from eyes like those of Lieutenant Adams. She awoke at the moment when the glittering eyes and huge wings of a great black bird swooped down to smother her. Sometimes she woke to sounds that weren't there, the sound of footsteps outside her door, the sound of something banging in the wind, the sound of weeping, sounds which ceased as soon as she sat up, her heart thumping.

She got out of bed, shaking her head to banish the images and went to draw back the curtain. She looked up at the sky and the fells, which were bright and still in the morning light. What they had imagined about the Black Tarn seemed impossible.

There was a light knock, and Annot appeared with a cup of tea.

'You shouldn't — I ought to have come down by now.'

'I thought you might have a restless night, and when I listened at the door, I thought you must be asleep, so I left you. It's only nine o'clock, anyway.'

'Did you sleep?'

'I fell asleep eventually, and then I was dreaming of that bottomless pool and Slee looking down into the water, and him — oh, I was glad to wake up to the sun this morning.'

'What do you think now?'

'Well, you didn't imagine that room. I went out to look in the outhouses. That bed's there, all rusted, and that chipped table you described. The leather straps have gone and there's no mattress.'

'Then we must find out what happened, if they — or just Bennet — did what we thought. I know it seems impossible now, in the light of day, but —'

'Let's not think that far. Let's find out if Raven was here. We'll look at Bennet's papers. Everything's in that room. I never looked. Just his scribblings, I thought. He was supposed to be writing another book on the history of Raven's Gaze. He was always nattering on about ravenstones, gibbets, and so on. I didn't take much notice. The will and the bank records were with the solicitors in Hawes, but there might be other things Bennet wanted kept secret. I mean, if Raven Lestrange was brought here, he came from somewhere.'

'A hospital, perhaps.'

'Maybe Bennet took him back because they couldn't cope with him — those leather straps you saw —'

'Yes, it makes more sense to think that Raven died in hospital and that there is some record of that up there.'

'And there'd be a funeral and a burial wherever he was — they'd not want to bring him back here.'

'But what a secret to keep — never to speak of him. They were guilty of something — of pride — and cruelty. They kept him in that room. It was a kind of murder.'

'It was — it was cruel. I'll leave you to get dressed now, then come down for some breakfast. There's a lot of stuff in boxes we can search through. Grizel will give us a hand.'

'What about Clemmie? She might be upset about the room.'

'Joe's taken her to school — grammar school in Kirkby Stephen — so she'll be away all day, and Joe'll be about the dale, visiting the farms, so we'll have the place to ourselves.'

Annot threaded her way through the boxes piled high on the bare floor and opened the shutters, and Catherine stood at the door with Grizel. It all looked perfectly ordinary — just a room in which to keep unwanted things, but when Catherine stepped in, she could feel the same icy cold as she had felt before and, though it was fainter now, the atmosphere of suffering still lingered in the stale air.

Grizel looked at her anxiously. 'All right?'

'Yes, it's not as bad as before. Daylight helps, but I can still sense it. I know terrible things happened here.'

Annot was brisk. 'Then, let's get on. Here, Catherine, these boxes near the window are full of papers from his desk. Grizel and I will look at what else there is.'

'When Mrs Whitenow died, her room was emptied, too. I wanted to find a photograph of Louisa. I'd seen one in her room, which must have been of her and Raven — the child wasn't a newborn in the photograph, so it couldn't have been John. I wanted to see if Thomas was like Louisa. I wonder what happened to her things.'

'Not in here. The old nursery, maybe. I'll go and look while you two search here.'

Catherine sat on a trunk and opened one of the boxes, which was crammed with papers tied up with string. She looked at the first bundle and recognised some of the pages she had typed for Bennet Lestrange — the familiar names brought back the raven mark on his long hand and his long gaze under those darkened lids. She remembered him in the tower and his breath on her neck. She had feared him then, and if it had not been for Marjorie's death, she would have gone for good. Cruel fate, she thought, and cruel Bennet Lestrange. There must be some kind of justice for Raven, the lost son. His fate must be known. If he had gone mad, then the war had done that. It did not make him a coward.

She concentrated on the papers, discarding the ones she had typed. There was a sheaf of handwritten papers with the title, *The History of Raven's Gaze Hall*, a monograph by Bennet Lestrange, M.A., Oxon. She saw raven-black ink, the familiar handwriting, looped and curved, the pen deeply impressed into the thick paper. He had written about the Vikings, their standard showing the raven… She turned over. Ah, there was Byron and his ravenstone. *Nothing new*, she thought, turning page after page. Stories of the wild Clayburns, of course, and Jeremiah Whitenow. She shook out the pages, but there was nothing about Raven Lestrange.

Another box contained maps, old books and pamphlets on the history of the house, and photographs of the dale and the outlying farms — black and white images, now rather cracked. She could hear Grizel's breathing as she turned pages, but Grizel didn't speak. Catherine's next box contained the deeds of the house, and marriage and birth certificates.

While she was reading, Annot came back. 'Anything?' she asked.

'Mr Lestrange's and Louisa's marriage certificate and John's birth certificate, but not Raven's. It's as if Mr Lestrange wanted to leave no trace of him.'

'Well, he didn't succeed. Look at this. It was tucked inside Mrs Whitenow's Bible, hidden in a box. I saw the ribbon and wondered what it was.' Something glinted in Annot's open palm.

Catherine went over to look at the silver cross, which was about two inches long and suspended from a purple and white striped ribbon. 'It's a Military Cross,' she said. 'Awarded for gallantry.'

'It's Raven's. There was this bit of newspaper with it.'

Catherine read the printed words aloud: '*The Military Cross has been awarded to Lieutenant B.R. Lestrange of the Loyal North Lancashire Regiment for conspicuous gallantry in the action at La Boisselle on the fifth of July. During the attack, Lieutenant Lestrange was wounded when he and a company of men took over an enemy machine gun and held off the enemy until reinforcements arrived. He has at all times set a fine example of courage and determination...*'

'A hero then,' Annot said. 'How could they not recognise that?'

'Mrs Whitenow kept the medal and the newspaper, but she couldn't accept that he had been broken by the war.'

'There was this, too — it was between two other pages. Grizel, is it Raven? It looks like him — from what I remember of him.'

Grizel stood up to take a photograph from Annot, at which Catherine looked over her shoulder. It was the photograph of a schoolboy in an Eton collar, a lock of hair fallen over his brow, and a slight upturn to the corner of his mouth, as though he was about to break into laughter.

'That's James Whitenow,' Grizel said, 'but Raven Lestrange looked like him — same hair, the way it used to fall over their brows, though Raven had a reddish tint to his hair.'

'Like Clemmie,' Annot said. 'I remember that. I saw him and John in the lane sometimes when they were back from school. Raven would give us a wave, but never John, who always walked on.'

'Clemmie's eyes are brown, and I mind now, those boys' eyes was pale green — unusual, but always a glint of laughter there.' Grizel turned over the photograph. '1880 — that's right. James Whitenow would have been fifteen. It was the year he died. Terrible thing, it were.'

Catherine looked at the boy who had no idea that in a few months, he would be dead. He looked like the fine boy Mrs Whitenow had told her about, and down the long perspective of years, she understood something of the bitterness of that old woman's loss. And then she'd had to see her grandson ruined, he who had been for her a replica of the lost boy. Her answer had been to banish him — wrong, but in a way understandable. She thought of how grief had changed her after Thomas's death, how she had banished herself and withdrawn from friendship and love. She had one chance now to redeem Mrs Whitenow's loss, and perhaps her own. But she could not forgive Bennet Lestrange.

'At least Mrs Whitenow kept something of Raven's. The medal meant something to her, but Bennet Lestrange erased him from his life. It's monstrous.'

'I haven't found anything else in the old nursery, so we still don't know what really happened to Raven after that, only that Mrs Slee told Grizel that he had been killed — and that was in July 1916.'

Catherine looked at the scrap of newspaper. 'He served with Loyal North Lancashires. We know where he was wounded and that he was awarded the Military Cross. I know someone who can help us find out what happened to Raven after he had been wounded.'

Catherine had corresponded with Pat Sinclair over the years. She was Mrs Rhodes-Smith now and she and her George lived near London. Catherine had visited occasionally. Pat always seemed to be pregnant, and the big, untidy house was, as she had foretold, filled with children whom the colonel adored without necessarily recognising each one, a failing which made his wife laugh. He was a good-hearted, patient man, Catherine reflected, who would help his wife's old friend. The colonel still worked for the War Office. She could telephone and ask for him. Surely Colonel Rhodes-Smith could find out about a lieutenant who had been awarded the Military Cross.

She explained to Annot and Grizel and they went downstairs. 'We'll make some tea while you do it,' Annot said.

Catherine dialled the exchange in Hawes and asked to be connected to the War Office, Whitehall, London. Eventually, a female voice announced that she was through. Catherine gave her name and asked to speak to Colonel George Rhodes-Smith, emphasising that it was an army matter and that she was an old friend of the colonel's. He would certainly wish to speak to her.

A series of clicks followed. George spoke her name warmly, and she gave him the details from the newspaper.

'I want to know what happened to him. He was John's brother, and I think he disappeared. At least, no one ever spoke of him and there is no memorial to him, even though he got the Military Cross in 1916 at La Boisselle.'

'The Somme,' he said. Not a question. A statement of a horror and a courage he understood.

'Yes.' She knew he would help.

George Rhodes-Smith didn't need to ask anything else. 'I'll find out what I can. Give me your number and I'll ring you back when I know. The Loyal North Lancashires, you say?'

'Yes, Lieutenant Bennet Raven Lestrange.'

'Got it. It shouldn't take long. I know the commanding officer of the regiment, and I'll get onto the War Pensions people.'

Catherine went into the kitchen to tell Annot and Grizel. 'Good,' Annot said. 'After we've had this tea, we'll keep on looking. We might find something else before your colonel rings back.'

'An' I'll get some food on the go. We'll finish that soup at dinner time an' I'll make a pie for tonight.' Grizel smiled at them. 'We'll need summat fortifyin' after all this.'

Catherine and Annot found more papers relating to the history of Raven's Gaze, deeds, contracts of sale, receipts of purchase, servants' wages, valuations — *Goods in ye House £4 5s; Goods in ye Parlour £2 2s; Husbandry Gear £2 2s; Livestock, Beasts and a Horse £16 5s; Hay and Straw Bigg and Oats £7.* Dame Abigail Clayburn, wife of Raven Clayburn, paid her maid, Gennett Pepper, eight shillings for the year. The will of Margaret Clayburn excluded her son, Garth Clayburn, for having married Thomasyn, a daughter of the barbarous Scarr family. No Scarr should ever have benefit from Margaret Clayburn — the quarrel would, no doubt, last for generations.

'Just like those old families to bear a grudge till Doomsday,' Annot said. 'Oh, and listen to this one. Benjamin Slee, a labourer, was hanged for the theft of a silver cup. I'll bet Esther hasn't forgotten that hanging.'

Catherine laughed. 'And here's the record of the death of one Jasper Clayburn, found drowned with a dagger in his side — murdered, I'll bet.'

They looked at the pile of papers, many dating back to the seventeenth century, dusty, yellowing parchments with cracked red seals, nibbled by mice and beetles, telling of the house's long history, and conjuring the vengeful Clayburns, their properties, their lands and money, their quarrels, and their eventual decline.

'You'd think he'd have learned from all this,' Annot said, rocking back on her heels and tossing another paper onto the pile. 'The last of the Clayburns, Elizabeth, signed away her property to Jeremiah Whitenow. Nothing but a pair of spidery signatures on bit of torn paper. They came to naught, and neither did Bennet.'

'He learned nothing from the war either, nothing of courage, or duty, or loyalty. Well, his lost son must not be forgotten.'

Annot was still staring at the papers. 'Clayburns and Whitenows, but nothing about the Lestranges. Who on earth was he and where did he come from?'

'Mrs Whitenow called him "the stranger". Bennet Lestrange said he came from Ireland. He talked of a grandfather and a country house. John didn't tell me anything, but at one time he was supposed to be in Ireland on business. I didn't believe it. I thought he was with his French lady.'

'And there's nothing about our Raven in this lot.' Annot looked round at the piled-up boxes. 'Dear Lord, where do we look now?'

Catherine didn't answer. She was reaching under the table for a small black lacquered box, which she dragged out and examined. 'It's locked.'

Annot looked. 'A small lock for a small key. I have all the keys to the house doors, but they're big ones. Bennet kept the keys to the tower in his desk. I'll see if there are any other keys in any of the drawers.'

Catherine gazed at the box while she waited. Probably more ancient documents, she thought. Bennet Lestrange would have covered his tracks, his secrets gone with him to the grave.

George Rhodes-Smith would find out, though. The Loyal North Lancashire Regiment would have records of Lieutenant Bennet Raven Lestrange.

Annot came back with a ring of keys, but none fitted the black box. She held up a penknife. 'Our Joe's. I'll have to force the lock. I want to know what's in it. Bennet's not getting away with his secrets.'

Catherine smiled, recognising the fierce light in Annot's eyes. She wouldn't give up. Annot tried to force the tip of the blade into the lock and when that didn't work, she worked at prising open the lid. With a sudden snap, a bit of lacquered wood split and the lid flew open just as Grizel came in to tell them that their soup was ready.

'Oh, my, what's all this?'

Annot was holding up a velvet bag. She emptied the contents onto the table: a collection of diamond rings and a brooch.

'Mrs Whitenow's,' Catherine said.

There were some sovereigns in the other bags, as well as some gold rings, a pearl necklace, and a gold watch on a chain. There was a little leather box containing a wedding ring and another diamond ring, and lastly, another box with another wedding ring and the ruby set in diamonds which John had fumblingly placed on Catherine's finger at their engagement.

'Thine,' Grizel said, 'I remember them.'

'Bennet Lestrange said the ruby was a Lestrange family heirloom. I didn't want it, and I had no use for a wedding ring after —'

A rustling sound interrupted Catherine. Annot was holding up a single sheet of paper. 'Look at this.'

It was a birth certificate from the country of Eire, which told them that Bernard Michael Lestrange had been born on the 1st of October, 1865, in Dublin. His father was Desmond

Lestrange, a bank clerk, and his mother, Bridget Mary, a lodging-house keeper on Barracks Street.

'Well, well,' Annot chuckled, 'the aristocratic Mr Bennet Lestrange of Raven's Gaze Hall was just Bernie from Barracks Street.'

'With his rich Norman blood,' Catherine said, remembering Bennet Lestrange looking into his glass of red wine, 'and his family heirlooms.'

'Mr Nobody — a stranger, indeed.'

'The Irish part was true, but I don't believe in the grandfather's country house. He even had a name for it — Rosemount.'

'He made that up,' Annot said. 'Just what he would do — Rosemount, my foot.'

'You have to laugh, though,' Grizel said. 'A lodging house — '

They looked at each other, laughing. *Friends*, Catherine thought. *How much I have missed them.* Something had been rescued from those dark times. Then the telephone rang, and they were serious again.

'Oh, my, thy colonel,' Grizel murmured.

'Run,' Annot said.

Catherine fled downstairs. Annot and Grizel waited in the hall, straining to hear the murmured words. They heard Catherine place the phone back on its cradle, waited in the pause that followed, and imagined her taking a deep breath to steady herself. Then she came out from the little room under the stairs, looking very white, the writing pad in her shaking hands. She looked down at the pad and read the notes she had written.

'Lieutenant Bennet Raven Lestrange, wounded at La Boisselle, on the fifth of July. He was missing for twenty-four hours. His wounds were treated at a Casualty Clearing Station; then he was transferred to a military hospital in Boulogne and from there sent to Number Four London General Hospital for specialist treatment for shellshock. It was from there his father brought him home in August.'

'And he could just do that?' Annot asked.

'Colonel Rhodes-Smith told me that under the terms of the Lunacy Act, servicemen discharged for shellshock or other mental problems could not be forced to have treatment and if Raven's family wanted to look after him, then they could. An officer's family — the army would take his father's word. They would have no further interest in him. The colonel contacted the Ministry of Pensions...'

'Is he dead?' Annot asked quietly.

'His death was reported to the War Pensions Department on the twentieth of September, 1916 — by his father —'

'Can it be true, then — what we thought? That Raven is buried —' Annot couldn't say the words.

'Kitchen,' Grizel said. 'Hot tea.'

'Sit here, by the range.' Annot put Catherine into the big chair while Grizel filled the teapot. Catherine thought she would never be warm again. She had not wanted to believe it. That poor boy, she thought, who probably had not known what was happening to him, and then to be thrown into some black hole up there or tossed into that fathomless tarn... No prayers, no bells, no holy glimmers of goodbyes. She was too shocked to speak.

Grizel placed the teacup into Catherine's hands. 'Drink that. There's sugar in it.'

'And brandy.' Annot had slipped out to get the bottle and she poured some into each cup.

'I didn't want to believe it,' Catherine said eventually. 'I thought this morning that you were probably right about their taking him back to a hospital — but Mr Lestrange told the pensions people that his son was dead in September. Yet we have found no records or letters which show where Raven was, or that he even existed. No birth certificate. No death certificate.'

'An' Esther Slee told me he'd died in July,' Grizel added. 'She lied — so did Bennet Lestrange lie about Raven's death? Perhaps he didn't die in September —'

'Bennet brought him home in August … but he could still have taken Raven back to a hospital where he died,' Annot said. 'I can't believe that Bennet just…'

'Esther Slee must know what happened,' Grizel said.

Catherine roused herself. 'Then we must ask her. We have to know the truth. So, when do we go?'

Grizel looked doubtful. 'She's that hard. I don't know as she'll tell thee.'

Annot's blue eyes flared. She was there again, the defiant girl in the cracked boots not wholly hidden beneath the woman in her pearl necklace. 'Then I'll damn well make her, even if I have to beat it out of her.'

Grizel smiled. 'Annot Syke of Starvecrow, eh?'

Catherine laughed shakily. 'Just what I was thinking. But I don't think we'll need to beat her. We have the War Office right behind us. This afternoon, then.'

Annot looked out of the window at the gloomy sky and at her watch. 'No, it'll be almost dark by the time we get there. Tomorrow morning — we'll get Joe to take us as far as he can up the road to Black Tarn and then we'll have to walk along the lane.'

'She'll be a bit surprised,' Grizel said wryly.

'Maybe I'll take one of Bennet's shotguns — to persuade her, in case she forgets her manners.'

18

'Bennet Lestrange brought me here once,' Catherine said, as she and Annot turned into the lane, having left Joe and the car parked by Rattenrow Cottages, which looked completely derelict now. 'I thought it was a frightening place. We stood at the edge of the tarn, and he said it was a place for drowning — drowning oneself or somebody else.'

'I know he was peculiar, but surely he wouldn't have done that if they'd put Raven in the tarn. It would be —' Annot looked up to where the tarn was — 'I honestly don't know how to describe it — sort of enjoying himself —'

'Oh, he would have been, because he liked knowing what others did not know. When he talked about drowning, I think he could have been enjoying a secret that I would never know. It was power he loved. He taunted Mrs Whitenow with the name "Raven", knowing full well that she would hate it. He was capable of any cruelty — even getting rid of his son's body.'

Annot was silent then as they made their way up the track to the farmhouse, where a forbiddingly scarred door confronted them.

'I'd best knock, I suppose, though you'd think the place was deserted. It looks that wretched. What's she done with her money, I wonder?' Annot said.

'She's in there counting it. Go on, do it. I want this over with.'

Annot lifted the heavy iron knocker and banged it several times, the sound echoing in the silence. And they waited, listening to the reverberations dying away. Then they heard the slow grating noise of ancient bolts being drawn. The door opened with an unearthly creak and the whine of rusty hinges.

Mrs Slee looked the same, only shabbier. She had never been young, reflected Catherine as she looked at the thin face with its hard line of a mouth and the two hostile eyes the colour of dirty stone, which blinked at them when she opened the door. She would have slammed it in their faces had Annot not pushed back with some force. That took Mrs Slee by surprise, but Catherine could tell that she was recovering her natural insolence.

'Well, well,' she said, 'a visit from the gentry. Two Mrs Lestranges. Two grieving widows, eh? I don't think. Made for each other, ain't you?' She turned her stony gaze on Annot. 'I've nowt to say to you. I know what you are. Still Annot Syke with 'is bastard in 'er belly.' Her laugh was as coarse as her broken, yellow teeth. 'A fancy name an' a fancy coat don't change owt —'

Annot was unfazed. 'And I know what you are, Esther Slee, so let's not waste time. We want to know about Raven Lestrange.'

Mrs Slee blinked again, and when she stepped back in surprise at the name of Raven Lestrange, Annot pushed past her into the cramped hall. Mrs Slee and Catherine followed. They stood on the stone flags in a silence broken only by Mrs Slee's indignant breathing. It was so cold that Catherine could see her breath curling in the air — that bitter breath of hostility she remembered from all those years ago.

'Tha can both get out,' said Mrs Slee, having recovered herself. 'I've nowt to say about anythin' to do with that 'ouse.'

Catherine took some official-looking papers from her pocket and glanced at them as if to refresh her memory. Her voice was the stern, calm voice of Sister Catherine Sisley, addressing a recalcitrant junior nurse or a hapless young doctor who had got above himself.

'I have been in touch with the chief of the War Office, Colonel George Rhodes-Smith, who has information about Lieutenant Bennet Raven Lestrange, wounded at a place called La Boisselle on the Somme. I take it you have heard of the Somme?'

'So what if I 'ave? Nowt to do wi' me.'

'Very well, I'll continue.' Catherine looked at her papers again. 'Lieutenant Lestrange was hospitalised in Boulogne and London and then brought back by his father to Raven's Gaze Hall in August 1916. Bennet Lestrange reported his son's death to the War Pensions Department in September.' She looked coldly at the hostile face. 'Yet you told Grizel Knipe that he had died in July and that his body was not found, though there is no evidence of his life or death to be found at Raven's Gaze. However, Colonel Rhodes-Smith is willing to send an officer from the Military Police to investigate. The officer will wish to question anyone who lived or worked at the hall in and after 1916. You are the only one left who can shed any light on the fate of Lieutenant Lestrange, who was awarded the Military Cross for conspicuous gallantry.'

Another silence stretched out. Catherine glanced at Annot, who nodded in approval. Even in the damp, gloomy hall of Black Tarn, she could see that her eyes gleamed in triumph. She looked back at Mrs Slee, whose eyes were cast down and whose scarred hands were folding and refolding the edge of her grimy apron. *The grease of a thousand meals.* The scars were faded to white now but clearly marked against the big brown hands. Someone had given her those. Someone she had fought with and restrained. Mrs Slee lifted her head to stare at Catherine, but there was something other than insolence in her gaze. There was a hint of fear. Not that she was going to give in.

'I've nowt —'

Catherine ignored her. 'If you would rather speak to the military authorities, then, of course, we'll go and make a telephone call.'

'Or we can go into your kitchen, and you can tell us. You look as if you need a sit down,' Annot said, sweetly mocking.

Mrs Slee flashed Annot a glance of pure malice and pushed past her to open the kitchen door. They heard her mutter, 'I've done enough for that family.'

The kitchen was squalid and smelt of stale food and damp. The windows were cracked, and the place was freezing although a low fire burned in the hearth. Catherine and Annot sat down at the scarred kitchen table, on which a knife and some pieces of meat in bloodied newspaper lay. Catherine could smell the blood, but she fought down her sudden nausea. Annot shoved the paper away. They weren't going anywhere. Catherine watched Mrs Slee as she stood uncertainly in her own kitchen. She had never seen the woman show any emotion other than hostility. Betty's death and her sister-in-law's sobs that day at Raven's Gaze had produced only an expression of irritation. She had not said a word about Thomas's death, but she had caused it. Catherine was glad to see her mean eyes darting about the kitchen as if she thought to make a run for it. But when her eyes rested on Annot again, Catherine saw the flare of anger. *No*, she thought, *you are not getting away with what you have done.*

Annot saw the anger, too. 'You'd best tell us, or —'

'Or what? What will tha do, when tha's just an insolent piece of muck?'

Annot stood up so suddenly that Mrs Slee started at the scraping of the chair on the stone floor. Annot stepped towards her as Catherine stood, too. Mrs Slee's eyes widened in fright, then sullenness took the place of anger.

'Sit down then, if tha must.'

Annot got her own back. She reached out, grabbed Mrs Slee by the arm, and bundled her down into a chair. 'You can sit down, too.'

Mrs Slee shot another venomous glance up at Annot, then turned to Catherine, who sat down, placed her official-looking papers before her, and took a fountain pen from her pocket. Mrs Slee eyed the pen and paper nervously.

'Go on,' Catherine said. 'We're waiting.'

'It's true that Mr Lestrange brought him back. I don't think 'e realised how bad it were goin' to be. It was the nightmares, see. 'E, Mr Raven, was quiet enough during the day, but I did the night shift, an', well, 'e'd scream the place down. 'E was that violent I had to tie him —'

'I saw the leather straps on that bed in that terrible room.'

'Oh, aye, I knew tha'd been in. Mr Lestrange couldn't 'ave anyone knowin' — I mean, 'is son an' heir cryin' like a babby when 'e were supposed to be a hero —'

'But to tie him down —' Catherine began.

'What else was I supposed to do? 'E were that beyond himself. 'E broke the window and went for me with the broken glass. See, my 'ands — 'e did that —'

'Surely he needed a doctor — what about Doctor Hall?'

'Bennet Lestrange didn't want 'im knowin'. Raven were supposed to be dead, anyways. No one were to know, an' it got easier when we kept 'im under with the laudanum and then —'

'He died because you gave him too much, I'll bet,' Annot flared.

'Oh, aye, tha'd know all about that — 'ow much did thee give poor Ted?'

Annot flushed. 'Bennet told you.'

'Said tha'd plenty —' Mrs Slee turned on Catherine — 'from that hoity-toity nurse —' Her glance, triumphant now, shot back to Annot. "E said tha would if t'money were good enough, an' all of a sudden, Ted's gone an' so 'ave thee, so don't —' She stopped when she saw Annot's hand on the knife. 'Tha wouldn't dare —'

'Try me,' Annot said.

'The military authorities are only interested in Lieutenant Raven Lestrange,' Catherine interrupted quickly. 'What happened when he died? Where did you bury him?'

Mrs Slee laughed, a mocking, mirthless cawing. *A raven's laugh*, Catherine thought, watching as she pretended to wipe her eyes before she said, 'Tha means in the dead of night, me an' im diggin' a six-foot hole with that ol' woman lookin' on? Or dost tha think 'e's at the bottom of Black Tarn, ten fathoms deep? Yon officers'll not find him then, will they?'

Catherine was enraged at the woman's callousness and her horrible intuition about their imaginings, but she made her voice steely calm. 'They will arrest you and keep you in the cells until you do tell them. And remember, you've just confessed to unlawful imprisonment, neglect and cruelty. That's enough for a long sentence.'

Mrs Slee paled at that. Her triumph was over, and she knew it. Catherine watched her thinking it out and saw her make her decision.

'Raven ain't dead — leastways not so far as I know. He were took away to an asylum — for lunatics, madmen like 'im. Nowt we could do — an' it were Bennet Lestrange's fault, all of it. 'E didn't want a mad son — 'e wanted a man what'd give 'im an heir.' She couldn't help herself and sneered at Catherine. 'Tha fell for that one for all thy airs, an' tha failed, didn't tha?'

Catherine kept her temper, but her voice was cold. 'Betty Slee died of measles, and you did not tell me. I know perfectly well what you are capable of and so will the authorities. You have played a part in a serious crime.'

'Not just me — that ol' woman knew. I'll tell 'em —' She whined now. 'I ain't takin' all the blame. I'm only a servant, obeyin' orders — 'e made me —'

'Where did they take him?'

'Private ambulance come. Took 'im one night to a place by the sea.'

'Where?'

'I don't know. Never heard nowt again. They never spoke about it.'

'Did Mr John know?'

'Mr Lestrange told 'im that 'is brother were in an asylum an' that 'e couldn't be visited. Mr Raven didn't know no-one anymore. Best forget, 'e said.'

'And Mr Lestrange didn't tell him where Raven was?'

'I don't know. 'E might 'ave. Not my business.'

Catherine saw the shifty look in her eyes. Mrs Slee knew something more. 'Yes, it was your business. You knew everything, so think back. Was it a long way or somewhere nearby? You must remember something.'

'We're staying here until you do remember,' Annot added.

'There was a fellow that 'elped us get 'im, Raven, into the ambulance... I think 'e said summat like — they'd twenty miles or so to go, an' 'e hoped the young man would stay sedated — 'e'd 'ad cases where —'

Catherine stood up. 'Believe me, I know all about that and it's terrible. All those young men, their lives wasted and ruined, and if you'd had any shred of human feeling, you wouldn't have done what you did to my son or to Raven Lestrange.' She raised her hand as Mrs Slee's mouth opened. 'I don't want to hear it. We'll be in touch. The people in the War Office will want to question you. Don't go anywhere.'

Annot had the last word. 'You'd best tidy up a bit before they come calling. I'd be ashamed of the muck in here.'

Catherine and Annot walked out. Mrs Slee didn't move.

They walked down the lane in silence. It was impossible yet to speak of what they had heard and too soon to meet Joe. They stopped in the shelter of some trees near the end of the lane. Catherine's heart was thumping, and she could hear Annot breathing as if she had run a race.

Annot spoke first. 'The old witch — only a servant. Following orders — she was up to her scrawny neck in it. I gave her a fright with that knife, though. But I wouldn't have —'

'I wasn't sure for a moment,' Catherine said, but she smiled at Annot.

'She'd have deserved it. I hope they lock her up and throw away the key. We should go down and you can telephone the colonel.'

'What's the point? She won't say any more. The important thing is to find out about Raven. Twenty — thirty miles away — near the sea. Where, Annot, where?'

'Blackpool — but that's more than thirty. Grange-over-Sands. Nursing homes there. Morecambe.'

Catherine knew then. 'It's Morecambe.'

'How do you know?'

Catherine told her about the dreadful visit she and John had made to Morecambe, how he had left her alone every afternoon, how he had abandoned her after the dinners to walk by himself, how he had been drinking — something he rarely did — and how he had lied to Mrs Whitenow about where they had been.

'Mrs Whitenow suggested Grange-over-Sands and when we came back, he pretended that we had been there.'

'But didn't you say?'

'I couldn't — I was so taken aback. In any case, I suspected that I was pregnant, and it was such a momentous thing that I didn't care about the lie. My only thought was to have my baby and leave as soon as I could, and then John left, and the news came that he was dead. I didn't think about Morecambe again, except for one thing, which was John's horror of a poor, mad ex-soldier we found on the beach. He walked away —'

'You think he visited his brother in Morecambe and that's why he left Raven's Gaze. He couldn't stand the pretence.'

'Unless he didn't go in to see Raven because he couldn't and that broke him — it was bad enough that he'd married me. I think he couldn't bear what he'd done and that's why he left. The fact that he couldn't make a life with Sabine made it worse — I believe that's why he killed himself. But, Annot, the secrecy about Morecambe is the only explanation for the lie he told Mrs Whitenow, and I presume he told the lie to Mr Lestrange who had told him to forget his brother.'

'So, we go to Morecambe to look for —'

'An asylum — for the insane. But it won't be a public asylum — Bennet Lestrange must have found a private one.'

'But wouldn't he need doctors to sign — I mean to say that Raven was mad? That old witch said Dr Hall didn't know anything about it.'

'He'd find a way — probably forged Doctor Hall's signature. I don't know how he did it, but he did it, and we must go and find the place because Raven could still be alive. Alive, Annot, and in need of us.'

Annot caught Catherine's passion. 'Alive — an' it matters. Clemmie's half-brother. We'll do it. I know — the post office in Morecambe. Joe can drive us, and we can just ask, or what about asking Doctor Hall? That'd be quicker. He must know if there are any private asylums in Morecambe or near there.'

'No, he'll remember me. He'll want to know why I'm back. We can't tell him what we've found out —'

'No, you're right — it sounds mad. Would he believe it? And Slee wouldn't talk to him. Oh, when I think of her — is she to get away with it?'

'Look up there,' Catherine said.

They looked back at the squat shape of the dark farmhouse with its sagging roof and broken chimney pots. Not a light showed.

'Think about her up there, sitting in the dark in that wreck of a place, counting her money and no one to share it with. Not a soul to give a damn about her. She's already got her just deserts.'

19

The following day, Catherine and Annot made the journey to Morecambe, driven by Joe. There they found a post office, where they enquired about private clinics in the area.

'You mean Seaview House, p'raps,' the woman behind the post office counter offered.

Annot pretended to look at the piece of paper in her hand. 'Oh, yes, it's on this list. Is that the only private clinic in the town?'

'That's the one for people what are convalescing — bad chests, usually. See, it's the air they come for. Is that what you're wantin'?'

'We want to have a look at it. Are there any other clinics?'

'There's The Grange —' The woman looked at Annot closely, and then at Catherine standing beside her. Two young women in good black coats and hats. Her glance darted to the door, where she could see the car waiting and the chauffeur wearing a cap, standing at the car door. 'But you'll not want a place like that. It's for them as is not right — in the head, I mean. Mental cases, they call 'em.'

'No, indeed. Where is Seaview House? Can we walk there?'

'It's a tidy step. It's at the place called Bare, just before the park. Posh houses down there. Just drive down this road and if you turn right just before the park then go straight, you'll find Seaview on the left.'

Catherine and Annot went back to the car, where Joe was waiting. 'We'll ask at Seaview House,' Annot said.

*

The recently appointed chauffeur was sent into Seaview House to ask, Annot's theory being that the car with two ladies in the back and Joe's smile would be enough to get the information they wanted, and so it was. Joe came out grinning as he put on his cap again.

'Madam,' he said, leaning in at the back door, tipping the cap over his eyes. Catherine couldn't help smiling, too, despite the knot of anxiety in her stomach. Great-hearted, loyal Joe who cheered them on and of whom Annot was so proud because he had risen above his early troubles to become the fine man he was. She compared him to Bennet Lestrange about whose parents she had wondered. The lodging-house keeper and the bank clerk — not very prosperous, she imagined. Their son Bernard had left them behind and reinvented himself as Bennet Lestrange, and invented a grandfather from a country house who had left him his silver treasures. Bennet Lestrange, whose inheritance was in truth bitter cruelty and selfishness.

'Away with you,' Annot protested to Joe, laughing, too. 'I take it you know.'

Joe nodded, got into the driving seat and started the engine. They drove back to the main road, from where Catherine looked at the endless grey sea. There was the pier. She thought of the ragged man with the eyes of Lieutenant Adams and a shiver went through her. Then she felt Annot's warm hand take hers as they turned away to find The Grange and Raven Lestrange, she hoped.

The Grange lay beyond the town nearer the countryside, though Catherine could still smell the sea. Stone gateposts topped with stone birds led them along a winding, tree-lined drive to a grand-looking sandstone mansion with long windows, a columned portico, and a smartly painted front door.

'It's not what I expected,' Annot said as the car stopped outside. 'It's like a country house. I thought it'd be all bars and black stone.'

Catherine stared at the door and the iron bell, which she would have to ring in a minute or two. The place looked peaceful enough, a place inside which the patients might be well cared for by compassionate doctors and nurses. Well, it was time to find out. She and Annot had decided that Catherine should go in. She had her marriage certificate, and she was wearing a gold ring on her wedding finger — one of Mrs Whitenow's. Not her own — she could not have borne to wear it again.

Catherine went up the portico and rang the bell. She glanced back at Annot, who was looking out at her, raising her hand with a thumbs-up. When she turned back again, the door was open and a woman of about her own age in the familiar starched apron and headdress was smiling at her. Catherine explained that she was here to find out about a patient, and she was invited into a large hall laid with black and white tiles. There were flowers on a narrow table underneath a gilded mirror and an electric chandelier shedding a warm glow on the velvet sofa and mahogany table. It might have been a country house, except for the smell of disinfectant which underlaid the scent of lavender polish, the signs on two shining wooden doors which bore the legends, *Office* and *Director*, and the wheelchair at the bottom of the stairs. Catherine thought of Ted Syke and of how damaged Raven Lestrange might be if he were here. She looked back at the nurse, who was waiting in silence, and took a deep breath. It was time to explain.

'My name is Catherine Lestrange of Raven's Gaze Hall in Yorkshire. I am a widow and have found out quite recently that my husband's brother, who is called Bennet Raven Lestrange — known as Raven — may have been a patient here. The family had lost contact with him. I don't know why, but I feel it my duty to try to trace him — to find out if he is still alive and perhaps a patient here.'

'Raven Lestrange? An unusual name, and not one I recognise as belonging to one of our patients.' The nurse smiled again. 'And I know them all.'

Perhaps Raven died here, Catherine thought. Her heart plummeted, then she thought that it was possible this nurse may not have known him. It was so long ago. 'Are there records I could look at? Perhaps Mr Lestrange died here before you came.'

'That may be so. I came here in 1919. We do have records, of course. Can you tell me more about him? Do you know when he was admitted, how old he was?'

'He was seriously injured in the war in July 1916 when he was twenty-three. I do know that he suffered from shellshock and was treated in a hospital in London. An old servant of the family told me that he had been taken by his family to a private clinic by the sea, probably in September 1916.'

'We do have a patient who has been here since 1916 and was diagnosed as a shellshock case, but his name is Edward. As I say, he came before my time. I was serving in Flanders then.'

'So was I — CCS number seventeen at Lijssenthoek. Remy Farm.'

In the moment of silence which followed, Catherine looked at the face opposite. Not a pretty face, but there was beauty in its pale gravity framed by the white veil, and in the calm blue-grey eyes which looked back at hers in immediate understanding.

'Number three at Hazebrouck — not so far away — then the Somme in 1916; Grévillers until spring 1918, then trying to keep ahead of the Germans as they swept towards us — all those terrible train journeys.'

'I remember — we were bombed at Amiens. I was injured by shrapnel and evacuated.'

'All those men — I'll never forget — the Somme — Passchendaele... My brother died there...'

'My husband was wounded at Arras. A close friend was killed at Chemin des Dames — so many...'

'And just one you are looking for. I understand. The fall of a sparrow.'

Catherine felt tears prick at her eyes. 'Not one of them should be forgotten.'

'It is so sad that he seems to have been forgotten by his family, though I am sorry to say that it is not as uncommon as you might think. Some families do prefer to forget those who are mentally incapacitated — they are ashamed of them, and yet a young man who fought ... 1916, you say? That conjures many memories of the Somme. Poor Edward Syke, our patient, has been forgotten by his family, too.'

Catherine froze. *Admitted under a different name by Bennet Lestrange? It would be just like him to choose Ted Syke's name.* He had told John to forget his brother, and John had lied about coming to Morecambe. Had he discovered the deception? She looked back at the nurse, and with a calmness that surprised herself, said, 'I know that name, but the Edward Syke I knew died in 1920. His widow is outside in the car.'

'You think our Edward Syke might be —'

'I have every reason to think so. It is a long story, Nurse...?'

'Grace Marshall — Grace.'

She held out her hand and Catherine shook it. 'Catherine Lestrange, and my brother-in-law is definitely not Edward Syke. He is Bennet Raven Lestrange, and he has been lost for sixteen years.'

'I'm afraid that Edward cannot tell us who he is. He is perfectly tranquil, except for his dreams — nightmares, I should say, but he does not speak. He understands what we say to him and smiles and nods his thanks, but he only looks out of his window. I am very fond of him and so I wish I could help him. However, you will have to talk to our director, Doctor Ellis. He is a very compassionate man who served, too. He was with Number Forty-five at Vecquemont in July 1916. We met at Doullens in March 1918.'

'I was there then — before Amiens. It was dreadful.'

'It was. I worked with Doctor Ellis. He told me that before the war he had set up a private clinic which he would return to, and I said I'd work for him again. He will be able to tell you about Edward Syke. I will go and tell him. He will see you, I'm sure.'

'The Somme,' Doctor Ellis said simply, after Catherine had explained about her brother-in-law, Bennet Raven Lestrange, whom she believed was a patient at the clinic under the name of Edward Syke.

A code, she thought, the Somme, the single word which had prompted George Rhodes-Smith to investigate and Doctor Ellis to ask Nurse Grace Marshall to bring the file without commenting on the extraordinary idea that he had a patient who had been admitted under a false name. And those other codewords — CCS, Remy Farm, Hazebrouck, Passchendaele, Grévillers, Amiens — which Grace Marshall had deciphered and known instantly that she must help the visitor in search of the one who was lost.

'Yes,' she said to Doctor Ellis as they waited for Nurse Marshall to bring in the file. 'He served with the Loyal North Lancashires and was awarded the Military Cross in the action at La Boisselle.'

Doctor Ellis pushed his spectacles up onto his forehead and rubbed his eyes. She saw the pain of memory in them. 'Ah, yes,' he said, 'I remember. Eleven thousand casualties on the first of July. The Lancashires — part of the nineteenth division — were rushed up there. They captured the village on the sixth of July.'

'Raven Lestrange was wounded on the fifth of July.'

Nurse Marshall came back with a buff folder, which Doctor Ellis studied while Catherine sat in anxious silence.

Doctor Ellis looked up. 'These are the notes of my colleague, Doctor Percy Norton — he has retired now, but if we need him, I can telephone.' He looked at the papers again. 'Now, he says here that Mr Bennet Lestrange came to see him with the patient's mother. Apparently, the mother and son were tenants on one of the farms he owned in Ravendale. Mr Lestrange explained that Edward Syke had been treated in London, and that he had brought him home to his mother, but she was unable to cope with him.'

Catherine had an inkling about who the so-called mother might have been. 'Does your colleague give any impression of the mother or Mr Lestrange?'

Doctor Ellis looked at her curiously and then at the notes. 'Hm… He was struck by her coldness. He writes that he decided to take the patient because he was certain that the mother was more ashamed than compassionate. He — erm — he says that he did not think her fit to care for him, and that the young man seemed frightened of her... However, he does add that such cases are complex, and relationships do come under strain in those circumstances.' Doctor Ellis looked at Catherine. 'That is the often the case, Mrs Lestrange — patients turn against those who love them most.'

'And Mr Lestrange?'

Doctor Ellis looked down again. 'It seems that he was in charge. He had offered to pay the fees —'

'And are they still paid?'

'Oh, yes, through a firm of solicitors in Hawes — Huggon and Beale.'

Catherine remembered Mr Huggon reading the will and asking Bennet Lestrange about another matter. Bennet Lestrange's curtness. It was a private matter, he had snapped to mild Mr Huggon. So it had been, and now it wasn't. Bennet Lestrange's secret was about to be exposed.

'I remember Mr Huggon — the family solicitor.'

'Well, Mr Lestrange spoke for the mother, who hadn't much to say, but Doctor Norton put that down to the fact that she was with her landlord and no doubt —'

'She wasn't his mother,' Catherine blurted out. 'She was Bennet Lestrange's housekeeper, who is called Esther Slee, and she didn't care a farthing for that sick young man. Neither did Bennet Lestrange, who was his father. He wanted to forget that his maimed son ever existed.'

Doctor Ellis stared at her. 'Let me get this straight, Mrs Lestrange, if you please. You are telling me that Mr Lestrange brought his son here under the name Edward Syke with his housekeeper masquerading as the young man's mother because he, Mr Lestrange, wanted to erase all traces of his son's existence. It seems — incredible —'

'Not if you had known him, Doctor Ellis. He reported his son's death to the War office in September 1916, but I assure you there is no trace of Raven Lestrange at his former home — no birth or death certificate, no letters, no photographs, no grave, only the Military Cross, which was found in his grandmother's Bible. However, the former housekeeper, Mrs Slee, admitted that she knew that in September 1916, Raven had been taken to a clinic by the sea. I knew it must be here in Morecambe. I came to the town in 1920 with my husband. I thought recently that he might have come here —'

'I'm afraid no one has ever visited — but would your husband have known that his brother was here under an assumed name?'

'I don't know, Doctor Ellis. He never spoke of his brother, but I think — when I look back — that he felt guilty. He committed suicide in 1921 — he was wounded at Arras in 1918.'

Doctor Ellis knew that name, too. 'I see. But you never met the young man. How will you know if our patient is Raven Lestrange?'

'I am told that his hair had a reddish tint and that he had pale green eyes.'

Doctor Ellis looked at Nurse Marshall, who nodded as he said, 'Like our Edward Syke. But I must be sure, Mrs Lestrange, before I can discuss his future. Is there anyone at all who would remember Raven from all those years ago?'

'Edward Syke's widow is outside in the car. She knew Raven Lestrange. I will bring her.'

In the hall, Catherine told Annot the story of the patient whose name was thought to be Edward Syke.

'It was all part of the erasing of Raven Lestrange,' Catherine said.

'The devil. Why on earth would he choose Ted's name? Any name from one of his books would have done,' Annot said. Catherine saw her face change. 'Oh, Lord, but I do know. The dates, Catherine. Bennet brought him here in September 1916 when Ted was reported missing — presumed dead. I believed he was dead. Bennet thought he must be dead and that's why he thought he'd get away with it.'

'He did — for sixteen years.'

'And even when Ted was brought back, Bennet had nothing to worry about because Raven couldn't speak about anything and neither could Ted, and who in Ravendale would be going to a clinic in Morecambe? In any case, we all believed that Raven had been killed in July 1916. Only Slee knew the truth, and she wasn't telling.'

'And Mr Huggon, the solicitor, but I doubt he'd tell anyone. He was frightened of Bennet Lestrange, but the fees have always been paid.'

'Oh, aye, Mr Huggon would be scared to lose Mr Lestrange's business. And anyway, he died in 1925 — Mr Beale is the solicitor now — paying the fees for Edward Syke about whom he knows nothing.'

'I wonder if Mrs Whitenow stipulated the continuing payment in her will. After all, she kept the Military Cross. She must have felt something for Raven, and Mr Huggon mentioned another matter to Bennet Lestrange after he had read Mrs Whitenow's will, but Bennet Lestrange shut him up very brusquely. Maybe a trust for Raven which even Bennet Lestrange couldn't break, even though he thought he was above the law. Maybe he tried to cancel the payments, and even timid Mr Huggon wouldn't let him.'

'I'm just glad the fees have been paid, whoever arranged it. It's horrible to think that Raven might have been sent away from here — we might never have found him.'

Catherine shivered. 'A dreadful thought, but come, they want you to see Raven — to find out if you recognise him.'

After Annot had told her story about Ted to Doctor Ellis and Nurse Marshall, they took her and Catherine upstairs to Raven Lestrange's room. Nurse Marshall opened the door so that Annot could peep inside. She saw a man gazing out of the window. He didn't look round until Nurse Marshall gently said his name. And then they saw his face. Doctor Ellis closed the door.

'It is Raven Lestrange,' Annot said. 'I can see the boy he was.'

'May I go in?' Catherine asked.

'Of course — you have dealt with such cases before.'

'I have.'

Nurse Marshall came out and Catherine went into the room, where Raven Lestrange looked out of the window again. *What does he see?* she wondered. She sat down opposite him and waited until he turned to her with an uncertain smile. His eyes were as transparent as pale green glass and empty as the blank winter sky. She might have been looking at Lieutenant Adams, who had vanished from her sight, or the man under the pier who had vanished, too. Or any of those who had been consigned to their darkness…

But she was here, and she was still Mrs John Lestrange, and he was Raven Lestrange and therefore hers, part of the legacy of Raven's Gaze Hall. He was part of her Thomas, who might have grown up to look like Raven. He was hers to take or leave. She reached out and took his hand. He had milk-white skin and the delicate bones of a bird — a sparrow, perhaps, but he felt as cold and lifeless as marble. She kept his hand in hers until she felt his pulse beating there and the hand became warmer, as if his blood were returning. Something fluttered in her palm, the butterfly touch of a finger — a man recalled to life.

Doctor Ellis allowed Catherine and Annot to bring his patient back to Raven's Gaze two months after Catherine had held that fragile hand — two months in which, very gradually, Catherine, Annot and Grizel had spent time with him, asking nothing of him. Doctor Ellis did not know if Raven would ever recover his memories of the time before the war, or even of the war, but Grizel's opinion was that it didn't matter. 'In God's good time, my dear,' she had said to the surprised Doctor Ellis, who had looked at Grizel for a long moment and then said she was right.

During her visits to The Grange, Catherine had read to Raven — she had searched the old nursery to see if she could find any suitable books and came across *The Wind in the Willows*, *Alice in Wonderland*, *Tales of Robin Hood*, Beatrix Potter, and the poems of Tennyson from the book which John had given her. It was all she could do for Raven's brother, who had loved him, and whom she had forgiven when she had learned of his terrible death. She couldn't tell if Raven understood, but he seemed calm as she read quietly and showed him the illustrations. Sometimes she simply sat and held his hand. He seemed to like Grizel best. She sat still and knitted and from time to time patted his hand, and showed him the scarf or jumper, telling him it was for him. 'Dear lad,' she called him.

In the early spring Catherine brought him snowdrops, and when he saw them, he wept. When Annot came a day or two later, with her hair tied up in the old way, and dressed in an old coat, he said her name. Catherine saw the change in his eyes, as if a light had flicked on briefly, and she knew there was hope. And when Clemmie and Joe visited, they talked to him about the walks they took in the hills and dales, and how when he was better, they would take him, too. It was Clemmie who used the name "Raven" for the first time and told him she was Clemmie and his sister. This time, the light stayed on for longer.

Before Raven had been brought home, the door to the spiral staircase had been boarded up by Joe and Billie Moffat. The boards and the door to the tower were painted blue, due to Doctor Ellis's belief that this colour had soothing properties. Raven had the bedroom which Catherine had occupied after her marriage so that Grizel could sleep in the room next door, which had been meant for Thomas. When Raven woke in the night, Grizel was there to soothe her dear lad and sit with him until he slept again. And when the summer came, Joe and Clemmie took him out into the sunshine.

Seven months after Raven's return to Raven's Gaze Hall, Catherine stood with Annot and Grizel at the open front door. She looked back into the hall where Clemmie, her hair afire in the sunlight coming through the window, knelt before her half-brother, whose hair caught the same light and burned auburn. His hands, still thin, but browner now, held the twist of wool and Clemmie looped it round his fingers — she was teaching him how to play cat's cradle. Broad-shouldered Joe, who had carried him into the house seven months ago, leant on the back of Raven's chair, his strong hand resting lightly on his shoulder.

'Your miracle girl,' Catherine said to Annot as she watched the three of them in the sun-filled room.

'Aye, thank the Lord she's not like me — or Bennet.'

'He didn't fail at everything — she is his daughter.'

'Hard to believe — maybe she's a changeling,' Annot said.

Grizel laughed. 'A Deirdre, mayhap, in Ireland — a fairy child and she's back, but nay, tha's in her an' there'll have been an Annot long ago up Hawes way, a fierce little lass who could stand up for herself. But 'tis magic, wherever she came from.'

'And dear Joe is magical, too. You have wonderful children, Annot, and Grizel is right — they are like you. Maybe Raven is the changeling.'

'Our changeling, now.'

'Aye,' Grizel said, 'an' he'll become the man he was meant to be — in God's time, my dears. For love will do it, as it will for thee, Catherine. Don't be afeared. Look now.'

They watched as a car came along the drive and drew to a stop before the steps.

'There,' said Grizel, holding Catherine in her arms, 'time to go to your future. Tha's waited long enough. Let be and live thy life.'

Annot hugged her. 'And come back to us — both of you.'

Catherine Sisley went down the steps and looked a long way to the distant horizon and beyond to the dazzling sky in which there was not a cloud. Then Doctor Sam Meadows got out of the car and came to meet her, his hands outstretched to take hers.

EPILOGUE

Dorset, 1933

Catherine smiled as she read Annot's letter. All was well at Raven's Gaze, where Raven Lestrange was continuing to thrive. Joe and Billy Moffatt took him out to work on the farms with them. The outdoor life suited him, as did family life, though Grizel still kept guard over her "dear lad" through the sometimes difficult nights, when nightmares came. But they were all hopeful about the future.

And speaking of hope, Annot wrote, *your news has thrilled us. Grizel swears that she will come on the train when you need her. Yes, she knows that your Sam is a doctor, but she wants to be there when the time comes. I don't know that I can let her come all the way on her own, so, if you will have us both, then I'll come, too. Of course, we would love you to come to Raven's Gaze. I think it would be a very good thing if your baby could be born here — a new life, and as I say, new hope for the future. Grizel, who sees all things beyond this life, believes your Thomas will bless your child's birth here and you will be healed by being close to both your children.*

Catherine looked round the freshly painted nursery and at the new cot of white wood with its lace-edged pillows, the frieze of painted animals on the wall, the white-painted fireplace and colourful rug before it — all so bright and so very different from the haunted nursery of Raven's Gaze. Her child would be born into light and joy. Yet Raven's Gaze was different now that a happy family lived there. Catherine did not know if she believed in Grizel's words about Thomas. It was impossible to know, but perhaps it was right that her new baby should be born in the same place — and live the life that Thomas had never had. And the child would be born into a family which would cherish him or her. There would be healing in that.

She would consult Sam, of course. What he wanted was the important thing, but she thought how lovely it would be for her stepson, William, to meet Joe and Clemmie, and Raven. Joe and Clemmie would take him under their wings while the baby was born, and her attention was on him or her. William would love the place and the people — he would have a family, too, and he would be another new young face at Raven's Gaze. Catherine had not forgotten all that had happened, though Bennet Lestrange had dwindled into a shadowy memory. There was one thing she could do now to erase that shadow completely before her child was born.

She left the nursery and went to the spare room, where in a drawer she had put the few things she had brought from Raven's Gaze. She took Bennet Lestrange's book to the fire and watched as the gothic script which announced the *Devil's Dictionary* faded in the heat. The pages caught fire and crumbled to ashes, and with them all those names which had so disturbed her: The Devil's Pot, The Witches Pot, Devil's Bridge, Foulsyke, Sorrowsyke. *The devil and all his works gone*, she thought wryly. They were just places with odd names at which one might be curious or amused. Bennet Lestrange's twisted mind had turned them into sinister things to exert his power over her.

She burnt the photographs, too. The one of Raven's Gaze looking its darkest and most forbidding, with that single light showing. Well, that would never be lit again. She watched the wedding photograph sizzle and curl in the flames and vanish, and the newspaper cuttings which had told of John's suicide.

She had forgiven John long ago. Bennet Lestrange had destroyed him — and the war had, too. But she kept the photograph of John in his lieutenant's uniform. He had been a hero in battle, and that was how he must be remembered. Raven must have the photograph of his brother. Not yet, though. Grizel would know when the time was right.

And the photograph of Nurse Catherine Sisley? She would keep that to remind herself of the girl she had been and the work she had done. That girl was a stranger no longer. She was part of the woman she had become.

Catherine waited until there were only ashes in the grate, which she stirred with the poker until there was nothing left. She went back to the light-filled nursery.

HISTORICAL NOTES

The First World War cast a long shadow across the lives of not only those who survived but also those who grieved for those who were lost, either to death or permanent disability. The story of Raven Lestrange grew out of the books I read, in particular, *The Roses of No man's Land* by Lyn Macdonald (Penguin, 1980) and *Casualty Figures* by Michèle Barrett (Verso, 2007), both of which tell harrowing stories of those who suffered from mental illness. Lyn Macdonald's book explores the role of nurses in the war. Reading all about the nurses of the war, I was struck by their courage and resilience. Aside from the appalling physical injuries, the nurses dealt with shellshock cases, too. Their patients might suffer from total paralysis, hysteria, trembling, hallucinations, incoherent speech, and mutism, which is what happens to Raven Lestrange. It is true, too, that some families were ashamed of what was perceived as cowardice in some quarters, and some were confined to asylums for the rest of their lives.

It was true that under the terms of the Lunacy Act, servicemen discharged for shellshock or other mental problems could not be forced to have treatment. And since Raven was an officer, the army would accept his father's decision to look after him. In 1920 there were 65,000 men suffering from mental illness and receiving pensions. It is plausible that when Bennet Lestrange of Raven's Gaze Hall reported his son's death it would be accepted, and his pension stopped.

Women were essential to the world of medicine. Doctors Flora Murray and Louisa Garrett set up hospitals in France amid fierce opposition from the military authorities, but they were so skilled and so successful that they were asked to open a military hospital in London. The wonderful book, *Endell Street: The Women Who Ran Britain's Trailblazing Military Hospital* by Wendy Moore (Atlantic Books, 2020) tells their story. I also read *Nurses of Passchendaele: Caring for the Wounded of the Ypres Campaigns 1914–1918* by Christine E. Hallett (Pen & Sword History, 2017) and the unusual book, *The Nurse Who Found Herself in 1916* by Sally Lawton (2018), which gave me an insight into the day-to-day lives of the nurses and the treatments available. As well as the trained nurses recruited to the Front, thousands of young women volunteered for the gruelling work as VADs (Voluntary Aid Detachment) at home and abroad. In her book, *The Roses of No Man's Land*, Lyn Macdonald describes the 'gently-nurtured girls who walked out of Edwardian drawing-rooms into the manifold horrors of the First World War.'

Nurses served in Italy, Salonika and Serbia as well as France and Flanders, where they served in the stationary hospitals in the big towns, but also on the Front Line in the Field Hospitals and Casualty Clearing Stations such as CCS 17, where my character, Catherine Sisley, works, and where she meets John Lestange for the first time. The work was harrowing — the soldiers' injuries were appalling. Amputations were frequent and many men were mutilated beyond recognition. They suffered from gas-gangrene, trench-foot, trench-fever, dysentery, pneumonia, and tuberculosis, and there were no antibiotics. It wasn't until 1915 that Doctors Carrel and Dakin came up with their Hypochlorous Acid Solution, which helped to treat sepsis in the early stages. The conditions in the hospitals were often dangerous and unhygienic. Hospitals and clearing stations were often bombed and flooded, and the medical staff had to be on the move, especially during the Spring Offensive of 1918. They packed up their units and transported their patients by ambulance trains or barges, or convoys of ambulances and lorries, under fire. The stationary hospital at Amiens took in between four and five thousand casualties in five days and was bombed continuously. The chaplain wrote an account of his experiences, observing that 'the pluck of the sisters and VADs is simply marvellous.' They worked tirelessly through the nights by candlelight, with bombs falling about them.

During World War I, women were recruited into roles which were unimaginable before 1914, but as the enormous cost of the war in terms of manpower increased, women were needed on the Home Front for agricultural work in the Women's Land Army and in industry, where they worked in the dangerous munitions factories. They became railway workers, porters, bus drivers, conductresses, and even police officers.

They also played their part in government departments, taking over clerical roles that were traditionally the preserve of men, and they worked in the intelligence departments as cryptographers, translators and censors, and some, of course, went abroad as spies, as does Claire Mallory in my novel *The Secrets of Treasonfield House*, after her work as an ambulance driver.

The Women's Army Auxiliary Corps was formed in 1916, the Women's Royal Naval Reserve in 1917, and the Women's Royal Airforce in 1918. The women in these services became clerks, cooks, codebreakers, translators, drivers and mechanics. Over 100,000 women joined the Armed Forces during World War I.

My reading informed my account of Catherine Sisley's experiences in the spring of 1918 and led me to contemplate what her life would become after the war, and where she might find peace and happiness.

However, Christine Hallett points out that the terrible experiences and incredible courage of nurses were never fully recognised after the war, the emphasis of historians being on the masculine experience. Even though some things did change for women after the war, only women over thirty who were householders got the vote in 1918. It wasn't until 1928 that the Equal Franchise Act gave the vote to all people over the age of twenty-one. Many women continued to work for their living, but there was no equal pay and there was still the expectation that women should stay at home. Society was still a patriarchy, and it is in a world of class consciousness and concern with property and inheritance that Catherine Sisley finds herself and becomes a victim of Bennet Lestrange, who wants an heir to Raven's Gaze Hall and has no interest in Catherine's experiences as a Front Line nurse. Annot Syke is a victim, too, because she is too poor to keep her farm going and is of a lower class in Bennet Lestrange's eyes.

However, there is a better future for them. Annot becomes an independent woman, and her children will not be servants or factory hands. Catherine finds someone who knows what she endured during the war and will respect her skills, experience and courage. At least, I hope that you will interpret the ending as an optimistic one.

A NOTE TO THE READER

Dear Reader,

The title of this book came first, or rather, the phrase, "raven's gaze", which I thought of when I visited the ruined Pendragon Castle not far from where I live. It was a gloomy day in March with some very brooding clouds overhead and rain slanting across the hills against which the castle walls stood out, as well as the few stark trees. It is an isolated, haunting place; legend has it that it was built by Uther Pendragon, father of King Arthur. Though the castle was built in the twelfth century, it is believed to be on the site of a wooden fort built by Uther Pendragon. All very romantic, but the thing that caught my imagination was the name of one of the twentieth-century owners, Edward Raven Frankland, whose father Edward Frankland had written a book about the Arthurian legends. The black bird which perched on one of the trees may or may not have been a raven, but it was very large, and its glinting, beady eye was on me. I put the words "raven" and "gaze" together and thought what a good title they would make for a novel. Not that I had any idea of what kind of novel.

However, the name "Raven" stayed with me, and ravens came up again when on a visit to the Tower of London, I bought a book, entitled *The Ravenmaster: My Life with the Ravens at the Tower of London* (Fourth Estate, 2018) by Christopher Skaife, who was the Ravenmaster at the Tower. It's a fascinating book that contains all sorts of information about these birds, especially the superstitions associated with them.

According to Greek myth, ravens were once as white as swans, and it was a raven that told Apollo that Coronis, a nymph who was loved by Apollo, was faithless. The god shot the nymph, but, hating the tell-tale bird, 'blacked the raven o'er…'

The raven is a bird of ill-omen, said to portend death and bring infection because it followed armies to prey upon the corpses. Christopher Marlowe, in his play, *The Jew of Malta*, refers to the 'sad-presaging raven that tolls / The sick man's passport in her hollow beak [...] Does shake contagion from her sable wing.' Shakespeare's Lady Macbeth refers to their supposedly prophetic ability: 'The raven himself is hoarse / That croaks the fatal entrance of Duncan / Under my battlements.' They do croak with a sound that is reminiscent of a rattle — a sort of deep, rather sinister chuckle. Naturally, this was on my mind when I thought of Catherine entering beneath the battlements of Raven's Gaze Hall. The light she thought was a welcome was a warning. It is Bennet Lestrange's eye which stares from the tower. He is the raven — the bird of ill-omen.

There's a German proverb that says, 'One raven will not pluck another's eyes out', which seems to suggest loyalty among these thieving birds. Thus, Bennet Lestrange and Mrs Whitenow, despite their mutual dislike, are thieves of Catherine's life and happiness, joined in their plot to force John Lestrange to marry Catherine so that there will be an heir to Raven's Gaze Hall. Brewer's *Dictionary of Phrase and Fable* translates the saying to mean, 'You are not to take for granted all that a friend says of a friend.'

There are some beautifully poetic collective nouns for birds, for example 'a charm of goldfinches', 'an exaltation of larks', 'a murmuration of starlings.' But the corvids are very often associated with malevolent doings, as in 'a murder of crows.' There's an old rhyme which says of crows, 'Five is sickness; six is death'. Sometimes this is attributed to magpies, which can be 'a mischief' or 'a murder', and there is 'one for sorrow' and 'seven for the devil.' They are associated with theft, as in *The Thieving Magpie* by Rossini. Jackdaws are 'a clattering' and legendary thieves, too. Rooks are a parliament, which doesn't sound too bad, but ravens are 'an unkindness' or 'a conspiracy.' Conspiracy was on my mind, of course, when I invented the family at Raven's Gaze Hall and their conspiracy against Catherine.

I invented Ravendale in which Raven's Gaze Hall is situated. It is based on Grisedale, a remote dale, part of the larger Wensleydale. It became known as 'The Dale that Died' in a 1975 film because so few people lived there — harsh winters and the harsh land drove the inhabitants away and many of the properties fell into ruin, though there has been a resurgence in the population in recent years. There are some fascinating names still remembered. Rowantree, where my character Grizel lives, is still a ruin, and I came across East Cote Weggs, West Scar House, Mouse Sike, Blake Mire, High Flust, and, best of all, High Paradise. On my 1930s map, I found High House, which no longer exists, but it was high on the fell, and so I turned it into Raven's Gaze Hall and gave it the tower and battlements common to houses in the dales.

For a long time during the writing of the story, Raven's Gaze was my working title until I realised that Raven's Gaze Hall was a place of entrapment, and so the title became *The Prisoner of Raven's Gaze Hall*.

Reviews are very important to writers, so it would be great if you could spare the time to post a review on **Amazon** and **Goodreads**. Readers can connect with me online, on

Facebook (JCBriggsBooks) and Twitter (@JeanCBriggs), and you can find out more about the books and Charles Dickens via my website, jcbriggsbooks.com, where you will find Mr Dickens's A-Z of murder — all cases of murder to which I found a Dickens connection.

Thank you!

Jean Briggs

Sapere Books is an exciting new publisher of brilliant fiction and popular history.

To find out more about our latest releases and our monthly bargain books visit our website:
saperebooks.com